ELLE HARTFORD

Mermaid for Danger

The Alchemical Tales #3

*This one is for my family,
found family,
and friends.*

*Sometimes I can be just as obtuse as Red is.
Thank you all for your support!*

Contents

Welcome

Long, long ago, a coven of witches created a world just beyond ours—a realm of fairy tales.

In Beyond, humans rub shoulders with mythical creatures, and magic mixes with science.

There are only three rules:

Happily
accept that we share the same home

Ever
remember that what you take, you must also give

After
struggle will always lead to new beginnings

So, if you are ready . . . you are welcome here.

* * *

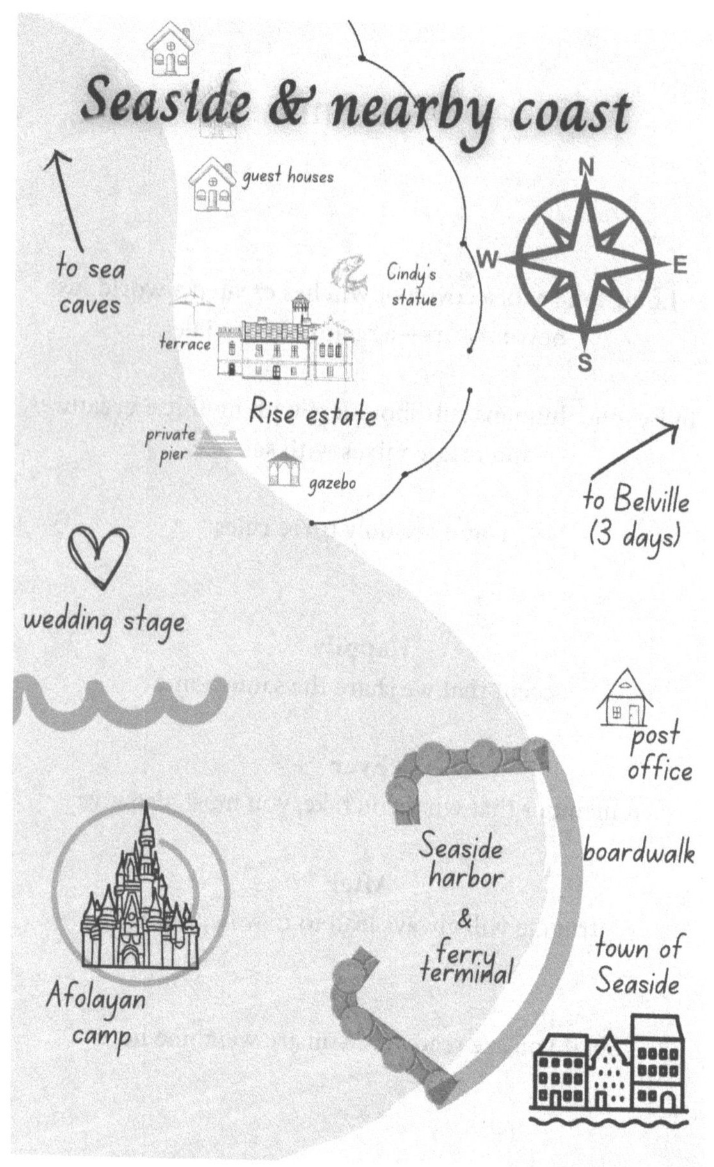

Seaside & nearby coast
guest houses
to sea caves
Cindy's statue
N
W
E
S
terrace
Rise estate
private pier
gazebo
to Belville (3 days)
wedding stage
post office
Seaside harbor & ferry terminal
boardwalk
Afolayan camp
town of Seaside

Cast of Characters

Seaside

Taiwo Afolayan: genderfluid merfolk; partner to Rei

William: canine familiar, capable of protection magic and plenty of sass

1

On the Road Again

"Welcome, welcome! Line for the ferry's to the right. No cutting, or the gods and goddesses of the waves will swallow ye whole!"

"If *I* don't do something worse first," my companion, William, grumbled. He lumbered at my side, his black doggy head as high as my thigh. His magic, a starry blue, glowed faintly as he prepared himself for the transition from land to sea. Though the afternoon around us was bright and cheerful, he clearly wasn't feeling charitable—especially now that our long journey down from the mountains had brought us to the ferry.

"Hush," I told him as he continued muttering to himself. The tiny ferry terminal was awash with people, mostly vacationers and locals, I guessed. Most were dressed in shorts or bathing suit cover-ups, the quintessential uniform of summer in Seaside. And most were also giving William and me curious stares. We carried too much luggage to be day-trippers; in fact, we were in town for a friend's wedding. While I was happy to see and support my friend, as I looked at the strangers in line with us I felt a familiar twinge of, well, strangeness. *Love,* I had once told one of my mothers—and she'd never let me forget it—*seems like such a hassle.* Strangers, vows, big public displays. Even the wiser, older me didn't totally get it.

I re-adjusted the strap of my canvas backpack self-consciously, trying to put my uncertainties about love and its trappings aside. In my year and more of running a shop, I'd forgotten that unique dichotomy of travel: on the road, it's easy to be invisible. But when you roll up in a new town or at a crossroads, you're an object of public interest.

We shuffled along in line as I thought. We *could* have taken a carriage or even caught a magitech hot air balloon from our home in Belville to Seaside, but William had convinced me to walk it "for old time's sake." Judging by William's demeanor now, I was guessing that the old times weren't as fun as he remembered them. Still, I *had* enjoyed a chance to collect a lot of great material along the three-day trip. Just before joining the ferry line, I'd sent a big box of flower stalks and even some malachite ore back home to Red's Alchemy and Potions, and I was already looking forward to getting home and using the ingredients—*after* the wedding, of course.

Come to think of it, Seaside's post office had been crowded too. Maybe that helped explain William's increased grumpiness . . .

I shrugged, letting his attitude remain *his* problem. Instead, I decided to enjoy the view. Seaside was a popular destination for tourists, the kind of city that still felt like a tiny harbor town. Long ago, some enterprising soul had realized that preserving the old wooden harbor, sparkling clean beaches, and vividly painted cabins would bring a lot more visitors. So, they'd had the good grace to hide their magitech train and balloon stations behind the hill that edged the back of town, and I swear they had a team of wizards on hand to ensure that all their window-boxes and tiny, sandy gardens bloomed plentifully. The ferry dock was particularly idyllic, even in line: as we waited patiently, lined up along a low stone wall separating us from the harbor, we could watch the seals playing in turquoise waves and hear children playing at the beach around the corner.

William, however, was looking firmly forward, toward the ferry captain. When two elves rushed up and joined their friends in line ahead of us, he growled.

"Need I remind you that we are in town for a *happy* occasion?" I whispered down to him.

"It's not the wedding yet." A serious undertone of menace laced his words. I rolled my eyes, but kept a more careful eye on the line, just in case William decided to do more than talk.

The ferry captain chatted amiably—and loudly—to each person in line as he took fares for the journey. I gathered pretty quickly that his name was Kye, that he didn't care for magic, didn't hold with technology, and didn't trust the weather, but that he had it on good authority that the wedding next week would be the event of the season. *Whose authority,* I couldn't help but wonder. *His fairy godmother's?* Though the joke made me smile, I hoped he was right.

"Name, destination, type of fare," Kye rattled off the familiar refrain as William and I stepped to the head of the line.

"I'm Red, and this is William. Oh, that's Cinnabar Sunset, if you need my *full* name. Full fare for me, half fare for him."

Kye nodded along thoughtfully, his weathered fingers skimming through his stack of tickets. "And that's William Sunset, is it?"

"Not a chance," William snorted. "Just William."

"And why does 'Just William' get half fare, tell?"

I nudged William with my knee, silencing whatever reply was on the tip of his tongue. To Kye, I said quietly, "He's an arcane familiar."

Usually I didn't like to explain as much to anyone if I could help it. Aside from William being touchy, it brought up a lot of awkward questions. Only sorcerers can create—and therefore own—familiars, which look pretty much like normal animals but often have a bit of magic (and a lot of attitude, in William's case). Technically, a familiar isn't truly alive; it's a spell. I'm no sorcerer, just an alchemist. And I certainly don't own William, as he likes to point out. As far as I can tell, no one does. He'd been with me for years, and never said a word about it. To say this was unusual would be like saying the sea is wet, but William is a loyal and beloved companion, no matter how grouchy he gets, so I never push him on the issue.

Fortunately Kye just nodded again, rather than ask prying questions. "That's alright, then." As he thumbed through his stack of tickets, he asked conversationally, "Here for a bit of sun, are ye?"

I glanced down at William, the shaggy black sheepdog, and then at myself. Underneath my tunic, leggings, and boots, my skin was as brown as ever. Copper, my mother used to call it. I wondered what prompted Kye to think that either William or I needed to work on our tans. Kye himself had gray, leathery skin, and he was so thin I thought he might be some kind of elemental spirit.

"Um, not exactly," I answered at last. "We're headed to the Afolayans' camp. Taiwo said you know where that is? She said you can basically see it from the harbor wall."

At my side, William chuckled. I nudged him, thinking he was laughing about my soon-to-be-married friend Taiwo, who has a tendency to exaggerate. This time he nudged back.

"You, and dozens like you," said Kye kindly. He handed over two tickets printed on blue water-proof paper and asked me for the fare. As I fished in my hidden coin purse for the correct change, he added, "Don't ye worry. I've added the camp to my route, just for the wedding. Folks've been coming in all week. It'll be our first stop."

I handed Kye my money, thanked him, and shuffled William and our luggage onto the dock. A short walk down the weathered planks took us to the gangplank for the waiting ferry, a boat named *Expedition*. I grinned as I looked over its white trim and blue paneling, thinking of the secrets this seemingly innocuous boat might hold.

"He's blind," William said, pushing past me to claim a spot along the railing of the front deck.

"Excuse me?" I followed, adding, "Hey, if you think you're going to get seasick, you might want to sit in the cabin."

"I'll be fine. It's just the transition I don't like. The *ferry captain*," William said, switching topics seamlessly and speaking as though I was about as quick as a snail. "He's blind."

"Oh. *Oh.*" I glanced back over my shoulder toward the shore, sighing as I rued my comment about "seeing" the camp. "You know I'm slow to pick up on those things whenever we're near the coast. I swear, it's like the light off the water scrambles my brain or something."

William chuckled again. "Sure, blame it on the light on the water or whatever. Even though that doesn't make sense, since you grew up on an *island*. If you ask me, it's because of the wedding."

"It is not," I protested.

"You've been distracted ever since we left Belville."

"I have not!"

"It's because you spend too much time in your lab with your plants and you're scared of *loooove*," William continued, tail wagging, drawing out the word "love" as though he was a child in grade school.

"I am not," I insisted, feeling more and more like a broken record by the second.

"If you say so." William shook his fluffy ears. "It's a good thing Officer Thorn isn't here to ask you to investigate anything, because a criminal could probably walk right past you and you'd be too busy complaining about 'light on the water' to notice."

"Alright, that's enough," I reprimanded him, looking nervously around at our fellow passengers to make sure they hadn't heard the bits about "criminal" or "officer." Officer Thorn was a dear friend, of course, and I'd been happy to help her in the past, but the last thing I wanted was for anything to go wrong for Taiwo.

As though he could hear my thoughts, William snorted. "You better hope nothing comes up at the wedding."

"Nothing will," I said, swatting his head playfully for having tempted ill fortune. "Besides, we're not here for trouble. We're just here to support our friends."

* * *

In Beyond, a lot of things aren't what they seem. It's basically the Golden Rule of the land—right up there with *always be kind to animals* and *if two bad things happen, expect a third.* No one knows why, exactly, not even the philosophers at the great universities. But it's a rule that seems to go hand in hand with the fact that old legends and fairy tales are known to repeat themselves—with unpredictable twists and turns.

William and I had learned that last autumn with a strange, beauty-and-the-beast-like encounter. And then over the winter at the local mine, Snow White's companions had turned deadly. Honestly, I was looking forward to a break from Belville. For being such a cute alpine town, it did attract a lot of mystery.

The *Expedition* had its own mysteries too, of course. But I'd expected those, so that was just fine by me.

Maybe, said a small, unbidden voice in my mind, one which sounded an awful lot like my mother, *that's your trouble with love—it's so often unexpected.* But I pushed the thought away; I was done with philosophizing for the day.

Behind us, Kye took the helm, and the ferry began to move. We glided easily through the calm waters of the harbor, passing numerous other boats—fishing boats, tour boats, even some traveling boats from distant lands. Some had sails, some were fitted with magitech engines; some even had oars. I wondered briefly what was making Kye's boat run. *Perhaps,* I thought, *he has an even more elemental connection to his job than I thought.*

My suspicions were proved correct as we exited the harbor gate. Once the rocks of the breakwater were behind us, the boat's prow began to tip down.

"Keep an eye out for the camp," I told William, as the water began to rush around us. I knew this was his least favorite part. "First one to see it gets the bigger slice of wedding cake!"

William grunted at me like I was the epitome of uncool.

I, meanwhile, grinned like a kid at a carnival as the waves continued rushing up, and up, until they closed above our heads.

I *love* that part of mer-travel.

When you get a captain who can do it well, that is.

The ferry which had seemed almost boring at the dock now soared along the sea floor, a submarine. The water formed a protective wall all around us, as though we were encased in a bubble. I forgot my contest with William immediately. Instead, my eyes were glued to the sands and kelp forests around us. A sea lion twisted past. A few manta rays glided overhead. The air was damp and salty, but the sunlight filtering through the waves was warming in a way that somehow it never was on shore. It was like the sun was gently hugging my shoulders.

"I saw it," William said. "Just so you know."

I laughed as I turned to look in the direction his snout pointed, just over the bow. Taiwo had been right: the camp was unmissable. It rose up from the ocean beds in a graceful, rounded shape, the walls and arches of the buildings glittering like jewels. Most of the communities of merfolk I've met are nomadic, but they know how to travel in style. Whenever they set up in a new place, they work together to create elaborate camps—sometimes even encasing them in air bubbles, as this one had been. Then, when it came time to move, the entire camp would be dismantled and returned to the sea floor in a matter of hours.

"It's beautiful," I said.

"Sure." William snorted. "You'd never know Taiwo's family is a big deal among the Clan of Yemoja."

This time I really did swat him. Though Taiwo's mother,

Jeannie, was the leader of their clan, they didn't care for ceremony or special treatment. "You keep your sarcasm to yourself, mister. The point here isn't politics, it's the wedding. If the number of exclamation points in Taiwo's letter were anything to judge by, they're absolutely over the moon about it."

"I know, I know." William grinned up at me, his tail thumping against the deck as the boat slowed. "I've never actually been to a merfolk camp before."

"I've never been to one as grand as this. It looks like they've even put an air bubble around the whole thing, probably to accommodate all the wedding guests. So you won't have to swim all the time. I'm sure they built in all kinds of pathways and cool rooms to explore, too. And just wait til you see the fish. Look, there's Taiwo at the dock!"

A small crowd gathered as the boat's prow poked into the air bubble around the merfolk camp, just far enough that passengers could disembark (or embark) before the boat sailed away to its next destination. I leapt over the railing and raced along the dock to give my friend a huge hug.

"Taiwo, I'm so happy for you," I said as I stepped back, grinning.

"Red, you are welcome and among friends," Taiwo greeted me with traditional words and a smile as big as my own before turning to William. "And William, you are welcome to enter our home. I'm so glad you two made it!"

"Yeah, well. Red tried to kill me on the way here," William mumbled, looking around at the gigantic bubble and gleaming buildings behind us.

Taiwo turned to me with wide eyes. A genderfluid merperson of the Yemoja Clan, Taiwo was taller than my five foot nine, with smooth black skin and long, beaded braids. When standing on dry land, as we were now, they sported a pair of legs covered in deep blue and purple scales, which peeked out from beneath their draping skirt. Their eyes, the same blue-purple and unusually large to accommodate watery light, never ceased to amaze me.

"He's kidding," I assured my friend. "It's his defense mechanism. Just ignore him. Tell us everything about the wedding!"

Taiwo laughed, a rounded, bubbly sound. "Oh, I will, don't worry. Come with me, I'll show you your rooms. Have you met Rei yet? No, of course you haven't. We'll go just as soon as you've set down your bag. Mother's looking forward to seeing you again too, Red. Everything's absolutely perfect so far. We're going to have such a lovely time!"

2

Something Borrowed, Something Blue

I first met Taiwo years ago when I was a traveling alchemist. I was going through a different sea port, Mystic, that summer when Taiwo and the other members of the Yemoja Clan made camp under the waves nearby. Most of the time, merfolk clans get along just fine with the folks on land; but that summer, Mystic was overrun by bad feelings, not to mention the grossest slime monster I've ever come across. It was actually the cause of the bad feelings, if I'm honest. Anyway, after we managed to get rid of it in what came to be known as "the Slime Monster affair," Taiwo and I became fast friends. We exchanged letters often, and when I set up my shop in Belville, Taiwo sent me rare shells and sea algae as a gift. (Maybe you have to be an alchemist to truly appreciate that.) My family growing up wasn't too different from Taiwo's—large, communal, and endlessly complex. That's probably why Taiwo felt like a younger sibling to me.

After William and I dumped our bags in a lovely room with

smooth shell walls and a window overlooking the sloped sea floor, our tour of the "camp" continued. And so did the nonstop narration. I barely had a moment to change my traveling shoes and shawl for their more respectable counterparts.

"We're lodging most of my guests here, of course," Taiwo explained as they led the way down an open-air hallway between little pods and spires of rooms. "Rei's guests are all staying in guesthouses on the grounds of his estate, or on their own boats. Have you seen the estate? Oh, right, you haven't met him. Well, it's *huge.* Rei's family is *super* important for local tourism or something. Apparently they've been here for generations. I personally can't imagine staying in one place so long, but I told Rei, of all the places to settle, Seaside's pretty nice. At least the waters are clean."

I exchanged an amused glance at William—or rather, I tried to, but I couldn't catch his eye because he was staring at the coral beds between the rooms. Everything beneath the camp's air bubble was dry, of course, but dedicated merfolk watered the corals the way landlubbers might water a garden. *Maybe William's hoping to see the fish I mentioned,* I thought.

"So, you *have* talked about the future with Rei?" I asked Taiwo lightly, making a note to ask about seeing the animal trainers as soon as the wedding fever died down a bit.

"Oh my waves, yes, *mother,*" Taiwo grinned back at me with the kind of exaggerated eye roll that only merfolk can manage. "I don't know why you all think I'm so impulsive. Like I can't be trusted or something."

"Remind me," I asked mildly, "how long have you known Rei?"

"Two seasons exactly on the wedding day," Taiwo said

promptly and without any trace of self-consciousness. When I laughed, they added, "Oh, come on, Red! When you know, you know. You'll know what I'm talking about some day."

"Uh huh."

"Or you won't. Honestly, I think the most impulsive thing you ever did was buy that shop in Belville."

"Well, running a shop is a lot *like* a marria—"

"It's not," said Taiwo breezily.

William shook his ears and decided to chime in. "The way Red does it, it is."

Taiwo tossed their head back and laughed. "I bet! Did she ever tell you that when we were together in Mystic someone asked her about me, like if we were *together* together, and she said—"

"Aren't we supposed to be meeting your mom?" I cut in, glancing around every new rounded corner.

"Yeah, and she loves this story. So, then this person asked *that* question about me, like, my anatomy, and Red was all 'why would I care about that?'"

Taiwo broke off in a fit of giggles. Even William, I was sorry to see, was prancing in his amusement.

"I still don't see why it's funny," I muttered. In my experience, it was relatively common for merfolk to get strange questions about their anatomy—and it was also common for them to be genderfluid, like Taiwo, preferring to use they/them pronouns. I'd always thought it was a neat echo of the fact that merfolk lived dual lives, both walking on land and swimming underwater. It'd never occurred to me to give it much more thought than that.

"That's why we love you, dear. An alchemist looks at the interior lives of things, isn't that so?"

From a large meeting hall to our left, Taiwo's mother, Jeannie, appeared and enveloped me in a warm hug. My embarrassment was somewhat assuaged by her comment about alchemy—and by the realization that I really had missed her. Jeannie's short, curly hair smelled like open ocean breezes, just as it had in Mystic, and her deep brown eyes always seemed to be smiling. Though she was perhaps an inch shorter than Taiwo, she was still a little taller than me, and the silver edging along her deep purple scales gave her an air of dignity.

"And you must be William," Jeannie continued, breaking away from me to kneel in front of my very pleased companion. Her golden robes swished around her and pooled over her knees, which I noticed she balanced on carefully: in the past year, I'd been sending her joint liniments to help with stiffness when she was in bipedal form. She told William, "Taiwo's told me so much about you from Red's letters. We're so pleased she has someone to look after her."

"It's a full-time job," he agreed, tail wagging.

"I seem to remember that we came here for *Taiwo,* not to gossip about me," I complained.

"We can do whatever I want, since it's my wedding," Taiwo proclaimed with a grin. "Mom, are you done talking about the stage? I was going to take Red and William over to see Rei."

"I'll come with you. I need to consult with the Rises, anyway." As we fell into step behind Taiwo, Jeannie took over the job of narrator. "Did Taiwo tell you that we're building a platform to have the wedding at sea level? It took some doing to convince everyone of the right spot, but we've finally got it. And not a moment to spare!"

William shook his ears. "You're building a platform—a

stage—with supports from the sea floor all the way up to the surface? And people are going to stand on it for the ceremony?"

"Or watch from small watercraft nearby, if they like," said Jeannie, amused. Ahead, Taiwo hummed happily. "It's not really as difficult a feat as you might imagine. In the area we've chosen, the water is only thirty feet deep."

I grinned, because I was familiar with merfolk building methods—and with Jeannie in particular, who had basically invented the "can-do" attitude. But William was having none of these reassurances. "How can you build it in time for the wedding? How could you build this *camp* just to use it for a little while?"

"Many hands make light work," Taiwo sang.

Jeannie smiled. "Our family found long ago that we could build twice as fast, and indeed twice as well, if we work with the sea instead of against it. Think of it more like growing than building. Besides, as I'm sure Red explained to you, we merfolk approach weddings a little differently. We like to savor them. After the initial feast tomorrow, there will be a week of festivities before the actual wedding takes place, so we have plenty of time. Why don't you come watch us work when you have a moment?"

"And that reminds me," said Taiwo, skidding to a stop. We'd come full circle and stood once again at the makeshift dock that extended out into the sea around us. "Are you both going to need the charm?"

"William could use some charm," I said, grinning down at him. "But not for underwater breathing. He doesn't actually breathe on account of being a strange magical creature."

"I think you mean *amazing* magical creature," he corrected.

I went on as though I hadn't heard. "And actually, Taiwo, I want to try out something I worked on back at the shop. I have it here." I held out a coiled shell pendant, hanging from a string around my neck. From my bag—because I couldn't go to a fancy estate without *some* conveniences—I pulled a vial of mint-green fluid. "It's an undrowning potion."

"Great," said William. "We come here for a wedding and you're going to celebrate by getting yourself killed?"

"I'm sure it will be alright," said Jeannie, who looked fascinated by the idea. "Taiwo and I will be right here if anything happens."

"I tested it out in my sink," I said, but even as I said it I wasn't so sure that it proved that I wasn't foolhardy. "I just put a drop in the necklace, and then drink the rest, so that it's both inside and outside my body. And then . . ."

I took a deep breath and pulled my goggles over my eyes. Technically they were alchemists' goggles, outfitted with all kinds of fun features like zoom and magic trace sensing, but they'd work just fine in an aquatic situation. Provided I was conscious and could work them. Before I could doubt myself, I walked the length of the dock and dove through the bubble wall into the water.

The feeling was incredible. It was a hundred times better than just swimming. When I swam I was always a little worried about being in, essentially, an alien element. But with my potion, I was completely at home.

Taiwo beamed at me as they joined me in the water, their long blue and purple tail swirling around me. To the side, Jeannie looked on approvingly, her robes floating ethereally in the still current. William's cold nose poked me in the rib and I laughed, then breathed in water once more. It was cool and light and *freeing.*

"Okay then," said Taiwo. Their voice cut through the water in a way that mine never would; no potion could match the way merfolk had adapted to their home. "Last one to Rei's is a rotten egg!"

* * *

"Rei's," it turned out, was nearly as big as Seaside itself. In fact, as we swam up to the massive bluff topped by a mansion that might have made King Midas proud, I half wondered if we'd ever been *off* the estate. The Rise property sported the kinds of manicured gardens, spotless boat docks, and banners floating in the breeze that simply screamed *we have enough money to buy this town ten times over.* The only thing that suggested any limits to the Rises' dominance was a white stucco wall that curved gracefully up from the beach along one side of the hill, disappearing into the distance, marking the line between normal life and the Rises' lush grass or impossibly shimmery sand.

As the merfolk led William and I to a little pier at the bottom edge of the estate, Taiwo turned back to grin at me.

"Yeah, I know," they said, correctly reading my expression of awe. "We're holding the opening feast here tomorrow. It's going to be *amazing.*"

"That's if we can make sure everyone has a place," Jeannie said, sitting on the edge of the pier to shake water off of her scaled legs.

"Mom's just not used to having other people set everything up for her," Taiwo explained to us with a teasing eye roll. "The Rises don't really take the same 'many hands' approach to work that we do. They tend to think more like 'too many cooks in the kitchen.'"

"What they tend toward is despotism," I thought I heard Jeannie say. But her head was down as she fixed her clothing, and she was clearly just muttering to herself.

I probably misheard her, I thought, falling into line behind my friends. As we climbed our way up an exquisite stone path—a path probably made of stone more expensive than anything I had in my shop in Belville—William quizzed Taiwo about the magical spells on the walls and estate grounds. I let my mind wander, knowing that William would tell me everything all over again later, if it was relevant. He liked lecturing about magic.

Thoughts of enthusiastic experts made me think of Luca, and I smiled. He'd offered to write me letters from Belville, and I found I was looking forward to checking in at Seaside's post office to see if any had arrived. Though William and I had stopped by the post office to mail a box, I'd completely forgotten to ask about letters—I was so used to not getting any, it hadn't even crossed my mind, and William had been too grumpy to remind me. *Of course, we've only been gone three days,* I told myself, *and Luca probably hasn't even had time to write. He's very busy, after all.* Luca was Belville's one and only scholar, a position that came with lots of duties and respect—kind of like being a town Witch. He ran the local book store, looked after the town archives, and helped anyone who needed to know something about town history.

He'd definitely have something to say about this place, though, I decided, chuckling to myself. Luca actually had a castle of his own, though it was more of a ruin. He was descended from a family of forest elves who had been cursed and eventually fled

Belville. As the last one left, Luca didn't talk about them much, but William and I had helped him solve a mystery about them the previous fall.

The path leveled out as we reached a broad patio beside the Rises' house, and I tried to focus on the present—not on my absent friend. *Taiwo, wedding,* I reminded myself firmly. *I wonder what Rei is going to be like . . .*

I have to admit, as Taiwo glided past guards down immaculate hallways, some misgivings crept into the back of my mind. I didn't even notice much of the house itself, because I found myself a bit worried about who exactly my friend was marrying. Taiwo loved Rei—that much was clear—but was Rei the sort of person who would be able to look beyond flashy appearances?

And we began climbing the marble staircase of a literal tower, my anxiety levels rose with us.

The spiral staircase deposited us at last onto squeaky clean tile. The room at the top of the tower was airy and bright, with windows forming a circle around the entire wall. Wherever there weren't windows, cushions and velvet curtains piled up against the wall, and bookcases filled with art supplies lined the floor. Between the dark wood shelves and the plush green and gold accessories, the room felt very much like a cozy den. In the middle of it all, a painter's stool sat amongst a little thicket of easels and canvases.

"Oh, Taiwo, love, it's you!" The speaker, a slightly disheveled young man, stood off to one side. He seemed to be struggling with some cushions, which he kicked furtively to one side.

"Rei!" Taiwo descended upon their betrothed with hugs and kisses, and I looked down at William, one eyebrow raised. Sure, I'd heard him call Taiwo 'love,' but still—this version of

Rei did not at all match the picture I'd had in my head.

Once the couple broke apart, Rei smiled at William and me—a bit anxiously, I thought. He was about my height, and he stood with perfect posture as he kept his arm around Taiwo. But his fine clothes were hidden behind a thick canvas apron splattered with paint, and his black hair was just a tiny bit too long, coming down over his ears. His skin was pale and it seemed to me that, as he turned to look up at Taiwo, there was something almost sharp about his face.

That said, his voice as he greeted us was anything but sharp: in fact, his tone was quiet and his words a little rushed, like he was shy or afraid of saying the wrong thing. "Red, William, of course," he said, as Taiwo made introductions. "How wonderful you could make it."

The phrase seemed a little pat to me, but William wagged his tail. "Nice view you have up here."

"Yes, isn't it?" Rei looked around as though he, too, were seeing it for the first time. "I come up here often to paint."

"Often! More like whenever you aren't absolutely needed for wedding business. Or family business," Taiwo said affectionately, ruffling Rei's hair.

"Oh, I'm not needed much for the family business right now, which is probably for the best," Rei protested vaguely. "The start of summer's always reporting season."

"Red was just doing that," William said, looking up at me.

This forced me to take part in the conversation, rather than suspiciously observe. A little embarrassed by my own reticence, I coughed and explained, "I own an alchemical shop in Belville. I just finished up my first year running it, so I actually went up in front of the town council for my official permits before we came. Wanted to make sure everything got done in time," I explained ruefully.

Rei nodded along and, seeing that we had found some common ground, Taiwo stepped over to the windows. "That sounds a lot like how things are done in Seaside, too," Rei said. "With provisional business permits for the first year, and so on. Of course, Rise Enterprises has been around a really long time. But Father always makes his yearly report to the town around this time anyway, and he's always starting up new ventures on the side that need to be approved, too."

"Like what?" I asked, curious.

"Trade, mostly," Rei answered. "Shipping, importing, that kind of thing. They say Seaside's a destination because the Rise family built the port. Recently, Father created a new express line of ships to carry passengers, too, not just cargo."

"Shrewd," William remarked. Then he looked up at me, one ear cocked. "Don't get any ideas. I am not helping you ship stuff all over Beyond. Dealing with your customers in Belville is enough."

I laughed at this, and to my surprise, Rei joined in.

"Oh, speaking of!" Taiwo exclaimed, still peering out the window, down several stories to the garden below. "I see Mom found Mr. Rise and Mara. That's the wedding planner," Taiwo explained for William and me.

"Strange," said Rei. "I thought my mother was spending the afternoon with Mara going over the final guest list."

"Well, anyway, I see them down there now, and they're with Cindy," Taiwo said, and again paused to explain, "Cindy's a friend of mine doing an installation piece for the garden, just for the wedding. I'm going to run down and talk to them, while they're all there. Do you all want to come?"

"I—I'll go in a minute," said Rei, uncertainly. "I just need to—clean up."

"William and I will help," I decided. "We'll meet you down there."

With a cheery wave, Taiwo was already halfway down the stairs.

In the silence, William shook himself and looked around. "Which painting were you working on, anyway?"

"Oh, um, it isn't one of those," Rei said, indicating the easels. "Actually I kind of had to hide it when you came up. But I have to store it properly. And if you two will promise not to tell . . ."

Without waiting for an answer, Rei reached for the canvas I'd seen him hide earlier. As he pulled it up in front of his chest, I saw what it was: a half-finished painting of Taiwo underwater, laughing, with shimmering bubbles among their long braids, and light playing off the scales of their tail.

"It's supposed to be a surprise," Rei said, suddenly bashful. "As a wedding present."

"Wow." I tugged at my ponytail, thinking, *serves me right for suspecting him of some kind of subterfuge. This explains why he seemed so shifty before!* "It's beautiful, Rei."

"I think it really shows the love I feel," he said, brushing aside the compliment to beam at the painting again. "It's love that makes it truly beautiful. That's what I think, at least. I know I—I'm not as outgoing or eloquent as Taiwo, but I feel just as strongly about this—about what we're doing. So I thought a painting would show that."

Rei looked at us, a little breathless, like he was simultaneously surprised to hear himself confess such things and looking for our approval. As one, William and I nodded.

"Good," Rei said, moving to stow his painting properly. "I

hope Taiwo likes it. I—I've been a little on edge, with the wedding, you see."

"Who wouldn't be?" I agreed sympathetically as William and I helped Rei tidy up his paints. "Weddings terrify me. All the details, the emotions—"

"I just meant I'm on edge about *this* wedding, since my family tends to make drama," Rei interrupted, his light brown eyes wide.

"That too," I said. "Aren't all weddings drama?"

Rei looked down at William, then up at me. A little shyly, he chuckled. "They're not supposed to be. They're supposed to be about *love*. I think, Red, that you must be a bit of a pessimist."

3

Something Old, Something New

"I am not a pessimist," I protested to William the next day, for perhaps the third time. "Am I?"

"Eh, I don't know if I'd say 'pessimist,'" he conceded. "But oblivious, yes."

"Hey, what does that mean?" I would have swatted at him if we'd been alone, but unfortunately, we were surrounded by the height of high society.

After a whirlwind of helping Taiwo get all the wedding guests settled at the camp, helping Jeannie deliver messages, and helping Rei soothe his nerves, William and I found ourselves seated and ready for the opening feast to begin. The concept was similar to rehearsal dinners I'd been to before, but in merfolk culture, it was known as the "First Wave Dinner." Apparently, it had been given that name because the night of eating and drinking kicked off a whole tide of wedding festivities, with one week leading up to the wedding itself, and another week of family-oriented celebrations afterward. Jeannie hadn't been kidding when she'd said that merfolk like to savor their weddings.

"Anyway, what you should be upset about is how Taiwo keeps racing us places," William said, without answering my question. "It wasn't fair," he added, as he sat in the extra-wide chair that had been provided for him at a round banquet table boasting real orchids in a room perfumed with the scent of fresh linens and fancy soup. "We didn't know we were going to the far pier this time."

"You're just mad because you're not very aerodynamic in water," I told him before changing the subject. "Can you believe this place?"

It was a classic—and very classy—wedding feast setting. The largest of the Rises' private piers had been converted into a banquet hall, with a graceful tented ceiling rising above us and pillars wrapped with lights and vines marking out the edges of the space. Through huge, crystal clear windows, the sea and the setting sun put on an appropriately lovely display. White linen curtains and tablecloths added a feeling of sophistication. While William and I were mingled in with hundreds of other guests at tables dotting the wide reception hall, Taiwo and Jeannie sat at one long banquet table on a raised dais at one end. With them was Taiwo's brother, Ige, and Rei and his family: Mr. Rise, Mrs. Rise, and Moe, Rei's adopted brother.

I hadn't spoken to the Rises or to Moe yet. But the Rise family in general appeared to be picture-perfect. Mr. Rise, the head of Rise Enterprises, looked exactly like an older, harder, more polished version of Rei in a tuxedo; the only adornment he wore was a tie pin with a jet black stone. By contrast, Rei's mother was all warm tones, her skin ruddy and her tawny hair flashing in the candlelight as she chatted with Moe, who looked exactly like a recalcitrant teen someone had stuffed into a suit. They all appeared to be average humans—but then, humans can hide all kinds of secrets; just look at me, with my Seer heritage.

"I'll believe it when they actually serve us the soup instead of making us smell it," William said, bringing my focus back to our table. "I'm going to starve."

"No, you're not. Can you imagine the coordination it takes to pull something like this off? And this is only the opening party. Oh, shh, something's starting."

All around the hall, voices fell to whispers. The fairy lights above our heads dimmed, leaving only candlelight flickering among flower petals on each table. From each corner of the room, music began, and then grew.

A sylvan quartet formed in the middle of the room, singing a classic love song.

Once the show was done, but before the spell was quite broken, Mr. Rise rose with his wine glass in hand.

"Welcome, everyone," he said, gesturing graciously with his glass. "And thank you for joining me as I celebrate my son's good fortune. To the happy couple!"

Obligingly, the crowd followed suit as Mr. Rise drank. We waited—even William was quiet—expecting more speeches to begin.

"I—I want to—" Mr. Rise paused. Maybe he, too, was overwhelmed by the spectacle of it all?

And then the glass shattered and red wine stained the table cloth as he fell.

I leapt to my feet among the commotion. "What happened? I have to get to Taiwo. Mr. Rise will need—"

"Red," said William, his starry magic wrapping around my arm and holding me in place. "Look."

I turned, frustrated. If Mr. Rise was having some kind of allergic reaction, he was going to need immediate help.

But then I saw what William had seen.

Just behind Mr. Rise, one of the white curtains had fallen across the exquisite cut-glass window. And with rays of the red sun lighting it from behind, the black ink on the perfect curtain was highlighted with a violent aura:

Ill winds blow on the house of Rise
Reynard the traitor now must die.

4

Something Wicked

"**S**it down," William rumbled at me—not quite a growl yet, but it would be the moment things got any worse. As if they could get much worse. "Sit down, Red."

"But Taiwo, and Jeannie—"

"No one's going to let you up there right now. Look."

For the second time, I followed William's direction. Glancing around the elevated table, I saw uniformed attendants—the Rise family employees—swarming the dais. They seemed to be setting up a perimeter, taking up positions at intervals as regular as a picket fence. *Whoa,* I thought. *This doesn't look like it's the first attack on the Rise family.* Every single one of the employees' faces was blank and serious, and they were already turning away anyone who wanted to "help" amid the chaos. A loud young woman with fiery hair was physically escorted away. Clearly, they meant business.

William was right. Numbly, I sat.

"Attention, please," called a voice from the dais. The speaker must have used some kind of charm to amplify their power, because the grand hall went still immediately. "We have all the medical assistance we require. The police are on their way. The one thing we ask all guests to do is remain in their seats until the police have arrived."

"What, just sit here?" I turned to William. Despite the reasonableness of the request, I was already itching to get up again.

"It's not like it'll take the police long to get here," he told me. "This is the fanciest estate in Seaside. I'm sure they've made it so that the police are never more than five minutes from—"

"*Police!*"

I jumped in my chair as the familiar call rang out. It wasn't Officer Thorn from Belville calling, but for an unsettling moment, I wished that it was. I could have used some of her bravado.

Instead, the individual who gave the standard police greeting turned out to be a captain, with two assistants trailing in his wake. He wasn't a massive half-orc like Thorn, but he *was* tall and steady; he seemed to be a coastal elf, with sandy skin and seaweed-green hair. He made his way to the dais with ease.

For a moment the room waited in tense anticipation as the police captain conversed in low tones with first the medical help, which was hidden from view by the banquet table, and then with the person who had told everyone to remain in their seats. I was finding that order harder to follow every second. My leg was jiggling like a leaf in a hurricane.

Finally the captain turned and addressed the crowd. "I want all wedding guests to form neat lines and exit via either side door. On your way out, you'll give your name to one of my assistants." Said assistants scurried to their posts, pens and notepads already in hand. I saw Taiwo speak up urgently from their place at the center of the dais, though I couldn't make out the words. Jeannie leaned in and spoke, too. The police captain cleared his throat. "All wedding guests, stay calm and exit now. Except for one alchemist named Red. Red, come up here, please."

* * *

"Very good. Now. You must know this is very unusual, Red, but the folks here insist that you might be able to help, and we're going to have to interview everyone anyway."

I sat across from the police captain, who'd introduced himself as Officer Ebb, in a cordoned-off corner of the reception hall. The dais was off to our left, and still bustling with strange activity. Out the windows over Officer Ebb's shoulder, the sunset had gone dark.

"I'm happy to help however I can," I insisted, shifting on my chair.

"Not that she actually saw anything," William added. He hadn't been given a chair; in fact, he had not been encouraged to stay, and yet he remained plastered to the floor at my side.

Officer Ebb gave the annoying talking dog a rather rueful look before clearing his throat again. "You're an alchemist?"

"Yes. I have a shop in Belville called Red's Alchemy and Potions." I paused, as Officer Ebb had started to jot the details down. His pen, I noticed, was not standard issue. It had a feathery top and very nice blue ink. I added, "I trained eight years ago in Brass, under the alchemist Paracelsus, if that helps?"

"I'm not doubting your veracity, Red," said the officer, with a telling look at my goggles—seriously, I'm never without them—and the slightly glowy pendant around my neck. "In fact I'm hoping you'll be able to fill in some gaps for me about what happened here."

"She didn't see anything," William insisted protectively.

Officer Ebb sighed and finally addressed him. "Even so, an expert's insight—"

"Don't you have alchemists in Seaside?" William interrupted.

For a moment, Officer Ebb seemed at a loss. I tried to cover my chuckle with my hand, but it didn't work.

"Sorry," I mumbled when they both looked at me. "It's not professional, I know. But Seaside alchemy has a reputation for being—um—more about tourism than about actual science."

For the first time, Officer Ebb actually smiled at me. "Thank you, Red. Very well put. I don't mind telling you that Seaside crime also tends to be more straightforward than poison. Most crimes here are confined to unruly meetings and graffiti—minor offenses. It's been a long time since we dealt with crimes of hate."

"Are you sure he was poisoned?" I wavered, but couldn't keep the rest of my questions in. "And you really think it was a hate crime? Why? Isn't the Rise family super influential around here?"

"Valid questions all, and we'll get to them in time, no doubt," said Officer Ebb. "But the—let's just say *spectacular*—nature of this crime has put the idea into everyone's heads. Not to mention certain old rumors and prejudices—but you wouldn't know about those, would you? Well, don't worry about it right now.

"Let's start with the facts," he continued. "How would you describe the events of the evening? The ones you could see," he added, cutting off William's protest.

"Everything seemed completely normal until Mr. Rise gave the toast," I said, shrugging. "William and I didn't have the best seats in the room, but we could see him stand up, start his speech, take a drink—and then he almost started talking again, but before he could say more than a few words, he started choking and he dropped his glass. Then he fell down behind the table, so I can't say anything more."

This all seemed useless to me, but Officer Ebb was busily writing it down. "And off the top of your head, can you name any poisons that might produce those effects?"

"Well—" I hesitated. "Jeannie and Taiwo might have . . . oversold my abilities. I don't actually specialize in poisons. I don't even work with them, usually. But I know the basic stuff any botanist or scientist might know."

"Such as?"

I bit my lip. "Well, there's cyanide or botulinum. Those are really common—I'm sure you know about them. They'd both work pretty fast like that. But cyanide has a distinctive smell. Given that we're by the sea, I'd also think about venom from a blue-ringed octopus—or devil's rope kelp or puffer fish— those are more specialized, and probably very expensive, but theoretically they'd be available around Seaside. Venom seems most likely because it's fast-acting and it's usually a liquid, but puffer fish—no, sorry, devil's rope—would be viable in a powdered form if I remember right."

"Good, good," said Ebb. "Anything else?"

"I suppose if it was a really fancy poison, it could be siren tears or something similar."

"And by fancy, you mean—?"

"*Really* expensive. And rare. Somebody would probably

have to make that in-house, otherwise it'd be really easy to trace who sold it to them."

Officer Ebb cocked his head at me. "I can certainly see why Jeannie recommended you."

Instantly, my brain switched out of "alchemist" mode. "How is she? Can I see them?"

"In just a minute," Officer Ebb promised. "Now, in looking over my notes, I get the impression that you think we could be looking for anyone with a marine connection, am I right?"

"Well—I don't know that I'd say it like *that* exactly—anyone determined enough could get hold of those venoms," I said. "And I don't have any idea how they got them to Mr. Rise, or why."

"Are you sure about that?" Officer Ebb eyed me speculatively. "Could any of these last for a long time in open air, for example?"

"You mean like if someone put them in the glass even before the party?" I paused, thinking it over. "I'm pretty sure the octopus venom is literally blue, or at least has a bluish tint, so someone would notice it. As for the others, I'm not sure. I don't want to mislead you here—I'm really not an expert."

"No," said Officer Ebb, "I can see that. You're a generalist, Red, which is even more useful at a time like this. How about putting any of these in the wine? What kind of dosages are we talking about?"

"Umm—it'd have to be a pretty big amount of any of them, given how fast it happened. Except the devil's rope," I added suddenly. "I remember that from an old book I have at home. 'Play jumping games with devil's rope, and before you land there'll be no hope.'"

Officer Ebb's pen paused. "That paints quite the scene. And

it's well-known, would you say?"

"I've heard it." William surprised us both when he spoke. "I used to hear it sometimes on the streets around Rote University. It's part of a song."

"And do you remember the song?" asked Ebb.

William looked like he might protest—probably he would refuse to sing—so I nudged him.

"Okay, fine," he huffed. "But I only really remember the chorus." After a moment, he began:

Devil's rope and devil's moss,
Just one touch and it's angels' loss,
Devil's rope and devil's club,
Two doses and it's looking up.
Who could all these devils be
Setting such ill fortune free.

"And that's all?" Officer Ebb scrawled over his notepad in an effort to get it all down.

"That's all," said William. "Never heard it anywhere else."

"Well." Officer Ebb snapped his notebook shut and looked up. "I certainly am glad I spoke to you two. We'll tell everyone this, but don't plan on leaving soon, okay?"

"Of course. Can I—"

"They're in the gazebo between here and the main house," said Ebb, kindly.

The gazebo, it turned out, was large enough to serve as a cabin—or would have been, if it had had walls; instead, ornately carved wooden pillars supported a tile roof. It was tucked neatly on a little cliff below the bluff that supported the main house. A carefully paved path lit with magic torches led the way straight to it. In about two seconds, I was at Taiwo's side. Along with Jeannie, Rei, and Ige, they formed a small, sad outpost overlooking the pier.

"Oh, Red," said Taiwo, immediately enveloping me in a hug.

"Who do they think did it?" asked Ige, Taiwo's little brother. His dark skin and dark blue scales blended into the night, but he made his presence known at once. In fact, I thought his manner rather abrupt for someone who hadn't spoken to me at all in years. But, he had just seen someone die. I shivered, and let it slide.

"We don't know that yet," Jeannie reprimanded her son. "Hush. This is a time to be together."

"You *will* stay, won't you, Red?" Taiwo asked breathlessly. Their face on my shoulder was hot and wet: they'd been crying. "You have to stay. We need your help. Rei has to look after his mother, and—and—"

"We're worried," Rei told me quietly. "If this really is some kind of hate crime like Officer Ebb says, then anyone in either one of our families could be next."

I looked between the two of them—Taiwo, my dear friend, and Rei, the forlorn painter. "I don't know much about Seaside, or about whatever history led to Officer Ebb's idea. But of course I'll help you both find answers. No matter how scary everything seems now, we'll get it all cleared up, don't worry."

5

Moonlit Blues

"Y ou can't actually promise that," Ige was quick to point out.

Taiwo glared at their brother. Rei opened his mouth like he might respond, but instead he just said, "I have to go up and check on my mother in the house. Why don't you all come, and stay with us this evening?"

"Of course," said Taiwo.

"No thanks," said Ige.

William and I did our best to blend in with the wooden supports of the gazebo.

Taiwo rounded on their brother. "We have to stay together, like Mom said."

"Sure," scoffed Ige. "Together with our *own* people. *These* people will probably stab you in the back."

"Don't be dramatic. You know everyone was searched on their way in," Taiwo retorted.

"Everyone except the Rises," Ige said, with a nasty look toward Rei. "Besides, there's lots of ways to hide weapons."

"Not *that* well," Taiwo said, exasperated. "You're just being ridiculous!"

"Not as ridiculous as you." Ige started walking off, muttering about money buying all sorts of things. His stride rolled like storm waves on deep blue scaled legs.

Taiwo turned first to Jeannie, then to Rei, fit to burst. Jeannie looked after her son, troubled.

Rei just mumbled, "I have to go to the house." He lingered for a moment, but finally walked off in the opposite direction.

"*Gah,*" said Taiwo.

"His father just passed," Jeannie said quietly, presumably meaning Rei. "Be patient."

"*You*'re coming at least, right, Red?" Taiwo asked, and without waiting for an answer, they rushed off after Rei.

Jeannie, William, and I were the last ones standing. We looked uneasily at each other.

With a sigh, Jeannie said, "I'm afraid Ige has always had a little . . . jealousy when it comes to Taiwo. I try to counsel him through it, but there's only so much a mother can do. I'll go after him and speak to him about his behavior. Red, William, you *will* stay with Taiwo, won't you?"

"Of course," I repeated. I wanted to offer more, but was at a loss as to what.

Jeannie nodded absently, her eyes drifting to the sea. "I'm glad you have agreed to help, Red. There is too much at stake."

Like Taiwo and Rei's lives together. Struck by uncertainty, I shuffled in my party clothes. "Jeannie, listen, of course I will, but I'm really not sure how much—"

"I trust you," she said, returning her gaze to mine and laying her hand on my shoulder briefly. Like most merfolk, she was incredibly warm.

Jeannie strode off after Ige. William whined as we were left alone. "Jeez, Red, what did you do last time that these people found so inspiring?"

"Nothing, really. It wasn't just me; it was all of us." I flailed, helpless to explain the sordid details. "I think honestly they were just glad I didn't run away when I could have. And Jeannie knows my mom somehow, both moms actually. I've never been able to figure out how, exactly, but I think they're all friends."

"Hmph. So these merfolk you met once years ago get to meet your family, but I don't?"

"That's really not our biggest problem right now," I reminded him wearily. "Come on, let's go catch up with Taiwo and Rei."

"If the guards at the house even let us in," William chipped in cheerfully.

Side by side, we climbed the stone steps that led up the bluff to the Rise family's meticulously manicured garden and enormous house. The walk wasn't an easy one, and I didn't envy all the caterers and event staff who'd had to cart everything down the hill to the dining hall . . . only to have to cart it all back up again.

We'd been in Seaside for just over a day, and my mind was already a complete mess. Not that I was feeling sorry for myself, exactly—but I had a lot of misgivings about getting involved in family affairs. Whether the Rises', or Taiwo's, both made me uneasy. And the idea of a hate crime just made everything worse. This was supposed to be a celebration of *love*, for goddesses' sake.

And William being snitty about *my* family on top of everything else was just gravy. It's not that I don't like my family— far from it. But they live on a literal desert island. There's not a lot of need for alchemy there. And there's not a lot of interest in it, either. My 'family' is actually a special clan of Seers—the kind of folks who can peer into the mystic mysteries of the universe, and whatnot. I don't have that gift, myself. That's probably why I've always preferred science. But I do love my mothers, and I felt a strong affinity for Jeannie. I knew, in my heart, that I would take on this case and try to help Taiwo's family in any way I could.

It's just that that *any way* part was ringing ominously in my brain as we scaled the darkened cliffs above the sea.

* * *

William had just been being snarky about guards at the house, but he turned out to be prescient. We had to explain ourselves no less than three times to a burly lady posted at the Rise's back door.

Of course it goes without saying that the Rise's back door was far grander than most *front* doors back home in Belville.

Tower aside, the Rise house must have been four stories tall, all shingled roofs and peaks and large windows that gleamed darkly in the night. Thanks to my own hesitation and William grilling me about Jeannie, by the time we made it to the back patio, Taiwo and Rei were nowhere in sight.

Well, I can understand why they wouldn't want to linger, I thought as the guard finally let us in. *Still, it would have been nice if Rei could have told his staff to expect—*

My internal gripes were cut short by wonder. The Rises' back door let into an enclosed porch which ran the length of the house, and from there into a large library, and from *there* into a brightly lit hallway which bordered a courtyard.

It turned out that one of the reasons the house seemed so massive from the outside was that, inside, it had a full garden with no less than *three* fish ponds and a living tree three stories tall. *How did we miss all this when we came with Taiwo yesterday? I mused. Oh, yeah. I was super worried about who exactly the Rises would turn out to be.*

"Where'd that lady say to go, again?" I mumbled to William.

"Just follow the sounds of bickering," he said, moving confidently toward the northern corner of the house.

"William, that's incredibly insensit—"

I shut my mouth abruptly as William stopped in front of an open door, and I collided with his furry shoulder. Whatever conversation William had overheard came to an abrupt stop as everyone in the room stared at us.

"Red, you found us," Taiwo said gratefully. I stepped over the threshold, glad for the welcome instead of an awkward reprimand about running in the hallway. Or saying rude things about a grieving family.

William's eavesdropping had got us to a comfortable, richly furnished room, the kind of place that might be called a "study." There certainly weren't the textbooks or lab equipment that might litter a study if *I* had one, but there were little tables with curiosities scattered among plush armchairs, a desk in one corner, and a fireplace crackling merrily along the outer wall.

Taiwo smiled from the middle of the room, as though on a stage. I couldn't help smiling back: Taiwo often did command the attention of everyone nearby. I could understand why Ige would be jealous.

Behind Taiwo, Rei and his brother—Moe—and a stranger, a gnome, stood clustered around Mrs. Rise, who reclined in a deep blue rocker.

"Hello," I said cautiously, not wanting to intrude—even though we *had* been invited. "I'm Red, and this is William. We're happy to help however we can."

"Red. We were just hearing about you." The gnome stepped away from Mrs. Rise to offer his hand, which I shook. This was slightly awkward, because he was about half my height. But from his business suit and shiny shoes, it was clear that he liked things done a certain way. "My name's Al Litely. You can call me Uncle, everyone else here does. Long time friend of the family. Kade is—Kade *was*—my business partner. I worked with him as an advisor for Rise Enterprises."

Behind Al, Mrs. Rise stifled a sob.

Moe greeted William and me with narrowed eyes. "Weren't the police talking to you?"

"Red is helping them too," Taiwo said at once. "She's a really clever alchemist. And she's basically family. Right, Rei?"

"Um," Rei mumbled.

Beside me, William sneezed.

I waved off the snub. The more I saw of Rei, the less backbone he seemed to have. *Again, family tragedy,* I reminded myself. *The poor kid's probably reeling.* In truth Rei and Taiwo were probably only five years younger than my thirty-ish, but I couldn't help thinking of everyone in this situation as young.

Including Mrs. Rise. When she wiped at her eyes and spoke, her voice warbled with emotion that made my heart melt. "A pleasure to meet you, Red. I'm sorry—I'm sorry that—"

"Please don't be sorry, Mrs. Rise," I assured her. "*We're* the ones who are sorry to intrude at a time like this."

"Oh, don't call me that. I insist you call me Lacey," she replied automatically, waving one pale, shaky hand. "And please, do stay."

"Okay. In that case . . ." I cast my eye around the room and spied a tea service table tucked beside the fireplace. "Can I get anyone some tea?"

Taiwo responded affirmatively, and the Rises mumbled acquiescences that echoed their mother's. While I busied myself with the tea strainer and cups, Al—I was *not* going to be able to think of him as "uncle;" he reminded me too much of a posh version of my friend Dusty back home—Al drifted to one corner of the room, speaking lowly into a magitech communication device as big as his palm.

But if he thought he could go unnoticed so easily, he had another think coming. I handed the tea around and ended with him in the corner, and after I gave him his cup, I didn't move. I'd promised Rei and Taiwo we'd figure this out, after all, and that meant I needed more information. Since the others were tending Lacey, that left Al for me.

He noticed my intent and politely stowed his comm device. I got straight to the point. "Rei and Officer Ebb seemed particularly concerned about a hate crime, but I don't quite understand why? Does it have something to do with that message about 'Reynard'?"

"Ah, the price of being new here," Al observed, thinking over my questions before he answered. Something in his manner suggested that under normal circumstances, he would be jovial and kind. But of course, the tragedy had taken its toll. With his voice lowered so only I could hear, he explained seriously, "I can't say for sure, of course. But the reference to Reynard is about an old prophecy in town. Nothing that was ever confirmed to be about Kade himself, you understand. But Officer Ebb is an old timer, like me. Together with Kade, we've lived here in town all our lives. Of course, over all that time, certain problems come up."

I didn't necessarily agree that time must bring problems, but I bit my lip and waited for him to go on. *Maybe he means business problems,* I thought. *He was Kade's business partner, after all. What if something went wrong between the two of them? Also, what kind of town has an ominous prophecy in its history??*

"I s'pose I should say, where Kade is concerned, problems were bound to come up," Al added with a sigh. He seemed genuinely sad as he went on, "Don't get me wrong, Red. He was my best friend. But that means I was one of the ones who knew him best. Rise Enterprises has a long history in this town of peaceful development. That wasn't the problem. But Kade himself, well, that was another story. He was brilliant at leading the business. Brilliant. Knew every detail. But he wasn't afraid of disturbing the peace. He used to tell me after every meeting that you can't make an omelet without breaking eggs."

"But how does that come back to the prophecy, or hate?" I asked, confused.

"It was more of a vicious rumor, if you ask me," Al said, with an undertone of vehemence. "It was a long time ago. There was a deal gone wrong, or something. I never knew the details of it. It started with the local Witch. Well, she *used* to be the local Witch, but she's in exile now. Before she left, she made a big talk about a curse on the town. Went on and on about Reynard."

Okay, so maybe "Reynard" was a sort of code name for someone, I thought. Hearing the name aloud rang a bell in my mind, and I realized why it sounded familiar. "Like foxkin?" I knew the name from my travels as a common title taken by foxkin—

that is, people with foxlike qualities, usually foxy ears or even a tail. There are all kinds of -kin in Beyond; for example, my neighbor in Belville, Gloria, is phoenixkin. There's nothing at all wrong with being -kin normally—it's usually the result of some magic, and as such, families consider it a blessing and honor their heritage, whatever it may be. But "Reynard" was often an outlaw or brigand's title, a sort of Robin Hood-meets-fox character. The name did have a certain unlawful reputation.

Al nodded, then sipped at his tea. "Most of 'em are just fine, I imagine. Foxkin, I mean. But this Witch, she talked about how someone with fox in their blood would be the destruction of the town. This was years ago. Ever since then, anyone who so much as whispers 'Reynard' or 'fox' still gets looked at crossways by most locals. It isn't—it wasn't—Kade. He was as human as you. But still, some people *thought* it was him. People who were jealous took it as an excuse to hate. It'd surface every few years, usually when Rise Enterprises made some new big move. Just a reaction more than anything else. But now, with the wedding—"

"Hum," I murmured, trying to think it through. *If the prophecy wasn't about Kade, though, that must mean someone else is in danger—or there's an extra criminal loose. Or it's all just a cover.* I decided to stick with Al's view of the situation for now. "So someone could have been out for Mr. Rise because they thought he was going to bring destruction to Seaside, because of his supposed heritage and what the prophecy said."

"But it was all just rumors, if you ask me," Al repeated. "Horrible reason for someone to die."

I ran my fingers through my hair. "It's unpleasant, but it's a little better than the alternative."

"What—oh," Al said, shifting to look up at me, "you thought it was something to do with the wedding itself? That someone was upset about the Rise heir marrying merfolk?"

"Something like that," I admitted, not saying that it could just as easily have gone the other way around.

Al looked across the room at Taiwo and Rei. "I don't think we have to worry about that, Red," he said. "At least, I hope we don't. Only guests could have got in tonight, and all the wedding guests ought to know how much Rei and Taiwo love each other. Who could stand in the way of that? Besides, there's never been any problem in Seaside with merfolk before."

Before I could observe—perhaps pessimistically—that someone *had* gotten in the way of the wedding, or at least of the opening feast, the device in Al's hand lit up. "A call," he told me, waving it so I could see. "It could be Ebb. Excuse me a moment."

I did so, drifting back toward the main group as Al took his call in the corner.

"We'll make it right, Lacey, you'll see," Taiwo was saying. The group remained clustered around the armchair where the widow slumped, clearly heartbroken. She'd forgotten all about her tea.

"But *how?*" asked Moe. Like Ige, he sounded querulous—but also incredibly weary. "How do you propose to do that, without suspecting all our newfound family *friends?*"

So Moe has realized the same thing Al said, that the culprit must have been a guest, I thought, coming quietly to stand by William. I wondered about Moe. Where Ige had been outraged, Moe sounded more bitter. *Something about the emphasis on 'friends' was off,* I decided. *What is he trying to say?*

I looked down at Lacey, but she said nothing. Perhaps she was thinking similar thoughts as her adopted son. It occurred to me that in everything I'd heard about Kade Rise, everyone said he'd been an excellent businessman. No one had said he was a particularly jovial host, or even a loving father, or anything remotely kind.

6

Howl at the Moon

"Alright." It was Al who broke the silence, coming back to join the group. He spoke with compassion and authority. "That was Ebb. Some of us are going to need to get down to the doctor's office where they're doing their tests."

Glances darted around the room as everyone understood what *tests* meant. The police were examining Mr. Rise's body, and they wanted the family to be on hand to approve the process.

"I'm not going," Lacey declared. Her grip on her teacup was bone-white.

Rei and Moe looked at each other until at last Rei said, "I'm oldest. I'll go."

"I'll go with you, if you like," Al said kindly, as Taiwo leapt up and clearly planned to do the same.

Lacey's gaze locked with mine. "Won't you stay, Red, William? You can distract us."

I wavered, but only for a moment. Sure, my primary concern was Taiwo, but I had every faith that they would be safe with the police and Rei; and besides, Jeannie had wanted me on hand not just to add protection, but to help. And this was a chance to learn more. When I glanced over at Taiwo, they smiled and nodded encouragingly. I reflected that nod back to Lacey.

"Moe," said Lacey after Taiwo, Rei, and Al had left the room, "there must be so much food left over, and Red and William must be very hungry. Would you go get them something, please?"

Moe shuffled. He hadn't yet moved from behind his mother's chair. "Couldn't you just ring for it?"

"Moe," his mother repeated quietly, "you know what an uproar the house is in. Please, just get it."

Obediently, the boy shuffled off. Something caught my eye as I watched him—in the firelight, his skin seemed almost to shimmer with a rainbow tint.

As soon as we were alone, Lacey cleared her throat. I took a seat next to her, understanding her intention. In some ways she reminded me of Jeannie; I could see how Rei and Taiwo might have things in common, with mothers so similar. But where Jeannie was soft and flowing, Lacey was intense. *But that is probably the grief,* I thought, remembering how warm she'd seemed when talking to Moe before the feast.

"Red," she began, her voice still emotional but quite firm, "I need you to stay until the others get back. We need the company."

"Sure," I said.

"You don't mind staying—despite any difficulties—perhaps very late into the night?"

"No, not at all. We only came for the wedding; it's not like we have anything else to do. And we'd planned to be here at least a week, for all the . . . festivities."

"Good." Lacey sighed, rocking slightly in her chair. "You must understand. I couldn't go see him—not like that. I couldn't even be waiting outside while they did those things. That isn't how I want to remember him. And I fear it would turn me . . . into something I don't want to be."

"That's understandable," I said, and I meant it. "Grief works in strange ways."

"Yes." Lacey's hazel eyes searched mine. Up close, I could see how reddened her eyes were, and how lined her cheeks had become. Auburn hair tumbled from her fancy updo in chunks and streaks. Her blue dress was rumpled and even torn along the sleeve, but she didn't seem to have noticed. I got the feeling that in the Rise family, Kade had been the one who really cared about appearances.

Next to me, William sneezed. "At least the magic in the house seems stable."

"You sense magic?" Lacey asked, her gaze flickering down to William.

"Did you sense anything about that curtain message?" I asked him, before I could think better of it.

William gave me plenty of side eye, letting me know he thought my timing was pretty poor. But the question was out there, and Lacey seemed to be interested in it, too. Finally he huffed and said, "Of course. It was thrown up there by a charm. The kind of gimmick kids use to write their names in the air at fairs."

"Huh," I said, thinking. "So it wasn't actually written on the curtain at all?"

"No." William gave me a look like he thought I was asking completely random questions, which, to be fair, I was. But I had a feeling the answers'd come in handy later.

"'Ill winds,'" Lacey murmured sadly. She didn't seem to mind our inconsistent sleuthing. In fact, she asked quietly, "Has anyone told either of you about the prophecy?"

"From the old town Witch?" I asked. "Al mentioned something just now, but he didn't remember the details."

"A Witch made a prophecy about this?" William asked, clearly put out to be the last one to know. "That's why Reynard was in the message?"

Lacey nodded, then shook her head, then set her chin on her hand. "I really don't know, to tell you the truth. Kade always said not to worry about it. But I do know—I always knew—that is, I know the prophecy. I'll tell it to you. I always had a feeling it would come back to—to haunt us," she said, wiping at her eyes again. "I'm sorry."

"We don't have to do this now," I said quickly. William glared at me.

"No, no," Lacey said, waving a hand. "I appreciate what you're trying to do, Red, I do. But it helps me to tell you. You ought to know, if you're going to be helping us. It went like this," she said, and after drawing in a long breath, she recited:

When Reynard rules Seaside
And none know his name,
And speaking the truth
Can only bring shame,
Then shall come the undrowned tide
To sweep away sickness and blame.

William whined. "That sounds a lot like a curse. You said the Witch who said it is gone?"

"She left a long time ago," Lacey said vaguely. "She renounced us, the whole town. But I'm certain she's still alive."

I thought. To up and leave an entire town—to leave an important post like being town Witch—sounded pretty drastic to me. *She must have had a reason for it,* I thought, and because I had weddings on the brain, I wondered, *Maybe it had to do with love? Al said it was a deal gone wrong, but he also said he didn't recall the details.*

I glanced at Lacey again as she continued talking to William. In the last big case William and I had helped with, the murder of several dwarves in a mining team, the murderer had turned out to be a friend. Someone so close that I had never really suspected them at all. I wouldn't make that mistake again.

Drastic moves like that are usually made by close loved ones, I thought. *And that includes murder.*

Lacey looked up and must have seen the troubled look on my face. "I hope I haven't frightened you, Red?"

"Oh—no, that's not it," I assured her. *I'm not scared of Witches, I'm scared that we may end up investigating those closest to you—and to Rei and Taiwo.* I bit back the thought, which was followed closely by another: *love and weddings bring drama, indeed!*

"Well, whatever it is, you're sensible, Red. Let your sense overcome your worries or feelings of propriety. There's no need for that anyway," Lacey said softly. A scuffle from the doorway announced Moe's return. Behind him came several waiters bearing trays of exquisitely chopped salads, aromatic noodles, and creamy soup.

William and I drew to one side of the fire as we ate. Moe didn't seem too chatty, and I couldn't blame him.

William, meanwhile, was full of opinions.

"Pasta," he grumbled so that only I could hear. "Why is every fancy dinner *pasta?* It doesn't have a flavor."

"You don't have to eat it," I reminded him quietly. "Hey, what did you make of Lacey's talk just now? About the prophecy, and propriety?"

"Nothing much to say about the prophecy until we know more about the Witch. As for Lacey not caring about propriety, that's not too surprising," William said after a particularly noisy slurp of soup. "Seeing as she's a werewolf."

"Excuse me?"

"It's all over her. Did you notice her amulet? No, of course not. Well, *I*, as a magical being, can sense these things. But still, didn't you wonder why she's so insistent about overnight company? And you could have picked up on her comment about 'turning.'"

"I just thought she meant—you know—when we get riled up, we do things we don't mean," I explained lamely. I knew other werewolves, of course—the baker back in Belville was one, and we'd met many on our travels. But most werewolves can pass very easily for "normal" humans. They might have extra thick hair or wolf-like coloring, but these days there are plenty of spells and conveniences that help them control the magic that makes them turn into wolves. For the most part, the days of werewolves running amok under full moons were over. But I could see how strong emotion might make Lacey feel like she was losing control of herself.

And furthermore, that was twice in two days William had got the jump on me. Normally I didn't mind, but seeing as we were now involved in a murder case, I was curious. "How about Moe and Rei?"

"Moe's adopted, remember?" William snuffled shaved radishes and curled beets. "Rei's something else. Must be something from his dad's side. I'm not sure what."

"Foxkin?" I asked in a whisper. When William gave me a bewildered look, I explained, "Al said the town think foxkin have to do with the prophecy. Because of 'Reynard.' And that message tonight . . ."

"I didn't think so," he said thoughtfully. "You're saying you think that message was *about* Rei?"

Fear pricked at my chest. "Shoot. I hadn't gotten that far yet—I was still thinking it might mean Mr. Rise himself. But if it meant Rei, then the family is still in danger."

"We're all in danger until the murderer is caught," William pointed out dryly. "I don't see any reason to jump to conclusions. But I guess I didn't look very close. Things like foxkin heritage can be hidden with glamours and spells, you know."

"I know. To me, they both look like pretty average humans," I said, sighing. "All the Rises do. Except I kind of think Moe glitters."

"Fey spell, probably. Can smell it from here. They aren't average," William said abruptly. "I don't know what Kade was, or what Rei is, or even what's up with Moe. But whatever it is, Red, I don't like it."

7

A Wedding Council

The next morning—that is, the morning after Taiwo's soon-to-be father-in-law was murdered and William declared that the groom and his family were some unidentifiable "magic I don't like"—I was out of bed before the sun had risen. We'd stayed over at the Rises' home with Taiwo. Rei, Taiwo, and Al had returned from the medical examination with very little to say. In fact, the whole evening had been somber. That was understandable, of course, but all that time in such a huge, echo-y house was starting to creep me out.

I did my best to tidy my long black hair underneath the hair scarf I'd donned last night to hide the glittery strands. (Yes, my hair has glittery strands in it—thanks, Seer heritage—and usually I try to keep it under the radar. And yes, I know, I should be the last one to look at Moe's rainbow glow askance!) After scrawling a hasty note to William, I tiptoed out of the guest room we'd slept in and began to search the house.

I actually wasn't searching for anything in particular. If Taiwo or any of the family was up, I wanted to help them, of course. But honestly, what I wanted most was a way *out*. I like my homes cozy and snug, like my little studio apartment in Belville. The mansion's expansiveness felt oppressive. The thing to do, I'd decided, was take a nice walk outside along the bluff. I might even stop by the guest houses that dotted the cliffs like sugar plums on a cake, just to do a little investigating. If I hadn't been in my party clothes still, I would've gone for a run.

Maybe I can even swing by the post office, I thought. *If they'll be open this early. Maybe Luca sent a letter like he promised—or Sir Rowan sent an update about the shop.*

I'd never had a shop before Red's Alchemy and Potions, and I'd never left Red's alone for more than a day. But I'd also never had a true part-time employee. Sir Rowan, who had shown up in town over the winter and decided to stay—in part because he'd happened to fall in love with one of Belville's residents— had worked for me for months now. Technically he wasn't a knight any more, but he was the sort of person who was so excruciatingly proper and respectable that everyone still called him "Sir." He was also an entirely competent potion-maker who probably was having no trouble at all managing the shop, but I still felt anxious about being gone.

More like I feel anxious about being here, I thought wryly as I turned yet another corner and *still* failed to find the house's front entrance. *How can I be lost in a house that is essentially a huge square?*

I did make my way outside, eventually, by asking the way from an anxious, pale porter I passed in the hall. He seemed a little surprised I'd noticed him at all—almost like he felt guilty for taking up too much space, which was odd because he was already short and very thin. When I addressed him by his name, he acted like I'd performed a suspect magic trick. Honestly, "Dale" was written in black and white on his lapel pin, probably as a convenience for the wedding guests. It hardly took much work on my part, yet it seemed like a big deal to him.

I'm glad not to live in a world like this, I thought, as I finally made it out into the fresh air. *So many invisible divisions between people, to the point where just* noticing *someone is considered unusual.*

Still, I did have to admit that as far as gardens and views went, the Rises had it pretty good.

And my mood, buoyed by the early morning light and scents of blooming roses, took another big leap up when I recognized Jeannie striding toward me, making her way up from the estate's front gates.

"I could have come in by sea, of course," she said, after giving me a hug hello, "but I've found that the Rises take their security very seriously. 'Unbreachable walls,' Taiwo tells me, is their ultimate goal. I find a straightforward approach from the direction they're most expecting it ends up working best."

"I believe it," I laughed. "How is everyone back at the camp?"

"As well as can be expected," she answered, though trouble flashed in her eyes. I could only imagine Ige was the source. But I didn't know him well enough to comment, so I let her move smoothly on. "I've come up with some supplies for you, actually. I didn't wish to go so far as to investigate your room—you must have your privacy, after all—but I brought you some of my spare clothes, if you'd like them."

"I definitely would," I said, accepting a small bundle in a waterproof bag. "But you didn't have to worry like that, Jeannie. It's okay if you want to go into my room." Seeing as

I myself had been planning on investigating other guests, it only seemed fair!

But Jeannie just gave me a knowing smile, rather than accepting my offer directly. "You have a kind heart, Red, and you know we all think of you as family. But until things have settled, bear in mind that you must stay safe, too. Be careful who you let too close."

* * *

After Jeannie's enigmatic warning, I didn't have much luck walking by the guest houses. I felt a little too skittish for proper investigating. And breakfast turned out to be *very* hit-or-miss.

William and I sat at one end of the grand dining table. I was wired after my morning activities, while William was snoozing into his oatmeal. The rest of the table could be divided along similar lines. Taiwo, Al, and Lacey were as jittery as I was; Lacey in particular seemed to be on her fifth cup of coffee, if the rings around her abalone mug were anything to go by. Meanwhile Rei and Moe were practically comatose, as though they'd given all their energy to their mother, and Jeannie was contemplative—no doubt reserving her opinions until they were called for.

At the other end of the table sat the most energetic of us all. As soon as everyone was seated—or slumped—and had some sort of food or caffeinated beverage in front of them, the newest member of the party began talking. In fact, she even got up to walk around the table, laying her hands on peoples' shoulders as she passed.

"I see some new faces! I'm Asmund Mara, wedding planner.

Just call me Mara, okay? Now, I know last night was terrible, and while that is still true, we also have some big decisions to make this morning! No doubt you all know that's why you're here."

Mara took her seat again and smiled at us—the kind of smile that didn't reach her eyes, which looked much more hollow than her words let on. After William had trounced me yesterday in the observation department, I was determined to do better. While the two families exchanged glances, I examined Mara closely. Her blonde updo didn't totally conceal the green tint to the ends of her hair, and her silk slacks didn't totally cover a smattering of pale green scales around her ankles. Half merfolk, then. But judging by her pale skin and the freckles peeking through her expertly-applied blush, she came from an entirely different clan from Taiwo and Jeannie. That might matter or it might not. While some clans and some races did have political opinions about one another, most didn't.

I kept looking, noticing the flash of gems on Mara's long fingers and all along her pointy ears. She had expensive taste in jewelry. But then, I suppose in a profession like event planning, your accessories become part of your marketing plan.

Come to think of it, my alchemist's goggles were probably playing the same role.

Lacey broke the silence around the table first. It seemed to me that, as wife of the deceased, that was her right. "I want you to make the right decision for yourselves, Rei, Taiwo. You can go ahead with the wedding—I know how much the date means to you. Do whatever will make you happiest."

Rei stirred. "But—what about the arrangements? For

Father? And what about the—the threat?"

"We can't give into threats," Taiwo declared.

"True, but we must make time for observances," Jeannie reprimanded her child.

"Why shouldn't the young folk do as they please," was Al's opinion. "We'll see to it that everyone's safe!"

"Maybe we'd be safer if we didn't have the wedding at all," huffed Moe.

I pursed my lips. *Moe and Ige really are of one mind, then.*

"Okay, I'm sensing some minor differences," said Mara brightly. She smoothed both hands over the air in front of her, as though ironing out the "difficulties" created by an untimely death. It still seemed to me that she was trying desperately to cover up how she actually felt. I remembered that Taiwo had spotted her the other day with Mr. Rise, and wondered. "We do have the wedding guests to consider as well! A wedding is for everyone, that's what they say. I know a lot of people have come a long way! But of course the most important people are here in this room. I'm sure we can come to an agreement."

"What's she trying to do," William grumbled to me. "Make this easier, or harder?"

"Mara's right," said Taiwo meanwhile. "All our friends have come out—"

"—all *your* friends," Moe muttered.

"—and we have to do *something.* Otherwise what? We send them all home, and try again—when? In months? Years?"

"I suppose we're just supposed to get over Father?" Moe's muttering this time was louder, and edged with pain. I felt for him, but I also couldn't help but wonder if he'd *ever* been on board with the wedding plan.

"Sometimes a celebration is exactly what you need to

remind you life goes on," Lacey told her son.

"Kade would have wanted the wedding to go on," Al added.

Of everyone, Al seemed like the only one willing to identify the dead man by name. Lacey shot him a grateful look, and I was glad she had support.

"We can do both. We can figure it out. After all, the actual wedding isn't supposed to take place for a week," Taiwo said, looking appealingly at Rei.

Rei looked uncomfortable.

Well, his dad *had* just died. I decided to give the kid a break. Clearing my throat, I asked, "Lacey, what kind of observation would you like to hold for Mr. Rise? Is it something that could be incorporated into part of the wedding activities, for example? Or is it something that would need to happen soon?"

Lacey and Jeannie both beamed at me. Funeral practices across Beyond vary widely, from none-at-all to month-long wakes. Given the different cultures at play in the wedding, I liked to think my question was valid.

"Kade," she glanced at Al, almost as though for support, as she said the name, "left instructions. He didn't want anything fancy—that isn't his family's way. And it isn't mine either. There is the business to attend to, of course—but everything else—he preferred a quiet, family matter."

Moe snorted. "Nothing ever stops business."

Ah. Clearly Moe's issues ran deeper than a sudden death and a wedding.

"We do still have a full week before the wedding was originally planned to take place," Mara chipped in, looking as though her smile had been painted on. The fact that she didn't acknowledge that Taiwo had *just* said that made me look at her askance.

"See? We can make it work," Taiwo repeated to Rei. "We can do something this evening. Right, Mrs. Rise?" When Lacey nodded, Taiwo added, "And we can add a tribute into the wedding ceremony, too. And by then, maybe we'll know who was responsible."

Rei's gaze darted between Al, Lacey, and Mara, as though he hoped one of them might make the decision for him.

William huffed, and I did my best to shush him.

"I guess that works," Rei said finally. "I guess—you're right, Taiwo. We can make it work. Right?"

"Of course, dear," said Jeannie gently.

"That's how life goes," Lacey added in agreement. "You have to take charge."

8

A Mountain Chorus

Shortly after the decision was made, the diners abandoned all notion of breakfast. In the awkward small talk and chair-scuffling, I hopped up and drew Taiwo to one side. We slipped out of the room by an exterior door (seriously, where had those been earlier?) and stood in the morning sun. The dining room and its adjacent brick patio was on the southern side of the house, with a wonderful view of the town and just enough of an ocean breeze coming in from the west.

"I just wanted to check on how you're doing," I explained. "And thanks for having your mom bring over spare clothes, by the way."

"Oh, no problem. Yellow looks really cute on you," Taiwo said, with a brief flash of enthusiasm, looking over the loose tunic and pants I'd put on. But that spark gave way to furrowed brows. "I'm so frustrated with Rei. Why can't he just make a decision for once?"

"Well, it *has* been less than twenty-four—"

"I know, I know." Taiwo waved off my rationalization. "But

he's always like this. Normally it's kind of sweet, you know, because he really just wants everyone to be happy, but now's not the time. You know?"

"He made the decision to marry you," said William, who had followed me outside the way a barnacle might follow a hull.

"Yeah, I guess that's true." Taiwo glanced down at William thoughtfully, and then smiled. "I know. I'm just impatient about all of it. It feels like—like people are trying to stop us, you know? And we can't give in to them. I mean, if we did that, then we'd never get married at all!"

"True," I said vaguely. I considered launching into a "potentially waiting a few days isn't waiting forever" sort of speech, but figured that was more Jeannie's job. Besides, Taiwo *did* have a point. "In the meantime, is there anything we can do to help? There must be so many things to do for the wedding, on top of preparing for the funeral."

"There's actually not." Taiwo tilted their head from side to side, soaking in the early summer sun. "Mara and Mr. Rise took care of pretty much everything. They've been working on this for moons now."

William, too, tilted his head. "Isn't it *your* wedding?"

"Yeah, but Rei and I just care about the getting married part, you know? And of course having all our friends and family there. Mara's a genius at parties, apparently. She's worked with the Rises before. And of course Mr. Rise had all sorts of ideas about what a fitting wedding for the future head of the family would be." Taiwo faltered, and then changed the subject with a small shrug. "Of course, Mom has ideas too. I think she's postponed building the stage until this afternoon at least, though."

"You were specifically invited to that," I reminded William

with a nudge and a smile. "Okay, so if we don't have to do any wedding tasks, I'd like to poke around a bit. What are you planning on doing this morning?"

"Honestly, just staying with Rei. And I'm sure—Mom and I will help Lacey with whatever she wants to do."

"In that case, do you mind if William and I run into town? I can count on you to stay safe of your own accord if you're just sticking around here, right?" I asked with a smile.

Taiwo smiled back and rolled their eyes. "Believe me, there's no place in Seaside safer than the Rise compound. It kind of makes you wonder about last night. Oh my waves, did I say that out loud? Sorry, I didn't mean to be morbid. But yeah, you do what you need to do."

"Great. We'll be back for lunch," I promised.

A call from the dining room interrupted Taiwo's reply. With another shrug and a thumbs-up, they disappeared back into the mansion.

"You got all your stuff on you already?" William looked up at me, panting. Seeing that I did, in fact, have my goggles and my nerdy tool belt which served as a purse, he leapt to all fours. "That's us excused from guard duty, eh?"

"Not exactly," I said, grinning as we fell into step. We paced along the length of the house, heading for the main driveway which would take us to the road into town. "I don't know Seaside very well, so there's some things I need to look into if we're going to really be of use to Taiwo and Jeannie."

William snuffled at the hydrangeas at the corner of the house. "Dare I ask what?"

"Well, I really want to know more about that Witch everyone told us about, and the prophecy. And I know I was dismissive of the alchemy in Seaside before, but I want to visit any alchemical or medicinal shops in town just in case. Not to mention get a feel for what other businesses are in town. Oh, and I do want to stop by the post office. That's personal business, though."

I looked down wryly, knowing that William had stopped listening to me as soon as I had mentioned visiting alchemical shops. "Isn't that the police's job?" he asked suspiciously.

"Yes, and I'm sure they're doing it, too. Especially since they know what actually killed Mr. Rise by now, hopefully. But I get the feeling Officer Ebb really only knows as much about the poisons as I told him, whereas *I* might know other things I've forgotten. Things which I might remember if I wander through a shop and see things that spark my memory.

"Besides," I added, lowering my voice, "I think Officer Ebb is really focused on that hate crime idea. Remember how he treated it with so much confidence last night? And I—well, it seems more likely to me that the murderer was someone really close to Kade."

"They say you're more likely to be murdered by someone you know," William mused.

I ruffled his ears playfully as we walked along. "Who says that? The kids singing morbid nursery rhymes at Rote?"

"Probably. There was some weird stuff going on there," William said. Then he shook himself. "But that's not the point. How come you're being so suspicious? You told me yourself we're in town for a happy occasion. That goes for all the other guests and close friends, too."

"I know, but," I paused, unsure how to explain my misgivings. "Obviously *we* wouldn't murder anyone at a wedding, but it's kind of the perfect opportunity, don't you think? Everyone's mingling, and busy, and distracted by the new couple . . ."

"We wouldn't murder anyone at *all*," William corrected me. "And does Luca know you're this weird about weddings?"

"Luca?" My footsteps faltered. "Why would he care? We're talking about Taiwo and Rei. And Mr. Rise. What we need to do is focus on them and their relationships."

William snorted. "You're lucky Officer Thorn isn't here to see what a busybody you've become."

"I didn't become one," I replied airily. "Jeannie *asked* me to be one. It's different."

"Sure," William rumbled. "Like the time someone asked you to find some books, or some ancient apple tree . . ."

"You like Sir Rowan," I reminded William lightly. I knew full well that he was referring to our two recent run-ins with murder, one involving my friend Luca, and the other involving my current shop assistant. "If you're lucky, we'll have had a letter from him today. Come on, post office'll be the first stop."

* * *

The wonderful—and sometimes frustrating—thing about Beyond is that it's a total hodgepodge of cultures, lore, technology, and magic. Nowhere is this more evident than at the local post office.

When I was a traveling alchemist, I enjoyed being almost unreachable. But now that I was *gasp* settled down and—*shudder*—*responsible,* I'd had to make arrangements for my friends in Belville to contact me if necessary. I refused to carry around magitech phones like Al (in my opinion, the only thing any magitech gadget can do consistently is break), and I have no magical or psychic abilities myself. (Aside, one could argue, from bad luck.) In a true emergency, our hometown Witch, Trent, would be able to send a message to William via magic. But for everything else, I'd told everyone to write to me at the Seaside post office.

Seaside's post office sprawled, not so much one building as a series of bungalows that managed to be both beachy and imperious at the same time. It was the first business we encountered as we came down the hill from the Rise estate. Even before we neared the front door of the main building, the sensations began: owls swooping, magical envelopes with little wings darting from one building to another or appearing suddenly in puffs of purple smoke, magitech systems buzzing and beeping, strange little breezes whirling past. I swore I saw a snake slithering by with a scroll tied round its neck by a string.

William harrumphed.

"You can stay out here if you want," I offered. "I'll just be a moment."

I took William's plop down on the sidewalk as an answer. Leaving him outside, I ran in and made my inquiries at the front desk, emerging moments later with four envelopes and a scrunched-up scroll.

"Those are from Sir Rowan," I said, handing the envelopes to William. The precise, archaic handwriting was unmistakable. "I'm guessing he took me seriously when I said 'write a daily report.' You look through those first—I'm going to open this one."

The pair of us drifted to a bench surrounded by fluff-topped grasses, absorbed by our mail. While William scanned the reports, holding them aloft with tendrils of starry magic, I un-crinkled the scroll to find that—as I'd expected—it was from a certain impulsive bookseller.

> *Hi, Red! I hope you got to Seaside okay. Did you make it? What was the trip like? Did you see anything neat on the way down the mountain? It's really boring here since you left. The other day Officer Thorn actually came by to visit, she was so bored. I think she misses having someone to argue with. Sir Rowan's too prim and proper, apparently. I haven't seen Trent in a few days but Thorn says he's trying to put a new roof on the Hut—again. Maybe he'll be done by the time you get back! Dusty said to tell you hello and that he still doesn't understand why anyone would want to travel so far on foot. How is the wedding? You've probably only seen the opening feast by now, right, and everything else is still coming? Lavender wanted to know what food they're having. I know you'll tell us about it when you get home, but you should write things now too so you don't forget them. And definitely write about your trip there, because we'll all forget to ask you about that when you come back, because we'll be so busy talking about the wedding. I hope it goes well!*
>
> *Luca*
>
> *P.S. While you're in Seaside you have to go to the bookstore there! It's really cool!*

"Red," said William gravely as I finished reading, "if you blush any harder at that piece of parchment, you're going to set it on fire."

"Don't be ridiculous. That's just the sun on my cheeks. Do

you want to read this? It's from Luca."

"Gee, never would have guessed," drawled my companion. "No thanks, I can imagine what it says."

He tossed the envelopes from Sir Rowan in my direction and started off down the street. I frowned after him, not sure what he meant.

"Well? Are we investigating or not?" he called.

Maybe Sir Rowan didn't write as much as he'd hoped, I thought, shrugging. I tucked all the letters into a narrow pouch on my belt and took off after William.

9

Seaside Piracy

The town of Seaside was like a tourism postcard come to life. Harbors and beaches hosted thongs of happy bathers, be it in sun or sea. A wooden boardwalk along the beach marked the beginning of town. The boardwalk itself was lined with booths and refreshment stands, more a carnival than a street. I knew from my travels that boardwalk businesses tended to be very seasonal and many changed from year to year, so I didn't have high hopes that anyone there would be able to give us information. Still, the boardwalk was a very logical place to start our investigation, because the streets of the town ran parallel behind it—essentially, by starting on the boardwalk, we'd be starting on one side of the grid.

"Plus," said William when I voiced these thoughts, "on slow days, the shopkeepers here have nothing better to do than gossip. I bet you they'll know a lot more than you think."

I bit back a grin—*of course William would think of the gossip,* I thought. Without any further argument, we strayed from the road onto the beach, and from the beach onto the beginning of the boardwalk.

Though it was still early summer, the sky was bright blue, the waves sparkled, and the happy children were in full force. The air was full of scents of salt and sugar as kids ping-ponged across the boardwalk, from cotton candy stalls to games of ring toss and fortune-telling to booths selling magical flying fish and back again. With the way the businesses were crowded up next to each other, there was no way we'd be able to talk to every single owner. Instead I took the lead, beckoning William into a slightly quieter stall jam-packed with colorful hats, charmed sunglasses, and shirts that read "Seaside is the only place to be" or "anything can happen at the beach."

Since I knew exactly what it was like to run a little business, I picked out a pair of woven sandals adorned with seashells— Jeannie hadn't brought me shoes, after all, and my own were a bit too fancy, since I'd been wearing them for the feast rather than for walking all over town. As the shopkeeper, an older woman with hints of troll about her wide, flat face and the scraggly pink hair atop her tanned head, rang up my purchase, I leaned in casually.

But I didn't even have to say anything.

"You're here for the wedding, I expect?" she said. Without really waiting for a nod, she said, "Haven't seen many of the guests come through, excepting the merfolk. Some of them came in for hats and glasses. You don't need a pair, then? They'll never be lost—the charm is 100% guaranteed."

I shook my head politely. The last thing I needed was to go around town wearing my goggles *and* a pair of sunglasses. *William would never let me hear the end of it.*

"Well, that's alright. So," she continued, as I counted out my change, "you must know all about the hullabaloo there last night, eh?"

I paused and looked up, taken aback by her choice of words.

Fortunately, William was not so hesitant. "We hardly know anything," he complained, hopping up to put his paws on the counter. The shopkeeper looked at him sympathetically; clearly, this had been the right complaint to make.

"All we heard was the police think it was poison," he went on. "And of course, we saw the message."

"I heard about that, too," said William's new friend. "Mind you, it shouldn't come as any surprise. Those of us who've lived our whole lives in town knew this day was coming. Say what you like about Rise Enterprises, but Mr. Rise himself was no peach."

"We heard he even chased a Witch out of town," William prompted, panting happily.

The shopkeeper nodded in approval as she deftly recounted my change and completed the sale. "Years ago, that was, but we all knew something bad would come of it. And now you think, it's really no wonder, is it? You mark my words, when they find the murderer—if they *ever* do—it won't be a person at all. My money says it's some magical minion from the Witch. They say she still watches us, to this day!"

On that rather ominous note, we seemed to have hit the end of what she knew. We lingered to say our goodbyes as I put on my new sandals, but soon found ourselves back on the boardwalk.

"Do you really think you should have said so much?" I asked William, worried.

"Please. None of that was anything she didn't know. You'd know how efficient town gossip is if you'd ever come out of your lab and chat," William informed me smugly.

"Well, efficient or not, we didn't learn much," I reflected.

"Are you kidding? We learned lots. Did you notice how she confirmed that the witch left town *because* of Mr. Rise?"

"Yeah," I said, although I really hadn't. "But what about the witch being the culprit? Do you think that's likely?"

William cocked his head. "She'd have to be a *really* powerful witch, to get past all the security spells on the Rise estate. But nothing's impossible if you know the right magic and will pay the price for it. Come on, let's see what more people have to say."

I was a little surprised at how easily William could talk about the price of big spells, because I knew from tales I'd heard that he wasn't talking about coins. The price of magic was often a sacrifice from the magic user—anything from a bit of spilled wine or an offering of herbs to the loss of a limb, or a voice, or years from your life. The very idea made me shudder. *At least in alchemy you always know exactly what the deal will be,* I thought before trailing after William.

For a while, our investigation was a candy-coated blur. The young boy who sold me a repurposed-fishnet bag to carry my fancy shoes informed us that everyone knew Mr. Rise had been killed because he was secretly a fox out to overthrow the town government; the beleaguered fairy at the lemonade stand spoke at length, as she prepared William's special lemon iced tea, about the different versions of the prophecy she'd heard. A group of animal handlers escorting some crabs to a touch tank told us that Rise Enterprises was about to go under, while a nanny looking after some children happily destroying a sand castle told us that Rise Enterprises was about to unveil a new secret product that would make it three times more profitable than before.

Interestingly, no one seemed to know very much about Lacey, Moe, or even Rei. It seemed Mr. Rise had dominated his family's public image.

As well as their relations with the witch, I thought when we had a moment of quiet. We'd nearly made our way to the opposite end of the boardwalk, and William had finished his tea. As we sat on a bench to catch our breath, I noticed him eyeing a display of magical taffy-pullers and cleared my throat.

"What we need is more reliable clues, not more sugar," I reminded him.

"You're no fun," he retorted. "I think I've earned a balloon animal, at least."

"What are you going to do with a balloon animal?" I asked, exasperated. "Unless it's a balloon witch, I don't see how it will help us."

"One balloon witch, coming right up," said a strange voice next to my ear.

I yelped and leapt to my feet, spinning around to face the speaker. My surprise only increased as I beheld a woman in ragged breeches and a loose white shirt beneath a garish vest, topped off with a red hair scarf. The whole outfit didn't so much *scream* "pirate" as sing the word at the top of its lungs in classic sea-shanty style.

She was even wearing an eye patch.

The piratical woman grinned as she vaulted over the railing behind the bench, landing in front of me with the tools of her trade—balloons—already in her hands.

"What kind of witch will it be? Pointy hat? Purple cloak? Or are you looking for something more unique?" she asked roguishly.

Clearly she's just a balloon artist and this is part of her routine, I told myself, trying to recollect my scattered nerves. "Sorry," I said, "we were talking about a *real* witch we're trying to find. It's—um—nothing. We'll let you get back to your work."

"Oh, I know," said the false pirate, nodding disconcertingly as she began twisting gray balloons in her quick hands. "You're looking for Clemency."

"Excuse me?" I stared.

"Clemency. That's her name. She lives in the cliffs way outside of town. She looks like this."

I goggled at the balloon figure thrust into my hands. Despite being made of charmed rubber, it was clearly a little woman in a gray dress, no taller than my forearm. She even seemed to be holding a crystal ball.

"Cool," said William at my side, since I had gone speechless. "Are you a real pirate, then?"

The balloon artist tapped the side of her nose, grinning down at my companion. And before I could think to thank her, apologize, or even pay her for the balloon witch, she disappeared into the crowd.

Still wordless, I thrust the string tied to the balloon creation's feet to William. With a wide, doggy grin, he accepted the string, using his magic to tie it around his neck. The little witch, enchanted by a spell embedded in the balloons that made it fly, bobbed in the breeze beside his head.

"That did *not* just happen," I informed him.

"Oh, come on, Red," he said, grinning back. "It's like those shirts said. 'Anything can happen at the beach.'"

10

Part of a Seaside World

Meeting a pirate—even one who'd traded knives and doubloons for balloons—was about as much boardwalk as I could take. Shortly after that, William and I turned away from the beach and began to walk the streets of Seaside.

Of course, said streets felt more like an extension of the boardwalk than, say, pastoral Market Square in Belville. The main roads, running parallel to the shore, were hard-packed dirt with stone gutters—no doubt put in place to cope with heavy coastal storms. The sidewalks were full of shoppers and lined with ornamental grasses, which helped keep some of the dust and sand at bay. The shops themselves rose only one or two stories high, all narrow wooden buildings with pitched roofs, some curvy, as though boats' hulls had been repurposed as building materials. Most of the buildings had decorative trim and bright colors, and their signs advertised all manner of mementos. We hadn't walked very far before we came across a sign shaped like a smoothie that sparkled with a promisingly refreshing pink light.

"Oh, sure," William muttered, as I made a beeline for the cafe, "we can't get taffy, but we can get *smoothies*."

"Taffy is bad for—your teeth," I replied, stopping myself at the last minute from saying "dog's" teeth, because William hated being called a dog. Even though he looked and felt like one. "Besides, I'm thirsty, and you didn't share your iced tea."

As we stopped in front of the counter, we set aside our bickering to contemplate the menu. The inside of the cafe was just as sparkly and pink as the sign had been, with furniture made from driftwood and painted in fruity pastels. I wasted no time in ordering a blackberry smoothie, while William opted for another iced tea, this one with wildflower honey and strawberries mixed in.

As we waited for our drinks to be made, we drifted through the little shop. There weren't any other customers, so I walked around the tables and chairs, looking at the art on the walls. It took me a moment to realize that it, like the furniture, had all been made from reclaimed materials.

"Pretty neat, right?" A young man in a cafe apron asked. He straightened up from where he'd been cleaning off a table and gestured toward the three-dimensional seascape I'd been eyeing. "A friend of mine, Cindy, is the artist who made all of this month's art."

The name rang a bell in my mind. "Is that Cindy who's making a statue for the Rises, for the wedding?"

"Yeah, that's her," the boy said, nodding eagerly. Then he laughed. "Although she's not really making it for the Rises. I mean, they're probably not going to like it. I doubt they're big fans of recycled materials."

"Oh?" I asked, intrigued by his casual insight into the Rise family.

"Not fancy enough, I'd bet," he confided. "But Cindy never works with anything but."

"Then why'd they choose her?" William asked, nudging past a stray chair to bring me my drink.

The cafe employee looked down at William for a long moment, prompting me to look too. When I did, I saw that his witch balloon had shifted so that it looked like the witch was riding on his back. I laughed and adjusted it, and our new friend laughed too.

"To be honest, they probably didn't," he said easily. "I think she's doing it as a favor for the couple, not so much for the family. Did you know she and Taiwo used to date?"

I almost dropped my cup. Of course, I hadn't thought I knew *everything* about Taiwo's past, but still, that was news to me. And the friendly way the boy said it made me think he knew about it firsthand, and wasn't just repeating gossip.

He saw my surprise and laughed again, leaning one hip on the table behind him. "Yeah, but it didn't last very long. Cindy wanted something more serious, but I guess Taiwo wasn't ready yet. And then of course Rei came along. They're all really good friends now, though."

And Cindy was on the grounds the other day when William and I met Rei, which means I bet she was invited to the opening feast, too, I speculated. *Hm.* Aloud, I said, "Wow, I had no idea. I'm a friend of Taiwo's, but I live pretty far away. My name's Red."

"Drew," said the young man, returning my handshake with an easygoing smile. "Feel free to stop in any time while you're here for the wedding."

Something in the lightness of his tone made me hesitate. "Have you heard the latest news?" I asked as I sipped at my smoothie.

"Oh, I did," he said, gathering up his cleaning cloths. "I'm really sorry for Rei, of course, but it's not like I knew the old man personally. It's just kind of a . . ."

"Shock?" I suggested as his voice trailed off. Most of the other shopkeepers we'd talked to wouldn't have used that word, but then, they probably also wouldn't have called Mr. Rise "old."

"Yeah," said Drew, after a moment of gazing at the art behind my head. He looked back at me and nodded. "That's exactly what it is."

* * *

"Okay," said William, one hour and three "gifts and potions" shops later. "I know you said you wanted to investigate the state of alchemy in Seaside, but we really need a game plan here."

I could see his point. So far, my plan of wandering the streets of Seaside looking for poison vendors had only turned up a bunch of sunscreen, sunburn oil, and "turn the water around you pink" gimmicks.

"Let's at least finish walking Main Street before we head back," I said. We'd made our way about halfway down the sandy street so far. Unlike Belville, which was tiny and compact, Seaside stretched along a curved bay. "How about we talk suspects while we walk? Then it'll feel productive."

"More like it'll feel like a police station," William muttered. Nonetheless, he launched right into the topic, oblivious to the herds of children around us—the early lunchtime crowd. "Tell me you noticed how weird it is that *Mara* was such good friends with Mr. Rise," he began, laying a derisive stress on the wedding planner's chosen name.

"You mean, because of what Taiwo was saying about how they planned the wedding together? I will agree with you it's odd. But then, it does seem like Mr. Rise would have been the most opinionated out of everyone concerned with the wedding," I said, dodging a small blue child with a lollipop the size of its head. "You think it could have been an affair? Lacey seems so nice—I'd hate to think that."

"Not to mention that anyone would be a fool to cross a werewolf," said William.

"Maybe she's a pacifist," I reprimanded him, mostly for the sake of argument. "After all, she's done her best to be very sage about her husband's death."

"She could be a suspect too," William was quick to point out.

"If we're going to suspect the family, my money's on—"

William beat me to it. "Moe. Yeah, I get that. And no, I am not going into that 'herbal tonics' store with you, Red. I have *no* desire to smell like an arboretum."

"I think arboretums are nice," I protested. Of course, ten minutes later after I'd literally had to run away from a sales attendant insistent that I try milky oat tincture, I was both no further in my quest and a little unsure of my earlier bravado. But I didn't say any of that to William.

"Red," he said, as he rose from his post beside a nearby streetlamp and joined me, "I had a thought. If we *are* suspecting family members, what about Taiwo's family? What about Ige?"

"I agree that his attitude needs work, but why would he kill Mr. Rise?" I asked, doing my best to keep my voice low as a family of gnomes passed. They made me think of Al, and I made a note to bring him up too—although, as with Ige, I couldn't think of any reason he'd want Kade dead. The strongest suspects seemed to be Clemency and perhaps Cindy.

"Think about it," said William. "The police think this is a hate thing, right? Directed just at Mr. Rise. But what if someone was angry about the *wedding* instead?"

"I had that worry too. But if they were, then they didn't choose a very effective way of stopping it," I said, thinking of Taiwo's determination.

"Of course not. But they also chose to murder someone, so clearly they're not the best at decisions," William said. "Maybe they believed the prophecy, or were just upset with Mr. Rise. Like Lacey might be, if she found out about an affair, or Mara might be if he wanted to end—"

"Hey," I said, cutting William's wild speculation short. I pointed across the street at a bright red storefront with an adorable striped awning. "That's the bookstore."

William wrinkled his nose. "I don't think they sell poisons at bookstores, Red."

"No, I know that. But Luca said we should check it out." When William gave me another dubious look, I said, "Let's just pop our heads in, okay? I'm thinking at this point we both could use a break from murder."

11

Once Upon a Now

Ignoring William's protests, I darted across the road and into the bookstore. A set of gold bells jingled as I paused on the doorstep. The brightness, dust and noise of Main Street had given way to a warmly lit haven that smelled strongly of lavender.

Back home in Belville, Luca's bookshop was renowned for being a higgledy-piggledy mess—the kind of place where you could find anything if you knew which pile to look for, and you could spend hours if you first excavated an armchair and didn't mind the dim light.

Seaside's bookseller had clearly taken a different approach—so much so that I was almost surprised Luca had sent me here. Orderly shelves reached the ceiling in regular intervals. Beyond them, at the back of the store, the ceiling opened into a bright loft obscured by a polished wooden rail and strings of fairy lights made from old glass buoys. Signs painted on driftwood saying things like "rain storms bring bright shells" and "catch the friends you like, wave goodbye to the rest" took up tasteful space on the pale blue walls. Everything felt freshly washed and new.

"I'm back here if you want anything," a voice called from the loft. "Be warned, the anti-theft charm is very enthusiastic!"

"We'll come up," I called back as William joined me, sniffing curiously. The voice didn't sound overly friendly, but I didn't actually feel the need to buy any books or scrolls, so I figured I'd try chatting.

Following a hand-woven rug in sea glass colors, William and I found a spiral staircase which led up to the loft. As we climbed it, I realized we were entering a different space entirely. The calming nautical theme was still present, but instead of novels and old sea tomes on shelves, the loft was full of wooden cases of drawers—the kinds of drawers in which newspapers and legal documents might be stored. I knew because I'd been trying to convince Luca to get some for months. Bookshops in Beyond are special places: they carry not only stories, but often serve as an archive for the local area. In Luca's case, he'd inherited a "put it on the desk and I'll do something with it later" sort of archive. But here was a person who really cared about their records.

"Oh, hello," said the person in question. "You know, most people don't come up here first unless something's gone wrong. You aren't in some kind of trouble, are you?"

* * *

". . . and a friend of mine suggested we check out your store," I said, concluding my convoluted introduction of myself and William, and how we weren't—yet—in trouble. Exactly.

"You're here for the wedding? Then you *are* in trouble," said the bookseller. "My name's Varsha, by the way. Thank your friend for me, for recommending my store. You know, I was just looking into Rise Enterprises when you came in."

William sneezed. "Does that really seem like a good idea?"

Varsha gazed at us impassively. She sat behind a desk which appeared to be made of the flat hull of an old rowboat. Its massiveness made her appear very small; I suspected she was already small to begin with. She wore dark scholar's robes, just like Luca, but her hood was pushed back to expose shockingly violet hair and black, cat-like ears over a tawny face. Her eyes, too, were catlike and magnified behind a pair of oversize teal reading glasses.

"The truth doesn't have to be safe," she informed us. "But it's always a good idea. Did you know that Rise Enterprises owns most of the land in town, including the harbor? *Anyone* could know that, if they took a moment to look at some of the maps I have. Everything I've collected is free to look at, by the way. It's all public knowledge. It's just that no one *knows* it. Did you know that Mr. Rise conducted all his business deals in front of a selected group of reporters?"

I decided that I already liked Varsha. Pursuit of truth is a big deal in alchemy—even if alchemists are usually talking about "truth" in terms of the biological and chemical makeup of things, rather than the details of human events. With a smile, I stepped forward and took a seat across from her desk. "I don't know much myself, since I'm from out of town. Have you found out anything else?"

Varsha shifted so that the ancient cash register on one end of her desk didn't come between us. "I only just started looking when I came in this morning. Everybody was talking about the murder at the cafe over breakfast. Is it really true that someone wrote a threatening message on the curtains?"

"Yeah. *Ill winds blow on the house of Rise/Reynard the traitor now must die*," I told her. "Does it mean anything to you?"

"It's not exactly a common phrase around here, if that's what you mean." Varsha paused, considering this new information. "Some of the fishers at the cafe were saying it must be from the old witch—because of the prophecy, of course."

"Clemency?" I asked. "That's her name, right?"

"I really couldn't say for sure. She changed it after she left, and she hasn't been in town in years. These days, she lives as a sea witch, but no one really knows where." Varsha answered as though she was identifying a popular whale, rather than naming a very powerful magical practitioner. "Some of my records indicate that, years ago, after a trial—the actual details of it are obscured—she was forced to leave Seaside."

This time William spoke. "'Obscured'?"

"Sea water. Sabotage," Varsha clarified. "All the ink ran together and the parchment is ruined. Anyway, people around here say that she can still be found if you're desperate enough. She'll grant wishes, they say, but at a very high price. And if you don't pay up, the sea will claim your soul."

"Poetic," said William, dryly. Under his breath, he added, "*Witches.*"

"You're lucky Trent isn't here to hear you say that," I told him. Because I didn't feel like explaining William's sorcerer-like prejudice against other magic users to Varsha, though, I moved on. "Well, Mr. Rise wasn't drowned or claimed by a wave, or anything like that. But I suppose you could argue that a lot of poisons are water-based, especially since he drank his. Although we don't know yet if that's *really* what caused his death."

"The message would be her style," Varsha said, "but it's clear you know more about this than me."

William scoffed. "Barely. Red just likes to speculate."

"*Excuse* me? You were the one who—"

"Tell me something," William continued over my protest. "If Rise was such a fanatic about being open to the public, did he also turn his will into a public show?"

Varsha tapped her nose, thinking. Her glasses slid down and, in a well-practiced move, she pushed them back up. "You know, that's a good question. I've only looked into the early days of Rise Enterprises so far. Maybe if we look through some of the more recent newspapers, we'll find something useful."

Standing, she threaded her way out from behind her desk and between the low filing cabinets that filled the loft. As William and I followed, I noted that I'd been right: Varsha was only as tall as my elbow, and seemed more robe than limb.

"You take this drawer," she said, handing me a set of file folders, "and you take these. You can look through them, right?" When William nodded, glowing, she went on, "I'll take these. That gives each of us a decade to look through. You can spread them out on top of the file cabinets if that helps. Just make sure you remember where everything—"

"Got it," said William. A clipped article levitated beside his head.

"Oh, I forgot about this folder!" exclaimed Varsha, reaching for it immediately.

While Varsha busied herself reading the article, I raised my eyebrow at my friend. "Did you use magic to do that?"

"What's it matter if I found it?" William asked smugly.

"Seriously, *how* did you do that?"

"I'm telling you—"

I gave him a pointed look.

"Alright, fine," he said, exasperated. "It's on the folder. See?"

I looked at the folder Varsha still held and read the label: *To Sort and Categorize, Rise.* Judging by the thickness of it, it was full of articles. Running my hand through my hair, I wondered aloud, "What is going on with that family?"

"This is it," Varsha announced meanwhile, as though she hadn't heard our bickering. "It's actually a hearing where Mr. Rise announced some pending updates to his will. It was—let me check—spring of this year. The equinox, actually."

"And?" William practically barked the word.

"Most of the family business still goes to Rei," said Varsha, skimming the article. "That's how the Rise family has done things for generations—the oldest child inherits the estate. So no surprises there. The purpose of the proposed update, it looks like, was to include a new business venture along with Rise Enterprises in Rei's inheritance."

"What's the new venture?" I asked.

"Let me see." Varha's eyes skimmed back and forth as she read. "Oh, I know this one. It's a new company in town—just got started last year, I think. I should have the paperwork for it somewhere. It's a small shipping outfit called 'Mountain Meet Company.' People around here call it MMC for short. Whoever runs it has always kept a low profile, though . . . I had no idea it was part of the Rise umbrella. Rise Enterprises," she said, closing the folder with a snap, "has a lot more to do with the fate of Seaside than most people think."

12

Salad and Kelp

As lunchtime was bearing down on us, Varsha promised to search her records for further mentions of Rise, MMC, or Clemency, and I promised to check in with her the next morning if I could. After all, even if Taiwo and Rei's wedding went ahead with no delays, we still had five days until the ceremony.

My suspicions were proved right when we caught up with Taiwo over lunch. William and I intercepted the couple just as they were escaping the house to eat their salads and canapes outside in the sunshine. They seemed relieved to see us and immediately invited us to join them at their picnic table. William's newest friend, the balloon witch, wobbled in the breeze as he affixed her to a nearby plant.

Taiwo filled us in as we shared snacks. "So the observance is going ahead for tonight, but like Lacey said, it's just for family really. And you two, of course. We'll have it at like ten or eleven because Lacey says the sun needs to be fully set. I think they're planning on having dinner with everyone first, though."

"Great," William mumbled through his mouthful of cheese. "More pasta."

I kicked him under the table and motioned Taiwo to go on. With a smile, they said, "The wedding's still on, just as planned, but we're really hoping the police will wrap up their investigation before then. Or *you* will. You *have* been investigating, right?"

"We have," I assured them. "So far it's just been a lot of information gathering, but we'll sort out the patterns soon enough, don't worry. Actually, everyone in town was really nice, too."

"Unlike here," William added unhelpfully.

"William!" I scolded.

Taiwo laughed. "No, it's fine. It *has* been such a mess, hasn't it?"

As they spoke, their dark hand went to Rei's pale arm. For a moment under the shade of the fancy picnic umbrella, the two lovers shared a sympathetic glance.

"We're both really glad you're here," Rei said quietly, turning to me. "It's good to have someone with . . . outside perspective."

"Sure," said William. "Sounds like the only perspective round here for years has been your father's." This observation was delivered with William's signature callousness, but fortunately, it seemed to be the right thing to say.

I watched Rei's gaze flicker, as though something inside him had been unlocked. "You're right," he said softly. "Mother has opinions, of course, but . . . they just always agreed, her and Father. If they argued, we never, ever saw it. They told me once you have to present a unified front to the rest of the world."

"That's fine, but your own children shouldn't count as 'the rest of the world,'" said Taiwo. The heat in their voice suggested that this conversation had come up before.

Rei bit his lip, and then nodded. I noticed he'd shifted to put his free hand over Taiwo's. "Moe used to fight with Father sometimes," he said. This seemed irrelevant for a moment before he continued, "Not about Mother—about—about the business. It's the only thing we ever really talked about. Moe would pick fights about it. Now, I—part of me wishes I had, too. Maybe then I'd at least have more to . . . remember."

"Better to go through life doing your best than thinking about 'would have' and 'should,'" I told him kindly. It was something my mothers had said to me when I left home to train as an alchemist.

"Red's right, Rei." Taiwo put an arm around his shoulders. "We just have to get through this one step at a time. And if you really want to, you know we can cancel everything in a moment."

"I know. But I don't want to," Rei said, smiling at Taiwo despite the wanness in his eyes. "Marrying you is the one thing I *did* take a stand on. It's like you said. I don't want to back down now."

William's nose lifted, his detective mode engaged. "Is there anyone you know of who *doesn't* want you to marry? Either of you?"

Rei hesitated, and I recalled his nerves when we'd first met in his painting studio. Taiwo waved one hand. "I mean, you saw Ige last night. He's really been a pill about it all. Even today, he was full of talk about how Rise Enterprises trades in weapons and they're dangerous and they have swords that can dissolve in water, or something really silly like that. But that's just how he is—it's not like he really doesn't want us to marry. He's just an alarmist. Everyone else has been just lovely."

"Well . . ." Rei paused, and then looked at Taiwo as he faltered.

"I mean, true," said Taiwo, just as though Rei had actually voiced his thought. For our benefit, they said, "*My* family's 'lovely' and the Rise family 'lovely' look a lot different."

I chuckled. "That's normal, as far as I can tell. But I have to say, Rei, it does seem like you have Lacey's full support."

"Oh, yes," Rei said, shaken from his silence. "Mother's always loved Taiwo. And everyone else—maybe they were happy about the wedding, or maybe not, but I don't think anyone cared enough to actually *kill* my—my father. I mean, why do *that* if what you want is to cancel the wedding? Why not—why not steal the rings or curse the stage or something?"

"Or target one of you," William said, adding to the rather creative list of crimes.

"It's a good point," I agreed. Thinking of the vagueness of the message on the curtain, I added, "Let's not draw any conclusions yet."

"Speaking of the stage, though," Taiwo said, "if you want to see it, William, I think Mom's going to go work on it now. She just came out of the house and headed for the dock."

"Where?" William leapt up, then turned back to me.

"Go on," I laughed. "I'm going to stay here. It'll be fine."

"Yes!" said Taiwo, beaming. "Red, come on. There's someone I want you to meet."

* * *

After helping Rei stack our lunch dishes, Taiwo took my arm and led me around the house.

"So, tell me," they said in confidential tones once we were alone in the garden, "what did you learn in town?"

I laughed. "Is that why you really wanted to go for a walk? Are we actually meeting anyone at all?"

"Oh, we are," Taiwo assured me. "She's working on a new art installation on the other side of the house. You'll love her. Now spill! What have you learned so far?"

"Not that much." I told Taiwo about the rumors regarding the prophecy, our bad luck with local alchemy, and meeting Varsha. I left out the rumors about Cindy, though, because I had a feeling I was about to meet the artist in person. Instead, I explained about the updated will and Rei's inheritance.

"'Mountain Meet Company,'" Taiwo said slowly. As our path wandered into the sunlight, they lifted a paper parasol painted with delicate swimming fishes and opened it to shield us. Merfolk, in my experience, tend to be sensitive to direct sunlight—no matter how much they love its warmth. "MMC for short, you say? Maybe someone likes Ms, huh? I never heard of a company like that, but I don't really pay that much attention to business, as you know. Maybe my friend will know."

I gave Taiwo a sidelong glance. Despite their cavalier tone, I happened to know that Taiwo had been the one to bring their clan's seashell trade into the new era with modern marketing and trade deals. They had a gift for bringing people together which I, as a reluctant business person, envied greatly.

"So, pin in that," Taiwo continued, excited. "And let me tell *you* what's happened. The police came by earlier—you know, Officer Ebb and his schoolies." I grinned; 'schoolies' was a common merfolk term for groupies or followers. "Turns out it *was* poison that killed Mr. Rise. I think it was something you had suggested, too—devil's rope kelp, I think it was? Officer Ebb was asking us all about it and said they only found it in Mr. Rise's cup, not in anyone else's. Lacey had every single glass tested, of course."

I pulled up short on the paved path. "Taiwo, are you *sure* it was devil's rope?"

"Yeah, it sounds even more right when you say it. Why?"

I ran my free hand through my ponytail, uncertain what to say. Devil's rope was a poison derived from kelp—kelp which grew deep on the ocean floor, if I remembered right. Deep enough that if it was available in Seaside, it was probably expensive, because it came from far away under the sea. And all these things pointed to a merfolk murderer . . .

What if the murderer did want to cancel the wedding? I thought. If they murdered Mr. Rise and made it look like a merperson did it, that might be enough to drive the families apart. And if they were mad at Mr. Rise anyway, maybe it was a 'two birds, one poison' situation . . .

13

Keep Your Friends Close

"Oh look," said Taiwo. "There's Cindy now!" In their excitement, Taiwo let go of my arm and darted into a nearby garden, parasol bobbing.

It could have been a person on the Rise side, I couldn't stop thinking, *but it also could have been a merperson trying to make things really obvious . . .*

"Red, come on! Where are you?"

I sighed and did my best to set aside my misgivings. Putting on a polite smile, I followed Taiwo's voice around a hedge of roses.

The hedge encircled a stone patio, it turned out—similar to the stone outside the dining room, because of course everything at the Rise estate would match. This patio, however, was raised up slightly and away from the house, giving it perfect views not only of the mansion but of the sea and sky beyond. And in the middle of the patio was a half-colored statue: a riot of reds and purples which looked at first glance like a fish swallowing the sun. And next to the statue, Taiwo had slung an arm around a fire sprite.

The same sprite who'd been escorted away from the wedding party's table at the feast yesterday. I recognized her at once.

Fire sprites are easily identifiable, even to those of us who aren't William. They generally have flame atop their head instead of hair. This one had a blaze of orange with yellow sparks, which mirrored the joy in her golden eyes. In fact, from her paint-splattered clothing to her comfortably rounded curves to her large smile, joy radiated from every aspect of her.

"This is Cindy," said Taiwo. For a moment, taken by the contrast between merfolk Taiwo and their fiery friend, all I could was laugh.

"Hi, sorry, it's great to meet you," I said, extending my hand for a shake. "I love your . . . statue?"

"It's a commentary on the over-consumption of sea goods and the water which birthed us all," Cindy said promptly. "Want my card? Here, I have one you can take!"

Cindy handed over a business card embossed with gold—gold which, the back side of the card informed me, had been sustainably grown in a lab and had led a happy life. The edges of the card singed my fingers. Amused, I turned it over to read the full inscription: *Cindy Spark: artist, activist, environmental advocate.*

Hmm, I thought. Maybe 'joy' hadn't been quite the right impression.

Not that I didn't agree with Cindy's basic premises. And after seeing her art in the cafe in town, I was hardly surprised. But I got the feeling I might need to steel myself to get through the rest of this conversation.

"Cindy and I met ages ago," said Taiwo. "Actually, I've known Cindy almost as long as I've known you, Red." Turning to Cindy, they added, "How did we meet, again? Was it at the beach bonfire, or the yacht gala?"

"We already knew each other at the bonfire," Cindy said, bouncing. "Remember, you helped me put out the fire when it got too big? We met at the yacht. I was liberating the caviar and you came up and warned me that the guards were coming."

"And that those particular eggs weren't going to survive in the Southern Sea," Taiwo added with half an eye roll for my benefit. I pressed my lips together, trying not to laugh.

"I still can't believe how easy it was to sneak into that gala in the first place," said Cindy, who very much looked like her idea of fancy dress was clean, sustainable overalls with environmental buttons on them.

"I'm sure people are eager to talk about your art," I said, successfully tamping down my giggles. "It's very . . . thought-provoking."

"I use only wild materials sourced from the sea that have already died," Cindy told me proudly.

I nodded along until that last detail about 'death' caught me up short. "Um, so, does that make you a scavenger of sorts?"

"The best kind of scavenger," Taiwo laughed affectionately. "Cindy, Red works as an alchemist. She gathers all her materials too, and even makes her own tools."

"Well, *some* things I make, but—" I hastened to correct Taiwo's praise.

But I didn't hasten fast enough. "I make everything," Cindy exclaimed. From behind her back, she brought out a paintbrush with bristles of very varying thickness, length, and attachment to the handle. I didn't know much about artist's supplies, but I was pretty sure that paint wasn't supposed to fly off the brush like that.

Of course, paintbrushes probably aren't meant to be shaken like that either, I thought. This time I couldn't help but chuckle—and back away to safety. "That's great, Cindy. I usually only resort to making something if I can't find the exact right thing on the market."

"Markets and business are just gigantic scams," Cindy announced.

I glanced at the Rise mansion behind us, feeling like a butler or guard might pop out of the hedges at any minute and ask us all to leave. "Well, I must admit I do run a shop . . ."

"Small local shops are fine," Cindy assured me. Apparently, she was strident enough even to take the conversational reins from Taiwo, who just stood back and looked amused at their friend's antics. "It's the really big ones you have to look out for. They have to be kept in check. The way some people brutally cut back beautiful hedges and make them maintain an unnatural shape—that's the same thing we have to do to big business, because otherwise they'll crowd us all out of the sun!"

"Wow," I said. "And here I thought we were just talking about paint brushes."

Cindy launched into another explanation, and behind her, Taiwo gave me a small, indulgent shrug. *We all have our passions,* they seemed to be saying. And while that was completely true, I couldn't help but notice that Cindy's passion put her pretty high in the runners-up for Most Likely Suspect in the murder of the head of Rise Enterprises.

* * *

Eventually I managed to detach myself from Taiwo and Cindy, mostly by insisting—whenever Cindy paused for breath—that I had my investigation to mull over. I considered the main house, but decided against it, opting instead to follow the garden path down toward the edge of the bluff.

As I walked and thought, I couldn't help but grow a little morose. Partly it was because Cindy had that energy that made the silence after her presence feel unnaturally quiet. But partly, too, it was because I could see that Taiwo and Cindy really were good friends—and my investigation might make things difficult for them.

Of course, it'd be Cindy who made things difficult, if she was the one who murdered Mr. Rise, I reminded myself. *The murderer's choices aren't my fault.* But still, I now felt the downside of suspecting one of Mr. Rise's close associates of having been the one to kill him. It wasn't a good feeling, throwing suspicion on friends.

And what does it say about me that I was so ready to pursue this line of investigation, I thought. *No wonder William's been making remarks about me getting 'weird' about the wedding and the murder.*

Suddenly, and rather unexpectedly, I wished for nothing more than my friend Officer Thorn. *At least I could bounce ideas off of her, and she'd tell me if I was being irrational . . .*

Instead of Officer Thorn, though, I came around the corner of the massive house to find Lacey reclining in a beach chair beside a spotless pool, staring out at the sea. Though she was outside in the sun on a pool deck, she wore a sleeveless black dress and her house slippers. There was a beach umbrella behind her, unopened, and a pitcher of ice water and some glasses on a little table beside her, untouched.

The *incomplete* feeling of the scene went straight to my heart.

"Hey, Lacey, it's me," I said, following the path on to the deck. "Let me get your umbrella. Nice view, huh? But I have to admit to you, I never really have understood the point of having a pool right next to an ocean. William would probably say I'm uncultured in that respect. I guess there's not much to be done for me now."

Lacey sat still while I bustled around her, setting up the umbrella and an extra chair for myself to sit in. When at last I did sit and grinned bashfully at her, she burst out laughing.

"Oh, Red, I just love you to pieces," she said, chuckling as she wiped at her eyes. I handed her a handkerchief from my belt, and she accepted it with thanks, adding, "I hope you don't think I'm silly for saying so. I know we only just met. It's the way I am—Kade used to say I have emotions for the both of us."

"Well, it's definitely been a time of strong emotion," I said sympathetically, smiling. "Might as well take the good along with the bad, right?"

"Yes. My thoughts exactly," she said, sighing as she settled back into her shaded chair. "And you aren't wrong about the pool. Kade's mother had it put in, rest her soul. She and I never did get along."

"Rei says you've always been a fan of Taiwo," I said, shifting to pour us both a glass of iced water from the tray. With all the tears Lacey had shed, I knew she must need something to drink.

"It's hard not to be, isn't it?" Lacey smiled, but she sighed again, this time more deeply. "I'm sure you've noticed, though, that in this household we are not always 'fans' of each other."

"You mean Moe?" I asked as I handed her glass over. "I

noticed his attitude, of course, but I figured it was all due to the stress of recent events."

"Moe, yes, but it isn't his fault," Lacey reflected, looking back out to sea. "Kade never did quite know what to make of children, bless him. And I, too, had my faults over the years. It seems, looking back, that somehow we were always too young for the responsibilities we were given. Too young, trying too hard to be old. And now I see my children facing the same mistakes."

"I think I know what you mean," I said carefully. As I thought it over, I could indeed see how the pressures of leading a business and maintaining an image might lead someone inexperienced—or "young," as Lacey put it—into becoming a person they weren't proud of inside.

Lacey glanced at me, her eyes swimming. "Do you know what 'Moe' is short for? Okurimono. Because he was a gift—that's what it means." She sniffed, and distracted herself by taking a drink. "I love both my boys, and I love Taiwo and Jeannie, too. They've been very good to us. I only hope that Taiwo and Rei do better than Kade and I did . . . better by Moe, too."

The phrasing of that struck me as odd, and I tilted my head. "Lacey, if there is something—some reason from the past—for Moe's resentfulness, I'm sure it could be worked out."

"Oh, Red." She reached out and put her hand on mine, her unusually sharp nails pricking at my skin. "Do you know anything about sirens?"

"No," I answered, surprised at what seemed like an abrupt change in the conversation. "I've never met one, I mean. I've just heard stories."

While merfolk live in clans and generally structure their

society around a deity, sirens are something else entirely. They have human characteristics, like merfolk, but they can't shed their tails in favor of feet. Some old stories say that that's the reason they're so violent—they're jealous of anyone able to walk on land. Of course, that probably doesn't hold true, certainly not for *all* sirens, but the fact remains that if a ship is attacked at sea, it's often because a rogue band of sirens decided to make a meal of the crew. In general, sirens are much more animalistic than most other folks in Beyond.

Lacey kept looking at me, meaningfully, and I frowned as I tried to put the pieces together. "You aren't saying Moe is one?" I asked, thinking of that rainbow sheen to his skin.

"No, no." She shook her head and pulled away, looking out over the waves again. "His birth family was killed by them. That's why we took him in. Unfortunately, he was just old enough to remember . . . and no child should have to remember something like that."

"Oh." I blinked, feeling very sad for the little boy Moe must have been. I could understand why such a memory might make assimilating into a refined family heading up a trading empire difficult. Some traders even dealt with sirens, if they felt they could protect themselves in doing so. But did this also mean Moe harbored distrust for Taiwo and the rest of the Afolayan clan? That hardly seemed fair, but it was conceivable.

"Red," Lacey said again, before I could ask any follow up questions, "you're a good friend, to Taiwo, to William, and Rei. Please don't let any of this get in the way of that. Don't feel like you ought to dwell in guilt, or 'shoulds,' or past mistakes. Just love your friends, and let them love you. No matter what may happen."

This advice sounded so similar to what I'd told Rei only

hours before, but it hit me like a bolt from the blue. I'd been able to give the advice, but not to hear it myself, it seemed. Lacey's sudden insight, right after I'd been thinking about friends and murder and what a mess the wedding might become, made me want to cry.

When I was silent, Lacey looked my way. Whatever opinion she had of herself as a mother, it was clear that she was a kindly enough soul to guess at my feelings. She smiled reassuringly and patted my hand once more. "Don't worry," she said. "You said it yourself: we will work everything out."

14

In Memoriam

After running out to the mer-camp to pick up William, shower, and change into my own clothes, I returned for dinner that evening and was surprised to see that not only was Cindy still around, Mara had reappeared as well. The Rises' formal dining room felt quite full with all of us in it, murmured conversation and uncertain looks filling the white-paneled, candlelit room.

Lacey, who was seated next to me at one end of the long table, must have seen the misgivings on my face. As she passed the salt and pepper, she leaned in close to my ear and said, "I couldn't turn them away at the last moment. It would have made a scene, and Kade hated those even more than he hated party-crashers."

Though her eyes were still red-rimmed and sad, she smiled at me as she pulled away. I smiled back. "You certainly don't need any extra worries on your plate."

"No, indeed. I don't think Whitestone left any room." She gestured to her actual dinner plate, which was heaped full of pasta (William had been right about the menu).

Whitestone was the family butler, whose name I had heard often in conversation but whom I rarely caught a glimpse of. I was almost convinced that Whitestone was invisible when not in action. But Rei and Lacey spoke of him with respect, tinged with a slight grandfatherly feeling. Between him, Taiwo, Jeannie, and Al, it seemed the family was well stocked for friends. The thought made Lacey's advice even more poignant.

I chuckled politely at Lacey's joke about her dinner and scanned the table again. Across from me, William was talking Al's ear off, though I couldn't tell what the topic of conversation was—he was talking too fast. Rei looked uncomfortable at the head of the table, and Taiwo kept sending him encouraging looks from the opposite end. Moe, I noticed, kept seeing those looks and scowling all the more. Meanwhile, Cindy and Mara were talking.

Cindy and Mara? That seemed odd. I let Jeannie take over Lacey's attention as I tried to surreptitiously tune in.

". . . has to be done," Mara was saying.

Cindy's high voice was harder to hear. Had she said something about "el resources"? Or was it "kelp sources"?

"Red. Red!" William barked at me from across the table.

It's not like they'd actually be discussing poisons at the dinner table, anyway, I thought, shaking my head. *Probably it's something to do with the statue.* "What is it, William?"

"Tell Al about desert thistle."

Confused, I looked toward the businesslike gnome, who grinned at me a bit sheepishly. "Desert thistle? As in *lion* thistle?" I asked.

"That's it," he nodded. "William here's just been telling me about your experiences out on the Shifting Sands. It's common there, isn't it?"

"I suppose you could say that. I was there as a kid mostly, so I didn't take too much notice at the time. Some of the other people in my clan talked about it as a weed, actually." *Oops.* The moment the word "clan" came out of my mouth, I regretted it. It invited questions I didn't want to answer. Especially in the midst of a bereaved, imperiled wedding party. "Varsha might have a reference book on it," I hastened to add, though I wasn't sure my attempt at a segue would work. "We went to visit her at the bookstore today—it seemed very well-stocked."

I glared at William, silently wishing I could telepathically convince him to push Al off his chair before he had a chance to ask me which clan I came from. William had his nose buried in pasta and didn't get the hint.

Fortunately Rei, of all people, came to my rescue. Frowning, he asked, "Uncle, why are you interested in desert weeds?"

Lacey heard the concern in her son's voice and reacted immediately. "You aren't leaving us for the desert, are you, Al?"

"Of course not, of course not," Al reassured them, though I wouldn't have blamed him if he wanted a fresh start. "It's only a new venture of mine. Kade and I, we were always looking for new things to trade for. Just a little whim, nothing to worry about."

"It'd be a racket," William declared. "Everyone here'd want it. It has flowers with multicolor manes."

"I *do* think it might thrive in this climate," I said, "provided that you limit the amount of—"

"I hope we aren't talking about importing invasive species into a delicate edge ecosystem which keeps millions of animals alive and thriving!" Cindy trilled from the other end of the table.

I winced. *How is it she heard us in this din when I couldn't hear her?*

Lacey sighed very deeply beside me, her head sinking into her hand.

From the gloom in the corners of the room, Whitestone materialized. "Dessert will be served in the parlor, if it pleases you."

* * *

We made it through dessert without mishap. This was mostly due to the fact that, as soon as we'd settled into plush armchairs and sofas around the fireplace with our chocolate mousses, Lacey asked everyone to share stories about Kade. After such a request, it was hard for even a determined warrior like Cindy to steer the conversation toward biological imbalances.

William and I listened—absently on his part, politely on mine—as one by one, the guests and family spoke. In fact, even the dark wood walls and stately chandelier seemed to listen in.

Rei, with great reluctance, went first. He talked about his dad's head for business and calm demeanor.

Moe nearly said nothing, but at the last moment shared a story about a "sea potion" which really didn't sound congratulatory. Lacey's hands were digging into her rocking chair as she listened. I made a mental note to look into what details I could. *It does sound like he's talking about sirens, not mermaids,* I thought, curious but not about to interrupt with questions, especially not after Lacey had let me in on Moe's tragic past.

In the end we learned nothing from Moe's story, and everyone moved on.

Taiwo told a story about Kade's generosity in planning the wedding.

Al told the story of how he and Kade had met as young apprentices at the local paper.

Lacey, too, told us all how she'd met Kade while on a summer vacation.

Mara followed with a glamorous tale of the first event she'd arranged for Rise Enterprises. I couldn't help but notice that the gleam in her eye was more competitive than nostalgic.

Jeannie commented very kindly on Kade's dedication to his sons. Rei smiled at her, but Moe scoffed.

I had expected Cindy to stay quiet, like me, but at the last moment she added a story about meeting Kade while helping Taiwo pick out the wedding cake. "He really had an eye for local organic flavors," she said. It seemed to be a compliment.

Mara looked at me expectantly after that, so I said, "I've only been here a few days, so I can't say much. But I can see very clearly how much of an impact Mr. Rise made on all of you. As my mother used to say, that is true immortality."

Of course, that can be a bad thing as much as a good thing, I thought but didn't add aloud. Kade didn't seem like a bad person—an absent father, perhaps, but not exactly evil. And in any case, no one deserved to get murdered, especially shortly before their son's wedding.

William added, "In town they appreciate how open he was with his business dealings."

Lacey smiled and appreciated this input. But, knowing William as I did, I could hear the undertone in his voice.

He was trying to smoke out someone who might feel guilty knowing that their deals with Rise Enterprises weren't as private as they'd hoped.

Not the move I would have taken, but all the same I looked carefully around the circle of faces. Rei looked as uncomfortable as ever—probably worried about the size of the shoes he was stepping into—and Taiwo and Jeannie looked bland. Cindy's hair sparked with ferocity, which didn't surprise me: she'd probably been to more than one of Mr. Rise's business deals, whether she'd been invited or not. I wondered if Varsha had any record of protests. Al was frowning thoughtfully as he watched Cindy.

"Thank you, everyone, for humoring me," said Lacey. Above her head, the mantle clock chimed ten-thirty. "Perfect timing. We just have one last request of Kade's to humor, now . . ."

She led us to the sideboard, which hosted a dozen or so paper lanterns and candles. The mood became solemn as we each picked one and followed Lacey outside.

The nearly-full moon was bright overhead, and the stars twinkled, same as ever. The light off the ocean waves was undulating and clear enough to read by. In the garden, little fairy lights bloomed among the flowers. Silent now, the party trailed in Lacey's wake as she made her way to the edge of the bluff.

There, several stories above the water, she paused for a moment and turned back to us.

"I suppose you all know what to do," she said. "I told myself I would stay calm—I told myself—"

She broke off with a sob. The nearest person to her, Jeannie, gently took her shoulders and murmured some reassuring words.

I glanced round at everyone else. We *did* know what to do, but no one seemed to want to move first.

"Shall we?" I asked William.

"May as well," he grunted. "Here, I can light them."

With a flashing spark and blue flame, he lit first my candle, then his own. Securing them inside our lanterns, we stepped up to the cliff.

"Let's go all at the same time," Taiwo suggested. Nearby, Cindy was already lighting her lantern.

"Kade would have liked that," sniffed Mara.

How interesting that we see a genuine emotion from her now, *of all times,* I thought. For a moment I struggled not to knock Mara's lantern right over the cliff. I'd had about enough of her mascara tears when poor Lacey was still unable to control her voice enough to speak.

Al took over lighting everyone else's lanterns for them, arranging us along the cliff as he went down the line. He winked when he got to me and William.

"Alright," he said, turning to the crowd, "on three. One . . ."

"Two," Taiwo, Rei, and Jeannie joined in.

"Three!" We all cried.

For such a dysfunctional party, I have to admit we moved perfectly in sync. As one, we leaned out, our arms extended. As one, we took a deep breath. And as one, we released our lanterns into the air.

I'd never understood the whole paper lantern thing until that moment. Back home, the winds are too strong to consider letting loose a small, flammable, *already on fire* object. But standing there on the bluff in the perfectly still night, surrounded by the scent of gardenias and the feeling of community that's the one silver lining to loss, watching the tiny flames make their way across the dark sky, I could understand why Kade had specifically requested this practice. There was something so sympathetic, and so heartening about watching the fragile lanterns fly.

And then in a sudden, roaring blaze, they all burned to a crisp.

"What?" asked Cindy, as we all turned to her. The sea breeze picked up and blew fine ash into our faces. Lacey sank to her knees.

I'd never, ever heard a gnome sound as angry as Al that night. "*What* was that?"

Jeannie tried to keep us calm. "Let's not blame anyone just because—"

"I had to do it," said Cindy, perfectly impervious to the doom that Jeannie was trying to avert. "Do you *know* how awful paper and wire is for ocean creatures? Have you ever seen a picture of a fish who mistook an old firecracker for a worm and tried to eat it?"

"Stupid fish deserved it in that case, if you ask me," William muttered quietly.

But not quietly enough. Cindy's eyes blazed. "None of you *care!* I'm the only one here looking out for anyone but myself!"

Taiwo spoke up, but didn't sound as confident as usual. "I think we all just need to go inside and—"

"Oh sure," said Moe, his voice laced with all the venom he'd been holding in all night. "We should just *move on,* shouldn't we? Because it's just *so easy.*"

"I didn't say—"

"None of you think about—" Cindy started to say.

"Kade wanted this and you *ruined* it!" Mara wailed.

I'm not actually sure what happened next. At first I thought

William had tackled Mara, and for a brief moment I wanted to congratulate him. Then I realized that William was still by my side. And that meant that the huge wolf-like creature rolling around on top of the wedding planner was a lot less harmless than my snarky companion.

"Lacey, no!" I cried. But by then, no one had a chance of hearing me.

All around me, dim shapes were fighting. Rei and Moe were on the ground, arguing. Jeannie was struggling to hold Taiwo back. Cindy was wielding fire and had already set a nearby tree ablaze. Al was simultaneously yelling at her and into his magitech phone . . .

"Come on, Red," said William, glowing. "Much as I'd like to let Lacey eat Mara, we'd better stop her and calm her down before the police get here."

"If we can," I agreed, hesitant. Mara was screaming like a banshee and Lacey in her wolf form was huge, nearly twice as big as William.

"No one else will," he said. "Here goes nothing."

15

A Rose By Any Other Name

It must have taken all the combined energy of Officer Ebb and his two trainees to pry everyone apart before we set fire to the garden and pulled down the mansion. Probably, Al should have told him to bring more help—at least one police member for each house guest, preferably. The eight of us were sequestered into separate rooms, with the exception of myself and William, and told sternly to wait our turn for questioning.

"I hope no one got seriously hurt," I remarked to William. After the mayhem of the garden, the house felt oppressively quiet. Maybe every person in their own room was straining to hear what the others were saying? But that was only a fancy on my part—in reality, the house was too huge for anyone to hear anyone else behind closed doors.

"You should be most worried about me," he grumped, and then admitted, "or Lacey's trees, maybe."

"The glow out the window's down, at least." Our guest room overlooked the bluff, and when we first came in we'd had a good view of one of the trainees trying desperately to quell the flames. He'd only succeeded because Jeannie had lingered to help him.

I cast a serious eye over William, for maybe the fourth time already. His fur was ruffled and sticking up around his shoulders on one side, and his snout was flecked with drool, but fortunately he hadn't actually sustained any injuries.

When I pointed this out—again—he said, "Yeah, well. To tell the truth, I don't think Lacey actually lost control."

"You're saying she planned that? She's pretty much the one who started the fighting, as far as I could tell."

William shrugged. "The physical fight, anyway. I'm not saying I know *exactly* what happened. I just think that maybe for a moment she snapped and changed, but after that she knew what she was doing. She was just putting Mara in her place."

"Mara's 'place' being a new mudhole in the lawn?" I had meant to keep my tone dry, but I couldn't help but chuckle a little. "She *was* being annoying, I'll admit to that. Still, we're lucky things weren't worse."

William shook himself thoroughly in agreement. "You know, sorcerers use werewolf strength as a measure for their spells."

"Seriously? Like containment spells and the like?"

"Or subduing spells," said William, his nose in the air.

"Well, we could have used some of that tonight." I heard a step in the hall outside, and paused until Officer Ebb poked his head through the open doorway.

"Please, *don't* add magic to all of this," he said wearily.

"Is it our turn to be interviewed already?" I grinned sympathetically at him. "Come have a seat."

Officer Ebb moved heavily into the room, turning a brocade

armchair from the fireplace so that he could look at William and me. We'd perched on the edge of the canopy bed, which had the best view of both the doorway and the window.

It occurred to me as I watched the officer that he moved and acted like he was old enough to be great-grandfather of most of the people present. He'd probably been hoping to spend his last years of active duty in peaceful routine . . . so much for that!

"You," said Officer Ebb emphatically, "are my last hope. Please tell me that as outsiders, guests, alchemists, whatever you are, *you* at least managed to keep your head during all of this."

"Let me guess," William panted. "Lacey won't talk, Mara's sobbing incoherently, Rei's mumbling, and Cindy's shouting about fish."

Officer Ebb rubbed one gloved hand over his face. He was still in his uniform, despite the late hour: it looked as though he'd been pulling all-nighters to work on the murder case. "Close. So far, Mara won't even come out of the bathroom. What kind of dog are you, again?"

William's amusement vanished. He growled, "I'm *not* a—"

I nudged him to be quiet. If Officer Ebb knew how independent and opinionated William was, we might find ourselves separated more often . . . not that I was hoping that being interviewed by the police would become a routine part of our visit. "I'm sure Lacey and her people know exactly how to handle her situation, Officer, but I still wanted to ask if she needs anything. I have a small traveling kit at the mer-camp, if she wants any herbs."

"Oh you do, do you?"

Shoot. I backpedaled. "Um, just *mountain* herbs. From

Belville, that is. Club moss, also called wolf's claw, is really good for calming lupinosity—or so I've heard."

Officer Ebb sighed. "It's kind of you to ask. We haven't spoken to Mrs. Rise yet; she's last on the list. When we do talk, I'll mention you brought it up. I'd appreciate it," he said, heading off my protest, "if the two of you keep to your room tonight."

William rumbled beside me. I bit my cheek. William just didn't like being told what to do; *he* wasn't the one missing his own clothes and accessories. At least I had my toolbelt. At this point, it was looking like I might as well move into the Rise mansion.

And I really liked Taiwo's camp.

I shoved aside the thought. It was a strange spike of self-pity, considering everything that happened to everyone around me. I shoved my hands in my pockets, finding the crumpled scroll from Luca at the bottom of one. I gripped it tightly as Officer Ebb began his questions.

"First of all, explain to me—as far as you understand it—the point of the lanterns."

"They're a remembrance ceremony for Mr. Rise. He requested it specifically in his will, apparently. It was meant as a symbolic letting go, I suppose? Lacey didn't mention anything about that, but it makes sense to me. It was actually really nice—for a moment."

"And the lanterns were supposed to *do* anything?"

"Um . . . fly off into the night? Not—catch fire."

"And not poison fish," William muttered.

Officer Ebb didn't bother commenting. "Uh huh. Walk me through the evening, please."

I did so, though I left out the conversation I'd heard between

Mara and Cindy. I had heard so little that to mention it seemed like slander. I *did,* however, tell Officer Ebb about Mara's emotional displays and Cindy's over-eagerness in the garden earlier.

"I think she's been riled up all day and looking for some kind of outlet," I said. I didn't mean to excuse her—just to try to understand why she'd do something so drastic. "Unless she's always like that?"

Officer Ebb gave me a look that said pretty clearly that she was always like that.

"Are you aware of the rumors about Cindy and Taiwo?" he asked.

"Rumors," I repeated, mostly just to stall for time. "Uh—yes, we did hear something in town earlier today. But I don't think there's much to it. Taiwo's devoted to Rei."

"Ah," Ebb said, wisely picking up on the protectiveness in my voice. "Forget I mentioned it. It was a while ago, in any case—bit of gossip from the younger set, that's all."

William snorted. "'Younger set' meaning Moe, I bet you."

I had a feeling William was right, but Officer Ebb ignored him. "You haven't noticed anything out of the ordinary about the two?"

"No, of course not. Taiwo's very happy with Rei and the wedding, as I said," I insisted. As I said it I knew I was right about Taiwo, but I couldn't help but wonder if maybe Cindy was having trouble with that.

Meanwhile Officer Ebb moved to the next question on his list. "What do you know of Cindy and Mr. Rise?"

"You mean, how they interacted? Nothing, really. She said something . . . almost respectful of him earlier. Something about organic cake. Nothing about meeting him during a picket, or anything. But I was thinking—well—this morning I met Varsha, over at the bookshop, and I was wondering if she might have some articles about any run-ins they might have had."

"Varsha Lin, yes?" for a brief moment, Officer Ebb smiled. "Brightest scholar Seaside's seen in decades. You were right to seek her out."

"Well, I didn't seek her out—not because of this, anyway—but we did talk a bit about the prophecy and Clemency, too."

"The witch?" Ebb cocked an eyebrow at me, momentarily distracted from his line of questioning. "How'd you learn about her?"

So he knows her new name, I thought. *I wonder if the police have been keeping an eye on her—maybe they know where in the cliffs she lives, too.* "Just picked up on some details from folks in town. That's where you're thinking the hate toward Mr. Rise might have originated, right?"

"Something like that." Once again, Officer Ebb appeared too tired to care. "Can you elaborate at all on the altercation?"

"Um . . ." William mentioning Moe *had* brought something to mind. I said, "Well, Moe and Rei were going at it pretty hard. More Moe than Rei, I think. And he—Moe, I mean—he said some pretty rude things, if I heard them correctly."

The officer's pen paused. "Rude things like . . . ?"

I shifted around on the cushy bed. "It was pretty loud, mind you. But I know the words I heard. It was stuff like— 'shame' and 'traitor' and 'sea rat.'"

"You're sure?"

"Yes." It felt bad to repeat the words, especially in light of the message on the curtain at the opening feast, but I knew I'd heard them.

"And have you heard language like this from the young Mr. Rise before?"

I tugged at my hair. I knew what Officer Ebb was driving at; Moe's language was pretty hateful toward merfolk. And it definitely mirrored the language used on the message emblazoned behind Kade's body. Still, I didn't feel comfortable sharing stories about him when I'd hardly spoken to him myself. "I barely know Moe at all, but he does seem to have . . . issues with the rest of the family. Rei and Taiwo in particular."

"I don't see how you could hear any language from Moe, with the way he mumbles," grumbled William.

"Uh huh," said Officer Ebb again, writing all of this down carefully—even, I think, William's comment. "Anything else? You said you two jumped on Mrs. Rise?"

"Only because we wanted to stop her from hurting Mara," I explained hastily.

"*Too* badly," William amended. I swatted him. I was starting to feel like we were putting on a bad comedy sketch for Officer Ebb.

"At first I actually thought she was William," I admitted. "I didn't see her change—it all happened so fast. And then everyone was yelling, and it seemed like Al was calling you, so . . . that was the most helpful thing we could think of to do."

"Helpful, indeed." Officer Ebb laid his pen down against his notebook. "You come from Belville, right?"

"Ye-es," I said, not sure what this had to do with foolishly tackling full-grown werewolves.

"Then you must know Officer Thorn."

"Yes," I answered more easily, though I was still confused. "She, um—she comes by the shop pretty often."

She also drags me into investigations and uses me as bait

sometimes, but hey, not every friend is perfect.

"She's earned quite a reputation in the guild," said Officer Ebb. "Perhaps you've heard."

"A reputation for—?"

"Solving murders," said Officer Ebb. "And not taking any of this guff while she does, either. Oh, I'm not saying *you* two have caused any guff. But you know what I mean. Talking to you has helped me come to a conclusion. As soon as I get back to the station, I'm calling her in for help."

William's head jerked off the silken duvet cover. "Why? Why would talking to us make you think we need *Thorn?*"

"Listen," said Ebb. For the first time that evening, he sounded downright cheerful. "I didn't get to where I am without knowing the value of top-notch assistance. You two have been a great help already. The way I see it, let's expedite the process and bring her in."

"Expedite the process of driving me away," William mumbled. Fortunately, I didn't think the officer could hear him.

"You're stuck here," I whispered, grinning. To Officer Ebb, I said, "Sounds good to me, Officer. Let me know if you need anything else."

"Suck up," whispered William.

"I appreciate that, Red. At this point, I just want this murder solved," said Officer Ebb as he stood to leave. "Mr. Rise would have been angry as a wet hen over all this fuss."

16

A Light in the Dark

The next morning after a tense breakfast, Mara hustled the wedding party off to try on their clothes for the final time. Watching Moe trail at the back of the group, I found myself glad that William and I had another morning to ourselves.

"I'm going to head to the post office and to see Varsha again, like I promised," I said, looking at my oatmeal-encrusted companion. Apparently, the Rises' cook made a mean breakfast cereal. "Want to come?"

"Might as well," he grunted. "Enjoy our last bit of freedom before Thorn gets here."

I chuckled. "Good point. I don't know how police officers usually travel between towns, but given the high profile of the Rise family, at this point I wouldn't be surprised if they had a sorcerer teleport her in."

William harrumphed at my attempt at humor, but we both got ready a bit quicker than usual after that.

As we strolled along the road into town, I took a moment to center myself. The sky overhead was pale blue, the birds chattering to one another cheerfully as they flew by. After the relative calm of yesterday's weather, a strong wind from the sea had picked up, and I was glad I'd picked up some of my own clothes from the mer-camp the day before. Merfolk clothing was nice, but it tended to be much more flowy—and therefore breezy—than my own standard uniform of close tunic and tights.

I let my hand drift through the tall grasses that grew alongside the road as we walked. They bent under my fingers, tickling the frayed edges of my fingerless work gloves, their young summer shoots still green and thin. The smells, sea salt and sand and fresh leaves, washed through me and made me feel clean in a way that my morning shower hadn't. It was nice to be away from the Rise estate.

"Remember," growled William next to me, "you have a shop to think of."

"What?"

"I know that look. That's your 'isn't it nice to be traveling' look."

"It is not. Right now, it's just my 'isn't it nice to leave murder behind for a while' look," I retorted, smiling. "And anyway, you know I wouldn't abandon Red's Alchemy and Potions for the road again. I'll admit I like little trips, but the shop is still my dream."

"Sure," said William, "not to mention some of the residents of Belville are pretty *dreamy* too."

"Well, now that Gloria's being more pleasant and Sir Rowan's working with us, we do have a lot of friends there," I agreed, unsure of what exactly he'd meant. "I have to admit I'm almost looking forward to seeing Officer Thorn."

William gave me a sidelong glance. "Are you sure you

wouldn't be happier if someone *else* from Belville came to visit?"

"To Seaside? But why would they?" I was genuinely confused by this, and William's dry look wasn't giving me any assistance. I finally resorted to laughing it off. "Maybe after this is all over, we can tell people to take their trips to the beach. But right now, Seaside seems a little too dangerous for casual trips."

"Only if your last name's Rise," William said dryly. "Tell me that after last night, you added Cindy to your suspect list."

"Oh, definitely. Though I'd feel bad for Taiwo if it were her."

"Maybe they're in on it together."

"William!" I reprimanded. "You know as well as I do that Taiwo and Rei are good for each other. No, what I'm still wondering about is the prophecy and the sea witch Varsha was talking about yesterday."

"Clemency?" William's nose wrinkled. "Why?"

"You know how all the lanterns caught fire at once? What if that wasn't just Cindy acting? What if someone else with magic—or a curse—helped it along? I doubt Cindy would admit that things got out of hand, and she makes the perfect scapegoat," I explained. "Maybe it's nothing. Anyway, here's the post office; you coming in this time?"

"Nope." William plopped himself down by the driftwood bench, leaving me to deal with the cacophony of letters being delivered, picked up, and sent out.

"One for you, and one for me," I announced as I came back. I handed him Sir Rowan's report. "You read it over first, okay?"

"What if it says something important?"

"That's exactly why you're reading it first. You're my filtering system. I can't handle the stress of deciphering Sir

Rowan's tiny print without knowing whether the shop caught fire," I said, grinning. Because Sir Rowan *would* write a lengthy report either way, I had no doubt. "I do read them, I just can't stand doing it right away. Besides, I have one of my own." I waved a scroll bent almost in half at my companion.

William panted back, his eyes sparkling—or perhaps that was just a result of his magic. "Another love letter?"

"I haven't gotten *any* love letters," I protested. "Honestly, the strife and turmoil of this wedding is enough to put anyone off the thought of love altogether. Except, of course, Taiwo and Rei."

I sat beside William and we settled into silence, reading.

Hi Red! I know I just wrote to you yesterday, and nothing has really changed since then. Except one thing did change! I put in a picture. I hope you can see what it is okay.

I unrolled the scroll and found that there was, indeed, a picture at the bottom. It appeared to be a pen-and-ink drawing of a . . . furry animal of some kind? *Sea otter?* I wondered. *How in Beyond would Luca find a sea otter in Belville?* I kept reading.

It's a mink!

I sighed, releasing nerves I hadn't realized had taken up residence in my stomach.

I found it yesterday after I wrote to you. It was a really slow day, and rainy, and I was just sitting there—actually I was thinking about how I didn't have anything else to write to you about, which is funny because then this happened. A mink showed up! Suddenly it was just sitting by my foot. It can talk, too. But I don't think it's magical; I think that's just because it's so old. You know how very ancient animals acquire logic and speech, right? It's written about extensively in—

Luca concluded this rather lengthy paragraph with, essentially, a list of tomes and scholarly references about talking animals. Often at home when he went into this "scholar mode" I could distract him with a mug of tea or some new alchemical gadget, but seeing as this was a letter, I read politely without really registering the meaning of most of the words.

Normal, bubbly Luca was back in the next paragraph:

Anyway, he's a really nice mink and now he's staying with me at the shop. Kind of like you with William! But my mink isn't as . . . grumpy. He does have a missing leg though, so if he was grumpy, he'd definitely have good reason for it.

I checked the sketch again and saw that what before I had taken as a fourth leg was actually the creature's tail. *What exactly is a mink?* I wondered. Then I smiled, because I had no doubt that Luca would tell me all about it the next time I saw him.

I'll tell you all about it when you get home. And you can meet him—he's really nice. His name is Frank—did I write that already? Anyway, I hope you're having a good time and that you're getting to visit with Taiwo, too, if they aren't too busy. I saw Sir Rowan last evening and he said everything's fine and that he writes you reports, and he offered to send mine too, but my scrolls don't fit in the envelopes he uses. I think he knew from the beginning it wouldn't work, but he was pretty nice about it. I haven't seen anyone else lately, except Lavender, who reminded me to ask you about the food and also to tell you to travel safe on your way back. I think you were planning on coming home in a week, right? It's really cloudy here but hopefully the roads will be okay by then. Okay, I have to go feed Frank. And eat breakfast.

   Luca

"I think Luca wrote this and sent it this morning," I said aloud, half chuckling to myself as I checked the scroll for a date. Naturally, there was none. "I wonder how he did that?"

"Maybe he uses mail charms," William said, his snout still pressed to Sir Rowan's detailed report. "Trent said that's at least fifty percent of what he sells to Belville residents. Or it was, until he got good at making healing salves."

"Yeah, literally turning people green isn't a great advertisement," I grinned. "I wouldn't have thought Luca sent enough mail to even know about mail charms. But thinking about it—advertisement, I mean—maybe we should look into any old ads run by Rise Enterprises. We looked at the articles yesterday, but ads might tell us about Kade's ideas towards magic or the environment, don't you think?"

William passed Sir Rowan's letter to me with a sigh. "It could work, but *you* have to be the one to bring it up to Varsha. She'll probably be offended you didn't trust her to think of that on her own."

* * *

Contrary to William's gloomy expectations, Varsha looked pleased to see us come into the bookshop. And as soon as she'd finished selling a stack of novels to a mom with deerlike antlers and her pack of young ones, Varsha listened to my thoughts and ideas with the professional excitement of a scholar on a promising hunt.

"I was only able to find a few things about Mountain Meet," she says. "They're not in the news nearly as much as Rise Enterprises, and they don't seem to actually own any land. Of course, by now they might be operating as part of Rise Enterprises, but I haven't gotten any updated records on that yet—my guess is the village council hadn't signed off on anything before the death. It's review season for local businesses."

"Yeah, I'm familiar," I said, because I could tell Varsha was sizing me up to see if she needed to explain herself. "I run a shop back home and just had to go through a review myself."

Varsha nodded in approval. "Normally it's just a matter of form, of course, unless complaints have been lodged about the business during the past year. That was rarely the case for Rise or any of its subsidies, but even so, the council in Seaside is not exactly . . . expedited."

"They run on beach time, huh?" I asked, grinning at her.

"They like to talk things over," she agreed. "At length."

While Varsha and I exchanged sympathetic glances about life as a small business owner, William moseyed through the neat lines of file cabinets, his fluffy tail visible over the furniture. "So what *do* we know?" he asked loudly.

I shrugged apologetically at Varsha. Fortunately, we were

the only ones in the store.

"Nothing more about Kade himself, or Rise Enterprises. MMC trades in natural goods, and seems to have fey connections," Varsha said promptly, adjusting her glasses on her nose. Today's frames were shockingly pink.

"What kind of connections?" I asked. A pit collected in my stomach as I thought of Moe.

"It was in an expose story on business deals in Seaside," Varsha said, pulling a notepad from her pocket. "Here, I have the names written down. Do you have a piece of paper?"

Normally, the answer to that would be yes. I make a point of carrying around a small lab book—usually for noting nerdy things like a new bunch of flowers I found or an idea for a new potion. But it wasn't in its normal pocket in the belt slung over my hips. After a moment of frustration looking for it, I set my confusion aside and reached into the pocket of my tunic, pulling out an old scroll.

"I'll write on the back of this," I said, more for my benefit than Varsha's. Her face was obscured behind her notes; she hadn't even noticed my frantic dance. She did look up as she read the names to me, though.

"Calamitous Seas of Port Blue, and Red Sands—I believe that's a weapons dealer, and—well—Silent Gray."

"'Silent Gray?' What's that?"

"It's supposed to be a pseudonym of the sea witch. In fact, it's what I knew her as primarily, until you came in yesterday calling her Clemency," Varsha said. Her fingers shook a little as she tucked her notebook away. "Anyway, that's all I've got so far. Oh—do you want a spare notebook? I can give you one for free. I've got tons."

"No thanks," I said, stuffing the scroll back into my pocket.

What's with Varsha and Clemency all of a sudden? Does she seem nervous? "I'll find mine soon enough—in the meantime, mail works just fine. How did you figure out about the pseudonym?"

"That's neat that your friends are writing to you here," said Varsha. Below us, the shop bell jangled. "I love writing letters. It gives me such a good perspective on things."

"Hey," said William, popping out of a nearby row of cabinets. "What if the 'deals' were just a front? What if MMC is actually run by one of those fey?"

"Do you have any shifter romances?" A voice called from downstairs.

Varsha hurried out from behind her desk. "Be right back."

As she disappeared down the stairs, I leaned over and whispered to William, "Did you hear her get weird about Clemency? She wasn't like that yesterday, was she?"

William's reply was cut off by yet another jingle of the bells. *The bookstore is busy today,* I thought. *What if someone—maybe even Clemency herself—paid Varsha a visit?*

Images of a sea witch bearing down through the bookshelves made me jump even higher when I heard the words,

"Cinnabar Sunset! Where have you got yourself into *this* time?"

17

Deep Waters

It wasn't Clemency. It was someone much more familiar. Officer Thorn stomped up the spiral staircase to the loft and emerged grinning from ear to pointy ear. "Thought you could hide, did you?"

"Obviously it didn't work too well," William muttered.

"Of course not. Everyone and their sister knows that the wedding couple's new protector and the funny talking dog went to the bookstore this morning," Officer Thorn said easily. "You two might as well wear signs. Now come on, I've got a lot to talk over with you, and I'm famished. I say we hit up the ice cream shop next door."

"You don't even know if we're done here," William protested.

"We are *not* eating ice cream for lunch," I pointed out.

"You can come back if you have more to do. And I'm sure they'll have some rabbit food for you, Red. Now hop to it! Time's a-wasting."

Officer Thorn wheeled and tromped back down the stairs with William and me in tow as surely as if she'd cuffed us. For the second time, I apologized to Varsha, although she seemed

129

more relieved than offended.

But Officer Thorn did tend to have that effect on people—that is, making them rather happier *after* she'd left. Though she's absolutely committed to justice and keeping her community safe, Thorn is notoriously avant garde in the way she accomplishes those goals. And her half-orc heritage makes her taller, broader, stronger, and greener than most of the people within spitting distance wherever she happens to be. Not to mention that her gorgeous black hair and expertly tailored uniform never fail to impress.

She was, in short, precisely the sort of person Officer Ebb desperately needed to deal with the Rise case and all its . . . complications.

"Came in this morning," she informed us without any preamble. We took our seats in a deep green booth at the ice cream parlor, which—ironically—turned out to have an alpine theme, with tree-slice tables, a tiled floor, and pine boughs kept fresh and smelly by magical charms. It also had sandwiches.

"Ebb's told me everything, of course," Thorn continued, barely pausing to place her order for a monte cristo and a banana boat. "Not that that amounts to much. Still, sounds like you two had some fun last night, eh? What do you make of it all?"

"The Rise family is creepy," said William. His tail wagged against the plush seat as he watched his french dip go into the oven behind the counter. "Taiwo'd be better off without them."

"*William*," I protested, "you can't just say that. We don't actually know if any of them are responsible. Besides, Taiwo and Rei really love each other."

His beady eyes gleamed. "Oho, is that Red the determined spinster taking the side of true love?"

"More facts, less bickering," Officer Thorn demanded. "What do we know about the Rises? The Officers around here are all starstruck by them and some old prophecy, from the sounds of it. Cowed by a bunch of hot air, as far as I can make out."

Thorn had a point, even if it was a punny one. I shared everything Varsha had told us about Rise Enterprises and its various side businesses—making sure to lower my voice. The parlor was full of shoppers on lunch break and families on vacation, but I still didn't want to take chances.

"That's a good start." Officer Thorn leaned back as our food was delivered, and then—after a thoughtful bite of half her sandwich—asked, "So have you made any sense of it?"

I shook my head, poking at my chips and veggie burger. "All this stuff about fey deals and corporations and pseudonyms might as well be magic as far as I'm concerned."

"And magic, like love, doesn't exist in Red's world," William quipped.

"I thought I was true love's champion," I shot back. "What is your deal today?"

"No, he has a point." Officer Thorn clucked. "I can't believe you haven't written Luca back, Red."

I dropped a chip and stuttered. *How does she know that?* "We've been busy, as you might have noticed. And why is everyone suddenly super concerned with my correspondence?"

"A good vacation gives you perspective," Officer Thorn said, winking egregiously at William.

Well, I thought, sulking, *I guess I'm not going to ask her if she's met this mink Luca was talking about.*

"In any case, it's a good thing the wedding party's busy," Thorn added. "I need you two this afternoon."

"Why's that?" William asked, suspicious.

"Because," said Thorn, "I already went up to the house with Ebb, and left him there. And I don't see why everyone's dancing around the primary suspect. We've got to cross *someone* off the list. Besides, maybe she'll be of some use."

"Oh, brother," said William.

"Who are we talking about?" I asked. Thorn's idea of a 'primary suspect' and my own often differed.

"The sea witch, of course," she replied. "Ebb knew exactly where to find her but hasn't even once paid her a visit, can you believe that?"

I balked. "Officer Thorn, you have to remember, not all Witches are as cool as Trent is, especially when it comes to the law and—"

"I've already booked the boat to take us down the coast," Officer Thorn declared. Seeing the dismay in our faces, she grinned. "What? Whoever she is, this Clemency's bound to be better than Mara."

* * *

It turned out that Officer Thorn's version of "booking a boat" was renting a rowboat from the ferryman, Kye, and making Jon, one of Officer Ebb's assistants, row us out of the harbor and along the coast. Jon communicated via sign language, commanding Officer Thorn's attention as she helped him get the boat ready. Stocky and silver-haired, with his brown skin laced by occasional scales that marked him half merfolk, like Mara, Jon seemed quite at home in the little rowboat.

Once we settled into a rhythm, slicing through the waves parallel to the shore, William perked up. He moved to the bow of the boat and sat there like a bit of art, embracing his role as pioneering wonder-dog, going where few but the truly desperate had ever gone before.

As far as I knew, anyway.

And after all, weren't we desperate too?

"Come on, Red." Officer Thorn sat heavily beside me at the back of the tiny craft, making it dip. Her usually loud voice was swallowed up by the wind and the sea so that only I could hear it. "Don't look so glum."

I eyed her warily. "Since when does it matter what I look like?"

"Since it means you might offend our suspect," Officer Thorn said cheerfully. "We want her to *like* us. Unless she's just going to fight us and have done with it."

"What a reassuring thought," I said dryly.

Officer Thorn tapped a sparkling pin on her lapel. "Trent made it for me—rush order overnight before I left. It'll repel the worst of any water-based magic."

"That's good for you, and William will be fine, but what about me?"

"Your defense is your knowledge," Thorn said, voicing a confidence I didn't feel. "And speaking of, why don't you tell me all about this sea witchery before we get there?"

"I don't know very much about magic," I protested, half feeling sorry for myself for having been dragged along on this venture, and half embarrassed that William's criticism of "Red's world" earlier might have been right. "You should have brought Luca."

"Oh I should have, should I?" Thorn's brown eyes gleamed

as she loomed over me.

"I mean, it's probably best you didn't, since he might get into trouble. But still, you know what I mean. I don't know very much about sea witchery. I can tell you a little about merfolk, if that helps."

"Actually, it would," Officer Thorn said, stroking her chin. "Am I right in thinking that Mara's merfolk too?"

"I bet she's only half, but you could just ask her. I don't think she's trying to hide it," I answered. "As far as I know—and I only know because of things Jeannie and Taiwo have said, and some things I picked up while traveling—there's seven different mermaid clans scattered all across Beyond. Each one seems to be devoted to a particular seafaring goddess— in Taiwo's folks' case, they're the Afolayan clan, and they're devoted to Yemoja.

"Jeannie's actually the head of the clan, as far as I can tell," I added, my heart warming toward my friends, "although they're not big on ceremony. They all have distinct cultures, you see. Most merfolk clans are nomadic, but some have huge cities built under the sea. The Afolayans are one of the nomadic groups, mostly known for taking care of harbors and estuaries, especially in warmer waters. In fact, Taiwo's father took it to an extreme—he's gone on some trip of his own. I guess that's how he's always been; I've never met him. Jeannie was saying that they sent him a message about the wedding, but they don't really expect him to show." I paused, thinking about the symmetry between Taiwo and Rei's absent fathers—whether the absence was physical or emotional.

Then I shook my head and moved on. "Judging from her coloring and the way she talks, I think Mara's family might be from a clan devoted to Ran, who's a mermaid goddess known to have a city in northern waters, but people usually don't go because—um."

Officer Thorn nudged me with one massive shoulder. "What?"

"Well, I hate to spread bad gossip, especially with so many things already going on, but it seems to be true . . . . Most traders I know won't sail near Ran's waters because her clan is known for . . . repossessing valuable items. Or, uh, possessing them."

"Thievery," Thorn said with a satisfied nod. "I knew there was something familiar about that name."

"But that's not saying *all* devotees or descendants of Ran are that way," I added hurriedly. "It's just some superstitions among traders, is all."

Officer Thorn seemed to take my hedging for granted. She abruptly turned the subject. "Is Clemency merfolk?"

"On account of her being a sea witch?" I hesitated. "I don't know. Varsha said she was Seaside's Witch a long time ago, but I guess she could have merfolk blood."

Thorn snorted. "It's a good thing Jon here knows where to take us. You and William have barely gathered any intel at all."

"I came here for a wedding, not to collect intel for the police," I retorted. "And there's been a lot to learn. Besides, even after what happened, I've mostly been around to make sure that Taiwo and Jeannie have the support they need."

"Tell me something," said Officer Thorn, shifting on the wooden bench beneath us. "Do you really think they'll go through with the wedding?"

"Yeah, I do," I said. Then I paused. Part of me was surprised that Thorn had felt the need to ask the question. But part of me was also surprised at my own faith that Rei and Taiwo would carry on.

Darn it, I thought. *William does have me pegged.*

It was to be expected, I supposed, after all the time we'd spent together.

"Even if there are more attacks?" Officer Thorn pressed.

I looked up at her. She was so much bigger than me that actually, she made a very nice windbreak. Still, I did feel a chill as I thought about that message—*Reynard must die.* "Well, you're here to stop them happening, right?"

"True, but all you have to do is read Ebb's notes from last night to realize it's a tempestuous group of folks."

I shook my head at Officer Thorn's nautical pun and smiled. "I believe Taiwo and Rei can make it through."

"Well, if you believe it, then it must be so," Thorn said, tossing her hair. "Too bad you don't use that belief in your own life more often."

"What, in facing Clemency, you mean?" I rolled my eyes. "Listen, not everyone is as bold as you or William."

"We're getting close," called William. "Jon told me so."

"Sure, if that's what you want to think." Thorn grinned broadly. "Time to put your game face on."

18

Cave of the Sea Witch

'Getting close,' it turned out, meant that our little boat was nearing a set of cliffs. Thorn stood, eagerly scanning the rocks, while I remained firmly on my bench and eyed the frothy waves. *Well,* I thought, *I do have my undrowning potion, and William will be okay. Presumably Thorn and Jon learned to swim in the police guild . . .*

The boat bumped and shuddered as Jon pulled up against a flat rock that just barely broke the surface of the sea. Each new wave washed over its lip. Still, it was clear that the rock had been flattened and put there on purpose: a little column had been erected for handy mooring. And at the back of the rock's flat top, against the sheer cliff, there was a ladder.

"We're going *up?*" I asked, risking a glance skyward. I couldn't see anything but cliff and increasingly cloudy sky.

"That's where the magic is," William confirmed.

Jon shrugged. Clearly, no matter which direction the Witch was in, his choice was to stay with the boat.

Officer Thorn rubbed her hands together. "Okay, me first. Then Red. Can you climb ladders?" she added to William.

"No," he said. "But I can hold on to Red while *she* does."

I sighed. "Great."

And so, the three of us set to climbing. It wasn't so bad really William, being magical, can actually weigh very little when he wants to. He went into his ethereal-familiar mode as he latched on to my shoulders and braced his feet on my toolbelt. Unfortunately for me, this more wispy version of William didn't provide any shelter from the wind, or from the sea spray and the few drops of rain that had chosen that precise moment to make an appearance. *Good thing I brought my gloves.* Fishing them out of my pocket, I donned the thin griffon-hide gloves and pressed the hidden buttons that closed off the tips of the otherwise fingerless accessories.

Officer Thorn was up the ladder in no time, of course. I don't have much of an issue with heights, but I *did* have an issue with the damp and slippery rocks all around us, so I took my time. About two stories up, the ladder gave way to a ledge in the cliff face.

A ledge which, in addition to Officer Thorn, supported a "wipe your feet" rug, an old anchor, and a potted orange tree.

My gaze drifted from these unexpected niceties to the door set into the cliff. Made of sturdy wood, with a porthole inserted for a window, it looked exactly like any of the front doors in Seaside. William leapt down and sniffed it carefully, glowing blue around the edges as he did so.

"Well?" asked Thorn.

"Well what," huffed William. "It's not going to catapult us into the sea or anything, if that's what you're asking."

"Good." Officer Thorn stepped up and rapped smartly on the misty glass of the porthole, calling, "Officer Thorn, Cinnabar, and William here for a visit!"

"Sure, fine, go ahead and tell the exiled witch my real name," I muttered.

William lumbered over and sat on my foot. "It's not that big a deal. Like fairies, a witch would need your *full* name before she could do anything, anyway. On the other hand, sorcerers—"

Noiselessly, the door in front of us swung open. From inside, a tense voice asked, "And is there a *reason* for this visit?"

"Just being neighborly," said Officer Thorn. I had severe doubts as to whether this would work, but apparently it didn't matter: regardless of Clemency's reaction, Thorn strode right inside.

William snorted.

I peered curiously into the gloom behind the door. I have pretty good vision in the dark, so I could make out the face of the person behind it—Clemency, I assumed. She looked more bemused than threatening. I figured it was safe enough to follow in Thorn's steps.

As William and I entered the sea witch's house, she closed the door behind us. With the rain and wind now locked outside, the inside seemed more cozy. It must have been hewn out of the rock, but it didn't feel that way at all. Instead, salvaged wood paneled the walls, and bright blue and purple tapestries hung everywhere. A fire blazed at the back of the space, and a kitchen waited off to one side while a bed piled high with blankets and furs stood against the opposite wall. The open floor plan was a lot like my apartment in Belville, and it made me suddenly long for home.

Thorn stood in the very middle of the room, dripping rainwater on a thickly woven rug. "How're things going?" she asked, quite politely, considering she'd just invited herself in.

"Things *were* nice and quiet. I had planned on a cozy afternoon," said Clemency. As she moved from the shadow of the doorway into the light, there was no mistaking her identity. Under layers of dark blue clothing and a long caftan, her skin was a dull gray, and her eyes were round and deep. I couldn't see her neck under her wild white curls, but I was willing to bet she had gills. *Shark-kin. I've never seen someone with those characteristics before.* I'd always heard that aquatic -kin preferred to live underwater.

Well, this is a liminal space if I ever saw one, I thought, looking around Clemency's space with new eyes. *Maybe she's exiled in more ways than one.*

"We'll get out of your hair soon," said Officer Thorn, still using her more gentle—that is, slightly less-loud—"talking to suspects who don't know they're suspects" voice. "Did you hear about the Rise family news?"

"No," said Clemency, eyeing us steadily as she crossed into her kitchen area. "I didn't hear about it. I saw it. But how, I wonder, did three strangers come to know of it?"

"Could've been the same way you did," said Thorn.

"Hmmm. I doubt it." Clemency's long, flat mouth curved up slightly in a cool smile. "I have my own methods, you see." She gestured to a cauldron standing in the corner. Most cauldrons are iron or some similar material, but when I glanced at hers through my goggles, it seemed to be black ice. I got the feeling that when it was full of water, it served as a scrying tool for Clemency. "I doubt my methods would serve you," she added, though her eyes settled on William as she said it.

William looked away and sneezed.

"On the contrary, you might be able to help us," said Officer

Thorn, still quite the professional. You'd never know that she once shook a criminal into a confession, or got into a fight with a tree. "We've been called in to help local police work on the case, you understand."

"Hmm. I do." Clemency's gaze swept up from William to me. Then she focused on Thorn once more. "My help is not something you want to bargain for. The goddess Sedna takes justice into her own hands."

William shifted, bumping my thigh. I didn't need his reminder, though. I recognized the name Sedna: she was the patron goddess of another merfolk clan, a communal group living even farther north than Ran's people. While Ran was known for having loose ideas of property ownership, and Yemoja and the Afolayans were known for looking after their waters, Sedna was known for seeking vengeance for wrongs and protecting outsiders. From the stories I'd heard, Sedna had become a sea goddess because someone close to her had drowned her.

No wonder Clemency's not worried about being a town Witch any more, I thought. *She's devoted to a goddess who sustains her magic.* While I wasn't entirely sure how witch magic worked—witches, in general, tended to be rather secretive—I *was* familiar with the concept of serving a god or goddess and receiving strength or magic in return. And I could certainly see how Clemency and Sedna might have a lot in common.

Meanwhile, Officer Thorn was unmoved. "Let's stick to talk, then. Can you tell me anything about devil's rope kelp powder?"

"Worked that out, did you?" Clemency's gaze slid to me. "That must have been your work. I noticed you at the opening feast."

William bristled. "What were you doing watching the party, anyway?"

"I make a point of keeping up with current events," said Clemency softly. "And what could be more current that the marriage of Seaside's prince of business and the heir of Yemoja? Hmmm. Perhaps you recognized devil's rope, alchemist, but it is clear you do not know of its use."

William's bristle became a low rumble. I spoke before he could say anything too offensive. "That's why we're here, Clemency."

Well, one of the reasons, anyway . . .

But I'd called her on her name, just as she'd called out my profession. This seemed to please her: her attitude shifted. "It is as well. Devil's rope is not so rare. But it is a difficult poison to use. The dose must be exactly correct. Too little causes only minor complaints, and too much does no harm at all."

Maybe that was the meaning behind that song William heard in Rote, I thought, recalling how the chorus he'd sung for Ebb had said that one dose was deadly while two was not.

"What exactly would the right dose be?" Thorn asked casually.

Clemency rolled her head on her neck, a gesture reminiscent of a fish moving through water. "The familiar knows what I am. I am not a healer. I do not work with plants. I have no desire to know about dosages of devil's rope."

"But the killer would have to," I murmured quietly. "They'd have to have special knowledge. Or be given the poison by someone who did . . ."

Clemency smiled her eerie smile at me once more. "It was no novice who killed King Rise. It is not only the dose that matters, alchemist. It is the time. Like many of the sea's gifts, devil's rope fades as it touches air."

"So it was put into the glass right before the speech," Thorn surmised.

Of course, I had already guessed as much, but the thought still made my stomach clench. The suspect pool was looking smaller—and closer—than ever. Only family members and Mara had been sitting at the raised table with Mr. Rise.

"Is this why you have interrupted my peace?" Clemency asked the officer pointedly. "To speculate about basic facts?"

"No," I spoke before Thorn could. She and William looked at me strangely, but I'd thrown my hat in the ring, so I decided I might as well follow through with it. "We—*I*—want to know your story, Clemency. I want to know what happened with the Rises, and your prophecy, and why you're living out here."

Clemency's round, dark eyes narrowed and seemed to shimmer suspiciously. For the first time, she walked toward us, coming closer to me. "That is a lot of wants, alchemist."

William growled.

"You chose to change your name," I said, trying my best to remain firm and neutral. "And to serve a new goddess. You chose a goddess with a heavy past, but you chose a name that means mercy."

This time, Clemency's entire body shimmered, like water was rippling over her skin. The effect was terrifying, because it highlighted the sharklike aspects of her appearance—and the power that sharks have underwater. I swallowed hard and held her gaze.

The water effect broke and Clemency smiled, like the smooth crest of a shark fin through waves. "Well argued, alchemist. I accept your logic as payment."

19

Clemency's Tale

"I will tell you the real truth of what you think you know," Clemency said, turning to pace slowly around our little group. William sparkled with blue magic, ready for anything, but Officer Thorn and I remained perfectly still. The sea witch continued, "It will not be as easy or as smooth as you would like. But you have paid for it by coming here and treating with me, and I do not suffer debts.

"I was once the town Witch of Seaside," she began, still watching us carefully. "The alchemist and the familiar knew this. The officer is surprised. Official Witches are supposed to be helpful creatures, aren't they? They are trained—they are tamed. So was I, once, decades ago.

"Dutifully I dealt with the townsfolk, tending to their wants and whims, healing scrapes and doling out charms. And in that spirit of duty, I gave my blessing to each new dealing of Rise Enterprises—and, therefore, Kade Rise.

"Kade Rise inherited the business from his mother before him. His mother had respect for Witches, for me, but little Kade had only ambition. If he could have, he would have

144

demanded rulership from me. When he could not, he began seeking it all over the world. A trident which could make the seas grow calm—a conch which could make its hearers sing to one man's tune—a stone which could reflect the appearance he wanted the world to see. He collected these trinkets, just as he continued to collect spells from me.

"And little Kade got exactly what he wanted. He was the youngest heir of the Rise family to negotiate a major new trade deal. The business flourished. He was more successful than his mother, more successful than his grandparents. He extended his power over Seaside and its council. And he took a lovely young bride.

"Little Kade could control business, but he could not control nature. He knew this. And that was why he still needed *me*." Clemency grinned darkly as she glided past William and me, continuing her slow pace around the room.

"When his first child was born, he came to me," she continued, her voice becoming more animated. "He wanted me to guarantee that his tiny child would be powerful, would be beautiful, would be just as successful as he was. He wanted his legacy to live on after he passed away. He *needed* it to. He did not make me a deal: he *demanded* that I grant these things. I was a dutiful Witch. I tried.

"But promises are not possible in magic, are they, familiar?" Clemency asked, wheeling on William. "Magic is the promise of possibility. It does not make any promises itself."

William rumbled, neither agreeing nor disagreeing, and the sea witch moved on.

"Under the light of the full moon, with every advantage I could think of, I did my best to weave my spells. I thought I was acting for the best. Little Kade Rise believed that his good fortune would benefit the town, and so the town believed that any misfortune to the Rises would mean its downfall. I had bought what Kade Rise was selling. I thought I was doing what must be done to secure the future."

Clemency paused—in fact, she seemed to hesitate, as if this part of the story pained her. William's rumble became a few quiet words. "The future can't be caught," he said, glancing up at me. "And it can't be bought, but it can be sold. My old sorcerer used to say that."

"Sorcerers, for all their uselessness, do know how to turn a phrase," Clemency remarked. Her disdain for sorcery so echoed William's disdain for Witches that I might have laughed, if the atmosphere in the room hadn't been so dark and serious. She cleared her throat and added, "No doubt the familiar has already guessed what happened. I stood on the bluffs and I called on all my power and I tried to bless the Rise child's future. But the future does not cooperate.

"Hungry Kade Rise had gathered the entire town to see the event. People lined the hills and coast like broken shells in the sand. They were supposed to witness the child's good fortune. And then I lost control of the magic and it ran through me, and what came out was pure prophecy. The prophecy the alchemist has come to investigate."

She stopped for a moment to stare at me, and then she recited,

When Reynard rules Seaside
And none know his name,
And speaking the truth
Can only bring shame,
Then shall come the undrowned tide
To sweep away sickness and blame.

"Perhaps you are unaware," she added, addressing Officer Thorn but also glancing once more at me, "that true prophecy is one aspect of magic which can not be controlled. You can not *choose* to prophesy. You can not *create* a prophecy. When a prophecy comes, it may even come to one without magic. The nature of prophecy is wild.

"And I, too, became a wild witch in that moment. Everything I'd been taught, the duties I'd upheld, became meaningless. Because in that moment while the magic was flowing through me, before I'd finished the last word, little Kade Rise pushed me off that cliff."

"He *pushed* you?" Officer Thorn interrupted, ever one to pause over a crime.

"Perhaps he thought he could stave off the future," Clemency said, continuing her slow circle with her hands behind her back, as though Kade's reasoning really didn't interest her at all. "Perhaps he believed I had betrayed him. And because he believed it, he made it so. The town believed him. I no longer had a place there. I hit the rocks, I hit the water, but I did not die. Instead, I found my goddess down in the depths, and She told me that I must be prepared to start a new life."

"So you came here," I murmured.

She turned on me. "I chose exile. I cut out the old and made myself new around the wound. And I am merciful—yes, I know you wonder, alchemist—I help the townsfolk who find me now. But only if they pay me. Because I have learned. I no longer give in to demands."

"But you admit to watching the Rises," Thorn said, sticking to the reason we'd come here in the first place.

"She has to," William said, when Clemency simply looked at the officer. "Because she's in the prophecy too. She has to wait to see how it ends, just like everyone else. It's like a curse."

I shuddered, thinking of the last time we had encountered a curse—the curse which had torn apart poor Luca and his family, and had left him with a strange affinity for shadows and the darker creatures of the forest to this day. Often he used a glamour to hide the effects, a darn horn protruding from his forehead and mossy tattoos all over his skin.

"The familiar is correct," said Clemency, with an especially shark-like smile. "I wait."

"Well," said Officer Thorn, rubbing her hands together as though dismissing a spell. "That's interesting. Any other insights you'd like to share, seeing as we're here?"

I noticed Thorn didn't thank Clemency for the information, which was a smart move. Sometimes when dealing with fey or magical beings, to acknowledge thanks was to acknowledge a debt. And debts to the fey—or to rogue witches—could take you to scary places.

Again, Clemency smiled. "My advice is the same as always. Look amongst yourselves. Betrayal always comes from the mouth that paints the prettiest pictures, and asks you for the greatest sacrifices."

William snorted. "Some turn of phrase."

"Be careful, familiar." Clemency's gaze went steely blue as she looked down at him. "You are ancient, but there are those who are more ancient still."

"That sounds like a 'no,'" said Thorn cheerfully. "We'll just be on our way, then. Enjoy your cozy afternoon."

And just like that, with four breezy steps, Thorn whisked herself out of the mess she'd gotten us into. But I paused on the doorstep. "Clemency," I said quietly, voicing a thought that had been forming in my mind throughout her story, "you loved him. Kade Rise. Or at the very least, you loved Seaside."

"Ah, the alchemist knows," said the sea witch, her vague shimmery-ness back in place. "She does not ask; she declares her findings. Very well. Since you have not asked, I will not answer. Instead, I will exchange an observation with you."

William whined at me, but I waited.

Clemency came very close to us at the door, and she did not smile. "To love is to drown. But if you are clever—if you are careful—if you are an alchemist—you become an undrowned one."

She reached out and nearly touched the pendant around my neck, the shell that held my undrowning potion. At the last second William barked, loud and sharp, and he pushed me out of the cave. The door slammed shut behind us.

"*That* was something," I muttered, automatically huddled behind Thorn on the doorstep. It was raining in earnest now.

"Not a word," William growled. "Not til we're in the boat. Get going, *now*."

Officer Thorn looked back at us with a grin. "Sure thing, O Ancient One."

20

Unfortunate Souls

We waited not only until we were down the staircase and in the boat, but a good distance away over choppy waters before anyone spoke again.

In fact *no* one spoke. The roar of the wind was interrupted by William buzzing.

"Haven't seen *that* feature before," said Officer Thorn, squinting through the sea spray at William, who was glowing bright blue.

"Ugh," he replied. "Shut up for two seconds, won't you? Someone's calling you."

"Someone's *calling?*" I repeated, astonished.

William gave me a look that could have cut glass. For a moment the glow around him brightened, and then it channeled straight up into the air. A globe appeared above his furry head. And in that globe, we could see half a mouth, a nose, and somebody's collar.

"Officer Ebb?" Thorn asked, shifting and setting the boat rocking wildly.

"Officer Thorn? Can you hear me?"

The voice coming through the globe was faint, but it was definitely Seaside's police chief.

William cleared his throat, looking very smug. "You're on a call. Hold the phone back from your face, Ebb. Everyone can see you."

"Oh. Oh!" Officer Ebb made adjustments on his end, as he'd been told, and came into view looking relieved. "I wasn't sure how this thing worked. I had to borrow it, you see. Officer Thorn, why have you been out of contact?"

"What do you mean? I haven't been out of contact at all," she protested.

Normally, I would have easily believed that Thorn—who often seemed impulsive almost to the point of roguishness to me—had gone *incommunicado* with her fellow officers. But the surprise and concern in her voice sounded genuine. My mind immediately leapt to a new conclusion.

"Clemency," I said. When it was clear Officer Ebb couldn't hear me properly, I added loudly, "We've just been to visit Clemency. Officer Thorn—and William and I—went right into her home. She probably had some sort of protection set up."

"Communication disabler," said William, nodding. The globe stayed steady above his head. I doubted Officer Ebb could see him, but he was clearly listening closely as William continued, "It's a standard ward. Probably Clemency wanted to be sure that Thorn wasn't recording or broadcasting her conversation."

Officer Thorn, meanwhile, had pulled her police-issue communication device from her pocket and was looking at it like it had suddenly turned into a live worm. "You tried calling me, Ebb?"

"Several times now," confirmed the other officer. "As soon as I realized what you were doing. What in Beyond did you go to Clemency for? Couldn't you have told someone?"

"Just a routine check," said Thorn, rather gallantly refraining from throwing Jon under the bus for being there with us. "We got some new intel. Seems like we're looking for someone very familiar with devil's rope, Ebb."

"We can talk about it later," said Officer Ebb, looking much aggrieved. "You *are* coming back, I presume?"

"Of course," said Thorn. "We may just make a stop or two along the way."

She signed off with her fellow officer and William grumbled. "Communication via familiar magic is probably *more* secure than talking in his archaic office in Seaside."

"Look who you're calling archaic,'" said Thorn cheerfully. "Just how old are you, anyway?"

"That's for me to know and you to never find out," William grumbled.

I chuckled, but something else was weighing on my mind. "Thorn, exactly what other 'stops' do you intend to make?"

At first she just shrugged. Then she turned, huddling in with William and me. "It's occurred to me," she said, "that there's one person who's been routinely uncooperative in the police reports, and who was up on that dais, near the wine glass in question. Ige."

"You don't mean that," I protested, aghast. "Plenty of others have been uncooperative too!"

"Sure," agreed Thorn, "but they didn't have as clear a shot, as I see it."

"And being merfolk, it's more likely he'd know all about devil's rope," said William.

"You don't know that at all. What if—what if—" I hesitated, and a thought came to me. "What if the poisoner has been trying for weeks?"

Thorn looked at me skeptically.

"What if the wedding was just a coincidence," I continued, gaining steam despite her disbelief. "What if the poisoner really doesn't know much about devil's rope, and has been trying various doses at all sorts of functions?"

"Doesn't seem likely," said Thorn doubtfully. "That's a lot of poison gone to waste."

"Maybe they're angry enough that it's worth it. Maybe they have enough money that they don't care. Maybe," I added, "it's someone who's been involved in the wedding planning! They'd have tons of opportunities. Someone like Mara, for example!"

"Or Cindy," said William. "She told that story about eating cake with Mr. Rise, remember. And she must be getting *some* money for her sculpture thingy."

Thorn pursed her lips at him. "Whose side are you on, anyway?"

William scratched an ear. "The right one."

"You can't narrow down the suspect list just yet," I insisted.

Officer Thorn heaved a heavy sigh. "Be that as it may, I still intend to take a look around the mer-camp."

"You don't *really* suspect Ige that strongly, do you?" I asked.

"Maybe. Maybe not." Thorn grinned at me. "*Maybe* I just want to see that mer-camp. I hear it's spectacular."

* * *

Officer Ebb was waiting for us when we got to the dock in

Seaside. It was raining seriously now, but neither the gray skies nor his violently yellow standard-issue rain slicker could disguise his displeasure.

"Officer Thorn," he began sternly as we clambered wetly to the safety of terra firma, "what possessed you to pull such a stunt?"

If Ebb was a disappointed grandparent, Thorn was a recalcitrant teen. "It wasn't a stunt," she protested. Unfortunately, the fact that William, Jon, and I were all a bit wild-eyed and shaken behind her didn't lend credence to this statement.

"*No one* is to disturb Clemency's peace," Officer Ebb said, looking past us at Jon. "Anyone from town knows that."

"That's why you needed me," said Thorn. "Someone had to go talk to her, or—"

"Wait," I said, curious. "You mean you're not staying away from her because you're scared of her, but scared of violating some agreement?"

Officer Ebb considered me dourly, like an ancient priest might have looked upon a disciple who thought to question whether the world was flat after all. "We have an agreement, yes. That the police of Seaside leave her alone."

I raised an eyebrow. I'd learned enough about Clemency to know that wasn't the whole story. "If that's half the deal, what's the other half?"

William shook himself. "Not persecuting Mr. Rise for pushing her off a cliff in front of the whole town, I bet. He gets left alone, she gets left alone."

Officer Ebb's expression went from dour to terrified, to guilty, to resigned.

"It's true, then?" I guessed, watching him.

"Keep your minds on the current case. We're not here to

judge the local history," Thorn warned us. She was so serious she even missed the opportunity to make a seafaring pun about "currents."

"You aren't here for pulling stunts, either," Officer Ebb insisted, obviously glad for a change of topic.

No wonder he's been so reluctant to share details about Clemency or even the prophecy, I thought. *And with the police being silent on the matter, and Mr. Rise being angry, no doubt, the town has had two decades or so to stew in fear of the exiled witch. I guess it makes sense why the prophecy might stir up strong emotions in everyone involved. Clemency talked about Kade being worried about his legacy—some legacy it's turned out to be! Poor Rei, stepping into that. I wonder how much he knows . . .*

At this point, the two officers began to hash out exactly what had or hadn't been a good idea, and I left them to it. Digging through my tool belt, I brought out a collapsible umbrella and unfolded it over William and me. We were already wet, of course, but it was comforting to have something to do. Meanwhile, Jon finished tying up the police boat and skittered off down the dock, no doubt grateful that their superior officers were otherwise engaged. I watched as Jon's escape was blocked by another figure in a dark gray rain suit that obscured all detail standing under a covered dock only ten or twenty feet away.

I guess none of us are escaping after all, I thought wryly.

"Isn't that right, Red?" Officer Thorn demanded.

I snapped out of my reverie. "Hmm?"

Officer Ebb sighed. "Officer Thorn believes that you have done some research at the bookstore that may be useful as well. Something about Rise Enterprises and Mr. Rise's will? I thought you were just looking into poisons."

The officers' voices were loud, bouncing around the deserted dock. William grumbled beside me. I did my best to take everything down a notch by saying, "I told you we were going to see Varsha, right, Officer Ebb? We didn't exactly find anything there about devil's rope, but she—we *did* find out that Mr. Rise had begun some new trading ventures lately. Maybe that's what Officer Thorn meant."

"It's not just what I meant, it's what I said," Thorn insisted, though she did lower her voice a bit. "Somehow all these things come together, Ebb. We have to be willing to chase down every lead."

Again, the local officer sighed. "I won't deny that you've been successful in the past, so this attitude must have some merit. But please, try not to go out of communication again, will you? The point of bringing you in was to increase cooperation."

"More like to let loose even more disruptions on the scene," William rumbled. I nudged him, but he refused to budge beyond the scope of the umbrella.

"Of course," said Thorn with the easy conviction of someone who has no intention of remembering this later.

"And where are you going now?" Officer Ebb's tired-parent voice was back again.

"The Afolayans' camp," said Thorn with relish. "Want to come?"

"I have to get back to the Rise estate. As it is, I feel I ought to be carting them all around with me wherever I go," Officer Ebb admitted.

William's ears perked up, and I have to admit, so did mine. "There haven't been any more threats or attacks, have there, Officer?" I asked.

"No, no. But it's three jobs together trying to keep them from arguing," he replied.

Officer Thorn shrugged. "It's a wedding. If it weren't for the poisoning, I'd say that's normal."

This surprised me into a chuckle—I hadn't expected to find myself in agreement with Officer Thorn about weddings. And at the same time, I could hear Lacey in my mind saying, *just love your friends, and let them love you.* This prompted me to speak up. "I'd like to go back up to the house with you, Officer Ebb. Officer Thorn, I'll meet you back at the camp later. William, do you want to come along with me?"

He shook out his fur again, grumbling. "I'd better. *Someone* has to keep you safe."

21

To Get the Witch

Along with Officer Ebb, William and I rode in a covered wagon of sorts, pulled along by a bicycle. This particular bicycle had been magicked to run by itself, which was for the best in such rainy weather. Tucked inside atop plush bench seats, the three of us were cozy, if a little crowded.

Officer Ebb spent the first two blocks staring hard out the window. Finally, he said, "How was she?"

"Clemency, you mean?" I glanced at William. "She seemed fine. A little intimidating, but she didn't do anything to harm us."

"Good, good. It's been years," he replied absently. "She, ah, of course she didn't confess to the murder, I suppose?"

I creased my eyebrows in disbelief. "If she had, Officer Thorn would've told you that right away."

"Right, of course." Officer Ebb resumed staring out the window.

Maybe he still can't believe we went there at all, I thought. I leaned forward and asked, "Do you still think the prophecy is at the root of the murder?"

"Must be—mustn't it?" Officer Ebb turned and looked at me, blinking as if he'd just realized I was there. "To tell you the truth, Red, I don't know what to think any more. That's why I brought in Officer Thorn. It'd be a relief at this point if it *was* just down to the prophecy, but then—"

"I really don't think Clemency had much motive," I told him. "She seems like she's done her best to wash her hands of Seaside and the Rises."

"Still, it could have been someone else who believed the prophecy was about Rise," William pointed out gruffly. "That's what the officer hopes. Right?"

"Well, insomuch as you can *hope* anything about a murder case," Ebb said, tugging at his uniform. "I, ah—I won't be able to stay with you once we get to the Rise estate. I've got to check with some of the guard. You'll be okay on your own?"

We agreed that we would be, and shortly afterward, the bicycle wagon deposited us at the Rises' front door. Officer Ebb hustled off. For a moment William and I stood under the cover of the front porch, watching him disappear into the rain.

"I know he's always been a little reserved," I said, "but didn't he seem—a bit odd about this whole thing with Clemency?"

"Obviously," William said.

"I guess he really didn't think Thorn would go see her."

"Of course not. But he probably did want her to," he said airily.

I cocked my head. "Huh?"

"You only got halfway there, Red," William replied, shaking water from his ears. "Officer Ebb *is* odd about Clemency. And he's probably about her age. He was around when she was active . . . and he's been shielding *her* as much as shielding *us* . . ."

"Are you trying to say Ebb has feelings for Clemency?" I frowned.

"Ding ding ding," William said, mimicking the "victory" noise from the games on the boardwalk. "That's what I'd bet, anyway."

I ran my hand through my hair. *At least I didn't entirely miss the clues on that one,* I thought ruefully. *I wonder if it matters? It would kind of give Ebb a reason to be upset with Mr. Rise.* Aloud, I said, "Is it just me, or is everyone around us falling in love with everyone else? I mean, it can't all just be because of the romance of the wedding, can it?"

"Oh, it isn't just 'everyone around us,'" William retorted smugly.

Before I could ask what he meant, the front door opened, and we were ushered inside the Rise mansion.

* * *

After our various drips and puddles were cured with the aid of a magical charm, William and I were shown into "the sitting room," where we found Lacey and Moe. The room was on the second floor with a wonderful view of the sea, full of comfy chairs, bookcases, and the occasional musical instrument or writing desk. However, none of those things were in use. Moe stood silently near one of the large windows, and Lacey had apparently been pacing—she walked over to us as we came in.

"William, Red, a welcome surprise," she said, giving me a quick hug. William she petted on the head; evidently, she bore him no ill will for his role in breaking up the fight last night.

"I thought you'd be out investigating all day—Officer Ebb told us all about your friend, Officer Thorn. I don't know if you've heard, but we've had a bit of a fraught morning."

"We didn't hear any specifics," I said, with a glance at William.

From the window, Moe grunted. "Do you even need to?"

"Perhaps it's best not to dwell," Lacey said, with a sad, tired glance at her son. She ushered us farther into the room, toward a tea tray, adding, "Rei's up in his tower, I believe. Please do feel free to visit him. But first, can we get you anything?"

"I'm fine with some tea," I assured her. "Lacey, I—I wanted to tell you that we've been to see Clemency. We went with Officer Thorn just after lunch."

Lacey's hand trembled as she poured fresh earl gray into a gilded cup. "It was only a matter of time," she remarked. "Did she—did she tell you much?"

I recalled that Lacey had said she didn't know the details of what had happened between Mr. Rise and Clemency, and I hesitated. *Surely she knows about Mr. Rise's reaction to the prophecy. Maybe she sensed there was more to it—since it does seem like there was a bit of a sad love triangle going on.*

"She gave her side of things," said William gruffly. "You ought to know she watches you."

"We—we did know that. Or rather, I do," Lacey answered, and I realized she'd fallen back on a habit of answering for herself and Kade for a moment. From the way Moe had stiffened over by the window, it seemed clear that he had not. "No matter what magical protections Kade put up, she always seemed to grow just a little more powerful."

"She does seem very devoted to her practice," I said neutrally.

"But I don't think she plans to do anything."

"Of course not," Moe broke in sarcastically. "Because that's the thing about devoted people, isn't it? They don't see anything beyond that one thing they love. No one else matters. Just like you with Father, and Father with his business."

With this cutting remark, he strode through the room and left, slamming the door behind him.

In his wake, Lacey sighed and sank into a nearby chair. "As you can see, we're still . . . still a bit . . ."

"Lacey, please, don't feel like you have to explain," I interrupted sympathetically. "A lot has happened in the past few days, and here we are stirring things up. If anything, we should be sorry."

"No, no, don't be. I told you that from the beginning," she replied, smiling faintly up at me. "It seems it's time for these things to be stirred up. Probably," she added, her gaze drifting, "we shouldn't have spent so long trying to keep them tamped down."

Next to me, William shifted. "Did Moe mean that? About Mr. Rise being devoted to his business?"

"Yes, I'm afraid so," Lacey answered. "They often fought about it—when Kade was alive. Moe always knew the business would go to Rei, of course. But more than that—he seemed to see what the rest of us ignored. That Kade was growing ruthless for the sake of his business."

The sake of his legacy, I corrected in my mind. *After the failure of the blessing for Rei, I bet he became even more intent on securing that legacy somehow.*

"But no one else noticed?" I asked, very quietly. From everything we'd heard about Kade and his power, it seemed obvious to me that he'd been—to put it delicately—ambitious.

"Not to the point of saying anything," Lacey said reluctantly. "I think we were all—well, we wanted to be as invested as he was. That was the thing about Kade, you see. He *was* devoted to Rise Enterprises, and he expected everyone around him to be just as passionate."

William gave me a look which seemed to communicate something like, *if you ever get that intense about Red's Alchemy and Potions, I'm not falling down that rabbit hole with you.* I tried not to grin back at him—obviously Lacey was feeling very somber—but it was difficult to think of an appropriate response.

"But you came to see Rei," Lacey said at last, rousing herself. "Don't let me keep you. It'll be good for him to see you—the two of you are like a glass of fresh water after too much briny sea."

We took our leave as politely as we could, and made our way down the hall to find the stairs to Rei's retreat.

As we walked the empty halls, William muttered, "It's weird she phrased it like that, right?"

"What, the fresh water thing? Maybe," I said, my hand going to my pendant. "It makes me think of the 'undrowned' thing again."

"It makes *me* think of poisoned glasses," William retorted.

"Oh, please. If anything, she was probably thinking of the fact that the last time I talked to her alone, I gave her some ice water."

"I think that's giving her memory too much credit," William observed. He looked up and nudged me. "What are you thinking now?"

"Nothing—just that when we *did* talk, last time, she told me something about friendship seeing us all through hard times.

Kind of the opposite of what Clemency said, when you think about it," I said, thoughtful.

"Or the same," William pointed out. "Clemency didn't say *not* to fall in love, Red. She just said that if you're aware and willing to change, then you have a much better chance of making it work."

I might have argued his point, but by then we'd reached the spiral staircase, and I needed all the breath I could get. Instead, I continued mulling it over to myself. *'Willing to change,' I could see how that's what she meant by 'being an alchemist,' because alchemy is all about transformation. And William would interpret being 'clever' as knowing what's going on at all times, I decided wryly. I think I get his idea. Not to be afraid of hard times, but to respond to them with the help of friends. It is kind of the same message.*

As we neared the top of Rei's tower, my thoughts shifted toward apprehension. I wondered how much to tell Rei about what Clemency had said. Over the winter, I'd caused some trouble by telling a young acquaintance, Snow, a bit too much about her own past. Maybe William was right—I *was* turning out to be a bit of a busybody. But people did keep asking for help . . .

We'll see how he responds and go from there, I decided pragmatically. By that point, we'd reached the top of the stairs.

We found Rei working on his portrait of Taiwo, swirling dark blues along the bottom of the canvas. He only seemed to look at it half the time—the other half of the time, his gaze seemed to be pulled out the window.

Classic pining, I thought, exchanging a glance with William.

I cleared my throat. "Hey, Rei. We just wanted to come by and . . . update you on everything."

"Red." Rei shifted on his stool, looking back at us. "Did Taiwo tell you what happened?"

"No, not yet," I said, with a mental note that I *definitely* needed to track down Taiwo after this. "We've been out. We actually went to visit the sea witch, Clemency."

Rei's brown eyes widened. "Her? I've only ever heard stories about her. I guess I kinda thought she and the prophecy might just be a fairy tale."

"Nope, both are definitely real," William said, trotting over to plop himself down on a cushion. "Haven't you ever thought of visiting her yourself?"

"Me?" Rei set his paintbrush down in a glass of cloudy water as he thought. "No . . . Father *really* wouldn't have liked that."

I took up a position leaning on a nearby empty easel. "What did he have to say about her?"

"Just that she was the reason Seaside was in danger," Rei answered.

William cocked an ear. "Seaside's in danger?"

"Just because of the prophecy," Rei said, sounding smaller and smaller by the moment. "That's why he always had to work so hard. Father, I mean."

"Huh. Rei," I said, realizing that now wasn't the time for a heavy conversation, "have you thought about talking to your mom about it sometime? Maybe after the wedding, and everything."

"Yes, I—I have," he said, looking up at me much as Lacey had. "I've always kind of wanted to, actually. But I always thought . . . I shouldn't."

William sneezed. "You're the head of a massive trade empire now. 'Should' doesn't apply any more."

"Or maybe it applies now more than ever," I said softly,

watching Rei shrink away from William's words.

After a moment, Rei sighed, just like his mother. "It feels like it does. And I don't know what to do. All I know is I love Taiwo, and I want to go through with this."

"Does Taiwo know that?" I asked.

"I—I think so," Rei said, twisting his paintbrush in its cup. "It's just been hard to get a moment alone. It's funny—remember before this all happened, when I was already nervous just about the wedding? And I thought *you* were pessimistic, Red. Now I feel like a pessimist."

"Hey, that's okay, Rei," I said, smiling at the memory. "You've been through a lot. Just don't forget that Taiwo could help you with that. And so can we."

22

Under the Sea

Shortly after that, we left Rei to his painting—and his thoughts. With a quick goodbye to Lacey and Officer Ebb, we made our way to the dock. I was starting to feel itchy about getting to the merfolk camp and learning what was going on. And I knew that if we swam there, our path would take us right past the building site for the wedding platform—and therefore, Jeannie.

Without needing to talk about it, William and I plunged into the water.

My undrowning potion had held up perfectly. *Clemency probably wasn't going to do anything to it,* I decided. *She was just making a point about the prophecy. She must think I'm involved in it . . . or maybe someone with similar skills is?* Either way, I knew better than to ask William what he thought about it again: he'd only be angry at me for letting the sea witch get so close.

Swimming under a stormy sea was much different from swimming through a clear, golden one. The lack of light from above made everything a bit cloudy and jewel-toned, and the waves above us seemed to tug at our shoulders as we swam. Even in the best of conditions, William was about as graceful underwater as a hare on a treadmill. And my super-speed on land did not help me in the sea. *Maybe when I get home, I should look into something that helps me walk and run underwater. Maybe some kind of weighted shoe? Of course, I wouldn't want to disturb the life on the sea floor . . .*

Thoughts of invention helped distract me from my worry—not to mention the physical exertion cleared my head. By the time we reached Jeannie and her team, I'd relaxed enough to return her smile.

"You're here looking for Taiwo," she guessed, turning to face William and me.

I nodded, since my voice couldn't carry as well as hers did underwater. I didn't want to embarrass myself by attempting a full sentence.

"Good," Jeannie continued, reaching out to help William float up to eye level without flailing about. "They could use a visit from their friends. But since you're here, how do you like our progress with the stage?"

We looked over Jeannie's shoulders and short, ruffled hair. Behind her, a busy group of merfolk—it looked like the entire wedding guest roster—swarmed around a set of pillars. Using their arms and fins, they stirred the water and gave direction—to each other, yes, but also to the teams of fish and shellfish which moved among them. Each small creature shifted sand and cemented shell to bring the ambitious plan into place.

The columns themselves, already tall enough to reach nearly to the surface, gleamed white and gold even in the cloudy water. Some distance away, another team of workers worked on a large, flat surface of shell which would be lifted on top of the columns. They seemed to be scouring the surface—no doubt working with all the sand in the water meant that plenty of impurities and bumps got into their construction. As an alchemist I was familiar with shell, or as it's known among scientists, calcium carbonate. A fellow apprentice of mine had been obsessed with it as a combination of elements: water, fire, earth. As such I had spent many, many evenings helping them clean up the lab floor. Shell is a beautiful material, and when you're merfolk you can certainly make it into anything, but it does have a tendency toward brittleness.

Seeing my glance, Jeannie pivoted, her long purple tail moving gracefully in the water. She must have intuited my thoughts, because she said, "Once the columns are in place, we'll be making struts and horizontal supports. Since the platform only has to support Taiwo and Rei and Arielle, who's doing the ceremony for us, it will be more than enough. Everyone else will watch however they please," she added with a smile.

Air bubbles tumbled from William's mouth, and I could guess exactly what he was trying to say. *It's for the best to keep everyone separated, given how this wedding has gone so far.*

I nodded and beamed at Jeannie, giving her two thumbs up.

"Thank you," she said graciously. "Will you take some of that enthusiasm to my oldest child, please? They're finding everything to be a bit of a strain. It's only natural for them both to feel that way, Taiwo and Rei, the poor things. They've had a small tiff over it. If I know anything about my Taiwo, you'll find them at the fish training barracks."

I gave Jeannie another grateful nod, and she waved us off. Her voice followed us as we started the swim toward the camp. "I feel better already knowing you're looking after Taiwo."

William grunted and nudged clumsily at my elbow, sending me drifting over a coral formation as we swam. I turned to frown at him, but soon divined his intent. He was trying to start a race! *He may be magical, but my limbs are better arranged for swimming,* I thought triumphantly, shifting into a quick breast stroke. Multi-colored corals and wary fish flew by— half the time, when I kicked, anyway. The race was not, I'm afraid to say, as clear-cut as I'd hoped.

But in good time, we both tumbled into the air bubble on the camp dock. William shook himself heartily, effectively drowning out anything I could have said about my victory. I grimaced and wrung out my clothes. Since my feet and all the rest of me were still wet, I opted to carry my sandals rather than listen to them squish as we walked through town. After all, the shell pathways were cool and smooth underfoot.

"You look like a vagabond," William declared as we began making our way to the barracks.

"It doesn't matter what I look like," I returned primly. "At least I don't smell like wet dog."

"I don't see how you can smell anything but salt, with that pitiful human nose of yours," he said, tail in the air.

I chuckled as he trotted ahead. Suddenly it came back to me that I'd promised him from the beginning that we'd see the training grounds, and we'd never had a chance to go until this moment. *Murder investigations take up so much time,* I thought to myself with a sigh. *What a pity to have to spend so much energy focused on something so sad.*

Of course, grief took time to move through, too. I wasn't surprised that Rei and Taiwo had had a "tiff," not really. But I'll admit I was glad that Jeannie didn't think it was too serious. Not serious enough to stop construction on the stage, in any case!

"Hey, slowpoke," William called back to me. "If you're any slower, the wedding'll be over before we even find Taiwo. Or worse, Thorn will catch us."

As usual, William's derision broke right through my thought cloud. I shook my head. And just like that, the worries were gone, replaced by irritation—and not a small amount of gratitude—for this grumpy arcane familiar.

His attitude *was* annoying and inappropriate, but it also was a great way to keep perspective.

"Getting ahead of me won't do you any good if you're going the wrong way," I replied. "Come on, the barracks are down this branch. Didn't you see the sign?"

Grumbling, no doubt about the artful inconsistency of signs in the merfolk camp, William lumbered over to my side and remained glued there. The path we followed took a dip, following the contour of the deepening sea floor as it curved behind the meeting hall. We passed a few more pods of guest rooms, and a bank of glistening yellow corals. Finally, with one more curve, the barracks came into view, nestled against the back of the camp.

I'd been in camps like this before, of course, and they seemed to follow the same logic. The barracks were always at the 'back' of the camp, nearest the open ocean. The air was quieter there, and the light a darker, more filtered blue. The ocean beyond was palpable in a way that slightly frightened me, a desert-island girl who had always been told that the worst fate I could suffer was to be swept away. However, I suppose to a mer-person or a fish that feeling of looming expanse was comforting.

The barracks themselves were an open-air building built

along the edge of the air bubble. A deck jutted out into the surrounding water. As we followed the path into the building, we found ourselves essentially walking under an awning. Stall after stall opened up on the right side, providing a sneak peak at the wall of water and a collection of some new kind of fish. It was like the most basic, most accessible aquarium.

And William, as I'd suspected, was all about it. He left my side and poked his nose into each and every stall, getting a good eyeful of whatever fish might be there—red-faced gliders, perhaps, or shimmering trout, or lovely angelfish, or sinuous eels. I actually had to tug at his tail to get him to leave the purple clownfish alone. Clearly, he'd forgotten all about Taiwo.

But I hadn't. I found my friend in one of the farthest stalls, sitting out in the water on the shell deck. Violently pink minnows crowded around Taiwo's hand and darted through their hair.

I stuck my arm into the water just far enough to tap Taiwo on the shoulder. While it would have been fun to sit with the fish, I wouldn't be able to say anything of use underwater. Besides, I was afraid William might drift away with his gaze glued to the fishes if I let him go out there.

"Oh, hi, Red." Taiwo shifted and leaned back so that their head and shoulders poked into the air bubble. They remained there, half in and half out, leaning against a column in the stall, not really looking at anything in particular.

Hmm, maybe Jeannie was a little too optimistic, I worried. I settled down with my back against the opposite side of the stall, facing Taiwo. William lay down between us, nudging aside my feet so he could stare at the bubblegum swarm of fish.

For a moment there was silence. I raised my eyebrow at Taiwo.

"I guess you heard," they sighed. "I hope you didn't come here to tell me to take back what I said. I know that's what Mom wants me to do but I told her, I have to draw a line *somewhere!* I said what I said, and that's that."

"What did you say?" I asked cautiously.

"Nothing that he shouldn't have expected!" Outside, in the water, Taiwo's deep purple tail flapped for emphasis. "It's all Mara's fault. She's beastly. She was angling for Mr. Rise, did you hear? Cindy and I saw her once at the bridal boutique absolutely making eyes at him over the lingerie. Cindy says that Mara was even asking him for 'business lessons.' She doesn't care about the wedding or Rei at all—she was just doing the whole thing as an excuse to get closer to *him!*"

I pursed my lips, running my hand through William's tangled fur as I processed this rather convoluted outburst. I'd never heard Taiwo talk that way about Mara, but of course William and I had had similar suspicions. Taiwo had every right to be upset, thinking that the celebration of their love with Rei was being used for such a purpose.

Not to mention for murder.

"Maybe you should start at the beginning," I said. "Tell me what happened, exactly?"

Taiwo heaved an enormous sigh. But then they shifted farther into the stall with me so that we properly faced each other, and explained, "Everyone was getting fitted for any last-minute alterations for wedding clothes at Something New, the wedding boutique—the owner there knows Mara, because *everyone* knows Mara! So anyway they're doing all the clothes, not just for me and Rei but for our parents and siblings too.

But of course Moe was dragging his feet about it and being rude, and Ige was an absolute *crab*. But that's just normal. That would have been fine! But Mara had been saying all morning how Mr. Rise would have been sad to miss this, and Mr. Rise this and Mr. Rise that, and I swear each time she said anything poor Lacey's face got tighter and tighter. And besides, it's not like we need Mara for anything any more. Everything's all set up. We know what we're doing. And we scaled it back a little bit because of the death and everything, so really, there's no use for Mara at all. Like, why is she even here, except to make Lacey's life miserable, and the rest of us too while she's at it?"

I nodded, working at one of the knots along William's back. He was so engrossed by the fish that I could have cut his fur off and I don't think he would have noticed. "Is that what you said that made everyone mad?"

"No. I mean, I *did* say that. Of course I did! Someone had to. We'd just got done with the fitting and poor Lacey just wanted to go home, and I wanted to have some time alone with Rei. I'd already said that. Everyone knew that's what I wanted to do, because Ige was even making fun of me for it, talking about how it might not be 'safe.' And then Mara comes along with some grand idea of how we're all going to go out to eat together. At the fanciest restaurant in town, of course! And then Ige, slug that he is, said something about her just wanting a free meal, and Al tried to tell him to just be nice, and Moe started getting upset all over again. And Mara was just standing there like this wasn't *all her fault*. So I walked right up and asked her that. Why she's still here, anyway. And she was all, 'you need me!' and I was all, 'excuse me, I don't need *you* at all,' and so she goes 'well I was hired by the Rises so only the head of the Rise family can fire me,' and everyone looked at Rei, and he—he just *stood* there."

"Ah."

"So then *I* said I wonder if he can even make the decision to get married in four days!"

"Oh." I hid a smile behind my free hand.

"Shut up, Red. I can see you trying not to smile." At first Taiwo was sulky and sounded very much like William, but by the end of the sentence, they lightened and even chuckled. "I know, it's ridiculous, isn't it? But I mean really, what *isn't* ridiculous about a man who can't even decide about being married?"

"Taiwo," I remonstrated gently, "you know that—"

"Don't! If you say anything about 'oh, Rei's poor dead dad,' I'm going to scream. I swear I will. I don't want to hear it any more. The man wasn't any better as a father than mine!"

"Taiwo," I repeated, and this time it was more of a question. Even William looked up briefly before returning to staring at the fish.

For their part, Taiwo shrugged and followed William's gaze out into the water beyond us. "I'm just saying. It's nothing Rei hasn't said himself. He felt like his dad was always gone. And mine *was* always gone, so . . ."

"I get what you meant," I assured them, "I guess I didn't realize how strongly you felt about it."

"I don't. I mean, I do, but for us at least it makes a kind of sense. My people are nomadic. It's just natural. But for Rei . . . it's more like his dad failed him. But he still has to step up into his shoes and take his place and run his business now that he's gone. It's a—it's like—"

"It's a legacy," I supplied, thinking of Rei and his feelings about 'shoulds.' "And not an entirely happy one."

"Right. So I don't see why we have to go around pretending that we're all beside ourselves with grief, when what we really are is totally confused and needing to make some decisions."

"I can see your point," I said, "and that gets back to what I was trying to say. I was going to say that Rei clearly has trouble voicing his thoughts when he's put on the spot."

"Oh. Well, obviously," said Taiwo, flicking their tail back and forth. "I mean, I know that. But this is *important*."

"Even so, not everyone likes an audience. Unlike you, some people actually find talking in front of others terrifying," I added, smiling.

"He's going to have to figure it out sometime," Taiwo muttered rebelliously.

"Yes, especially now that he *is* the head of the Rise family, as you pointed out. Imagine how hard that must be when it's not how you've been taught to act or how you're used to being," I said, doing my best to be tactful.

But again Taiwo, much like the insightful Jeannie, caught my meaning—and my eye. "I see what you're doing. I ought to help Rei out, since I'm so good at expressing myself already. And I know you're right, Red—of course you are—but it's just so *frustrating*. Weddings are about expressing yourself, not *learning* to express yourself."

"True. But I thought weddings are also the start of a journey together," I said. "Isn't that why you want to have the ceremony at dawn?"

"Whatever." Taiwo looked out into the water. After a minute, they sighed. "I know, I know. I just wish we were already married, you know? I wish none of this had happened. I wish everyone else would just let us be *happy*."

I reached over and put my hand over Taiwo's. "You *will* be happy. Whether or not everyone else lets you."

Taiwo hesitated a moment. And then, quickly, they leaned over William and pulled me into a hug.

"Hey! Can't a person watch fish in peace?" William protested.

Taiwo laughed. "No more than a person can sulk in peace, apparently. Not with Red around. But here, I'll make it up to you. Want to see them do a dance?"

23

The Seaweed is Always Greener

We stayed that night in the merfolk camp, at last. William got to ramble under the moonlit waves and watch schools of fish to his heart's content. And Thorn, who was given the pod next to mine (how lucky for me that my mer-neighbors had needed to leave early!), got to interrogate every single member of the Afolayan clan.

Actually, I have to admit, she was pretty good about it. When I'd first met her she could hardly hold a conversation without accusing someone of crime, but now, she just came across as an excitable—if somewhat morbid—fellow wedding guest. Maybe being in new territory had convinced her to feel her way a bit more carefully before leaping to conclusions.

Of course, that only lasted through the night. By the next morning, Thorn's good behavior—and my good luck—had worn thin.

At the communal meeting hall, Thorn and I met Taiwo and their family for breakfast.

"Good morning," Jeannie was the first to say, gesturing for us to take a seat at a long banquet table made of carved driftwood.

"Where's William?"

"He wasn't around this morning," I answered, grabbing a plate and eyeing the family-style serving bowls of kelp salads, melon, and fresh fish. "I figure he fell asleep last night at the barracks, probably dreaming of seafood."

"Well, he's missing out," Officer Thorn declared as she piled her plate with crab cakes. Most of the time, when they're living truly in the water—rather than creating air bubbles for the use of their land-dwelling guests—merfolk tend to favor food that is uncooked and full of liquid, since they don't often drink. But from what I've seen, many clans have happily adopted some landlubber twists on seafood classics.

I gratefully accepted some tea from Taiwo, who had remembered my preference; tea was unusual in a mer-camp. "I'll pick him up after this. But all that swimming yesterday left me starving, even after that lovely dinner last night."

Across the table, Ige grunted. "Why bother picking him up?"

"Ige!" Taiwo reprimanded from my side.

"I'm just saying, he's probably going to have more fun staring at fish than dealing with wedding prep. Especially since *someone* got their fiance to fire the wedding planner."

Thorn looked sharp. "Did he really?"

Taiwo grimaced. Clearly, this was still a sore point. "I don't know what he's done. He didn't mention anything about it last night."

"Oh, but you did talk to him? Good, good," said Jeannie, winking at me from Ige's side.

"Just for a little bit." Taiwo shrugged. "We're supposed to meet with Arielle this afternoon to make sure everything's ready for the ceremony."

"And we have that luncheon with Atargatis's priestesses,"

Jeannie reminded them, naming the goddess of another clan of nomadic merfolk. With a smile to Thorn and me, she explained, "The good thing about having extended wedding celebrations is that our friends from far corners of the seas are able to make it on time."

Ige scoffed. "The *only* good thing."

Thorn shifted beside me, and my breakfast started to sink in my stomach. "What do you mean by that?" she asked.

"Just that *some* people might not enjoy weeks on end of wedding nonsense," said Ige with a shrug. "But Taiwo's probably over the moon about it, aren't you, Taiwo? All this time as the center of attention? It doesn't even matter if someone dies."

Taiwo glared daggers across the table. "You know what *your* problem is, Ige? You never learned to think before you talk."

"Let's all try to be a little more reflective," Jeannie said, laying her hand on her son's arm.

But Thorn had found a lead, and she wasn't dropping it. "Would you consider yourself close with the Rise family, Ige?"

"How could we be? You saw what they had written on that curtain," Ige spat, conveniently forgetting that Thorn hadn't been present for the opening feast.

Traitor, I remembered. *Does Ige think that means that Rei is a traitor for marrying Taiwo?*

Meanwhile, the conversation—such as it was—continued. "The *murderer* wrote that," Taiwo protested hotly.

"How do you know?" Ige shot back. "It could have been anyone! Mr. Rise himself could have planned that!"

"And did he also plan to kill himself, then?" Thorn pressed, her food forgotten.

Ige shrugged, a look of disgust wrinkling his gorgeous blue

eyes. "He might as well have, after the way he botched his MMC deal."

"He *what?*" asked Taiwo, stunned. I echoed the sentiment, thinking, *this has taken an unexpected turn!*

"It's common knowledge," Ige said, backtracking.

"Hardly," I observed, "since the local historian didn't seem to have any knowledge about it when we looked into Rise Enterprises."

"Well it's common knowledge to me and my—friends. He was dealing with sirens, so no wonder he wanted to keep it quiet. And no wonder a man with friends like that would do such a thing!" For a moment, the four of us sat stunned by this strange twist in Ige's rationale. Feeling the weight of our stares, he asked, "What? It's not like Taiwo is the only one who can date fancy people in Seaside."

Personally, I had been more surprised to hear the sirens come up than to hear that Ige had friends in Seaside, but I wasn't the first to speak.

"Who's your contact?" Officer Thorn leaned forward, her hand itching toward the notebook in her pocket. "Who told you all this?"

"It doesn't matt—"

"It might matter," Jeannie interrupted her son quietly.

"Fine! It's Jon. Happy?" Ige grunted.

Taiwo leapt from their seat, knocking over their stool. "The *police?* You've been shacking up with the police, and you want to make fun of me about Rei?! How long has that been going on? What, did you meet at the crime scene? Oh, how romantic!"

"It's nothing," Ige protested, "just a one-time thing. And Jon isn't really with the police anyway!"

Thorn leaned so far forward that she, too, was in danger of tipping over her stool. "What do you mean, Jon isn't with the police?"

"It it's not like that," Ige said, his eyes going wide as he realized what he'd said. "I didn't mean it like that. I just meant Jon doesn't agree with Ebb about the case, that's all."

"Then what exactly does Jon think?" I asked.

"He thinks—I—I don't know! Why don't you go ask *him?*"

"We will," Thorn promised, standing. "And in the meantime, young man, you said something about William earlier. If I go to the barracks right now, will I find the dog free and unharmed?"

"Oh, my goddesses," I gasped, leaping up as I understood what Thorn meant.

Jeannie, too, stood. "*Nothing* could have happened to him here. This is a safe place! Right, Ige?"

Ige's eyes were now more white than blue. The last one sitting, he stared at us looming above him in an angry circle.

"*Please* tell me you haven't done anything, Ige," Jeannie added quietly.

"I haven't! I haven't done anything. For sea's sake, all I did was have a bit of fun with a random landlubber, and look what a big deal you all are making of it!"

"I thought you wanted to be the center of attention," Taiwo retorted.

"Ige," said Thorn, very slowly and seriously, "you've given me reason to think you may be dealing with a leak in the police station. And it's clear you know more than you've been telling me or Officer Ebb. Now, I'm just warning you, if I find out you know even *more* that you aren't sharing, you *will* be facing the law. And if I find out anything has happened to the dog, then there might not be anything left of you to face the law at all."

"Officer, please," Jeannie protested.

I, too, was torn. I reach up to put a hand on Thorn's shoulder. "I'm sure no one needs to worry. Because William is fine, isn't he, Ige?"

"Of course I am," said William as he trotted lazily into the meeting hall. "Why are you asking *him?*"

* * *

"I'm sorry," I said to Jeannie later, for the third time at least. "We're just a bit wound up."

"Everyone is," Jeannie assured me. She walked with her arm tucked under mine as we followed a little footpath among the coral beds. Taiwo had stormed off. At the edge of the garden, just outside the meeting hall, Thorn was interviewing Ige again. William was visible through the door of the meeting hall, stuffing his face with shellfish.

"And besides," Jeannie added, following my glance to the meeting hall with a sigh, "it seems no one was entirely wrong."

"Officer Thorn *can* be a little . . . sensational," I said.

"But she was acting in defense of William," Jeannie pointed out. This struck me silent; I hadn't even thought of it that way. For all their arguments, Thorn really cared about William. Jeannie patted my arm and added, "We all care for each other in our own ways. You like to understand your friends. Some . . . some people express their care through action. Even when they are confused," she sighed again.

"We'll get everything sorted out," I assured her. It was becoming a familiar refrain—wearing a bit thin around the edges.

"Of course we will. I just hope it happens before the wedding. Maybe I should be grateful we still have several days before the ceremony." Looking back toward the hall again, she added, "It looks like they are done now. Shall we go and hear their conclusions?"

"After you," I smiled, gesturing her through a narrow part of the path.

As we came up to Thorn and Ige, there were frowns, but no outright shackles. That seemed like a good sign. As Jeannie went to join her son on the bench, I sidled up to the officer.

"So, what's next?" I asked her.

"What's next is I call in to Officer Ebb," she said. "And my comm device's still not working. 'Scuse me while I go bother William."

She strode inside, leaving the three of us in her ominous wake.

"I don't know anything else," Ige said in answer to his mother's wake. "I told her that."

"Then I'm sure everything will be fine," Jeannie said.

"It was all a misunderstanding, right?" I asked Ige, trying to be friendly. "About William, I mean."

"Sure." Ige shrugged once more. I was starting to resent that gesture. "Though it wouldn't surprise me."

"Wouldn't surprise you if what?" I asked.

Ige turned his blue eyes on me at last. "If someone was looking for you two. It's obvious. You're the ones stirring things up."

"Us and the actual police," I protested, worried. *Of course, if the murderer already has a mole in the police station and is worried about loose ends, then . . .* Suddenly I recalled my lost notebook, the one I still hadn't been able to find after our visit to the bookstore yesterday. *What if someone is keeping tabs on us? On our investigation? Who would even be close enough to be doing something like that?*

Thorn came back out of the meeting hall at a run. "You're coming with me, Red. Now. Ebb's assistant Jon's gone, and Ebb just got word that the bookstore wasn't opened this morning."

24

An Ill Wind

Of course, hurry and command as she might, Officer Thorn still had to wait for the ferry. My aching muscles didn't mind the delay, I must admit, though I *was* worried about Varsha. As William, Thorn, and I stood on the dock, we couldn't stop turning the matter over and over.

"It must be Jon," was Thorn's prognosis. "I can't believe I didn't see it yesterday!"

"Jon is obviously working for someone," William decided. "Someone like MMC!"

"You both could be right," I kept saying, "but that *still* doesn't tell us the reason behind all of this."

Like an old folk song, these three choruses kept bouncing between us—not only on the dock but on the ferry ride back to town and even on the dock there. And when Officer Ebb met us at the bookstore, he added his own refrain.

"Such a smart young scholar," he kept saying. "How could something like this have happened?"

The two officers immediately began talking about searches

and radiuses. Apparently, some assistants—trustworthy ones—had already been dispatched to Varsha's house. Unburdened by knowledge of official procedures, William and I pushed past Thorn and Ebb, into the shop itself. There, we began poking around.

"I don't sense anything," said William, glowing blue as he checked for magic.

"I don't like this at all," I confided to him. We made our way up the staircase, safely ignored by the officers.

"Could be you're just overwrought because you have a soft spot for booksellers," he said, panting after me.

"I am not *overwrought*," I protested. "I'm being proactive."

"More like feeling proactively guilty," William countered. "Maybe Varsha just wanted a vacation. Or maybe she was mixed up in a shady crowd for some entirely different reason."

"Like Seaside has room for more shadiness than what was going on with Mr. Rise," I muttered. "I just really want her to be okay, alright? I couldn't forgive myself if somehow I got her in trouble by asking her to look into those records."

And, I recalled, *informing the whole family at the Rise estate that I'd done so.*

"Fine, fine." William glanced around the loft, which seemed perfectly normal, aside from being Varsha-less. "What do you propose we do?"

"Just look for signs of disturbance, maybe," I suggested as I headed straight for her desk. It was neat as always, even the cash register intact. I turned to the drawers.

"What, do you think she left her diary?" William scoffed as he sniffed through the rows of records.

"Well, no. But she *did* write a lot. She said she had a bunch of penpals, and besides, she kept notes," I explained as I searched.

"Maybe she wrote something that would help."

"That *would* be like a scholar," William admitted. "But, Red, if she didn't—or if we don't find it—you can't blame yourself, okay?"

"I'm not blaming myself yet," I said through gritted teeth as I continued to search. Paperclips, rubber bands, and an endless supply of pencils was all I'd found so far. "But everyone keeps reminding me we have to stick close to our friends . . ."

William grunted as he began sniffing around the window sills. "Fine time you pick to start listening to other people's advice instead of just *giving* advice all the time."

"Oh, come on. You like Varsha too. You're just as worried as me," I replied. Having found nothing but an old canvas lunch bag and a bit of string in the final drawer, I turned my attention to the desk itself.

"Maybe," William admitted. "Still not finding anything, though."

"We just have to keep at it, that's all. My mother always said—when you're in the dark, you just have to keep moving . . ."

My voice trailed off as my fingers slid over a piece of paper taped to the bottom of the desk.

Rather than remove it, I got down on my knees and took a lightstick from my belt, activating it and shining it up onto the bottom of the desk. For good measure, I tugged my goggles down over my eyes too. But I needn't have gone to all the trouble. In very neat printing, the note read:

Strange shadows following me on way to work. Pretending to go out for coffee. Going straight to Rise estate. If I'm missing, contact bookseller 222.

"Eureka," I said, grinning to myself. "William, you'll never believe this, but I was exactly right. The only problem is, I have no idea who 'bookseller 222' is. Maybe the scholar in the next town over? Did you know that scholars have numbers?"

"No. I always knew they were weird, though." William came snuffling up behind me, shouldering me out of the way so that he could read the note too.

"Hmph," he said. "Leave it to a scholar to be so orderly. Why can't Luca be this organized, too?"

I ignored the jab at my friend and stowed my light. "Come on, let's get the officers. Regardless of bookseller 222, we can at least head up to the Rise estate. Maybe we should swing by the coffee shop too, just in case. If we're lucky, we'll catch up with her and nothing will have happened yet."

"If we're lucky, sure," grumbled William as we scrambled to our feet. "You mean if the Rise family isn't some sort of mob organization. Which seems less and less likely by the minute, if you ask me."

* * *

Both police officers were relieved by my discovery—and both resolutely refused to split up. So all four of us set off at once for the Rise estate via the coffee shop Varsha had mentioned. It turned out that William and I had already visited Seaside's primary cafe, though we had elected to get smoothies and tea there rather than coffee.

"Hey," called the young man behind the register, as soon as I burst into the cafe just ahead of my friends. "Red, right?"

"Drew," I remembered, pulling up short. "Hi! Nice to see you again. Have you seen Varsha this morning?"

"Uh, no, I haven't," Drew answered, glancing over my

shoulder at the two police officers in full-on *looking for a missing person* mode. He seemed to understand the gravity of the situation at once. "She might have come by while I was in the back, though. Hold on, let me get the others."

Drew disappeared briefly into the kitchen, and came back with two companions—one a tall elf in a floury apron, the other a plump fairy in street clothes that suggested he'd been taking a break.

"They say they didn't see her either," Drew informed us at once. "Except—"

"Except," interrupted the elf in the apron, "I'm pretty sure I saw her and some friends walk by while I was restocking the bakery case."

"Some friends?" Officer Ebb asked.

"I *assumed* they were friends," the elf replied, showing uncertainty now that a police officer was questioning the memory. "They were walking awfully close."

"Which way were they going?" Officer Thorn put in.

"That way," the elf pointed along Main Street in the direction of the Rise Estate.

Okay, so she definitely was doing what she said on the note, I thought. *But she didn't think she had time to stop, maybe? If someone was following her that closely, she must have known . . .*

"Did you notice anything about them?" Officer Ebb added. Apparently, the two officers made a good tag team.

A good one—if a slightly overwhelming one. The cook blinked and faltered. "I, that is, no, I had dropped a muffin and I looked away . . . and then they were gone."

"So they were moving fast," Officer Thorn noted.

"All the more reason for us to move fast too," William rumbled.

"You're sure of all this?" Officer Ebb said, focusing on the elf. "And there's nothing you'd like to add?"

"Um—no?" answered the witness. "Is everything okay?"

"We hope so," Officer Thorn said. She turned and led the charge back out into the street.

Before I could join her and the others, Drew called out to me.

"Varsha isn't in trouble, is she?" he added.

"We're not sure," I said, not knowing how much to share.

"It hasn't got to do with the Rises, does it?"

"What makes you ask that?" I turned back to the cafe employees, even though my feet itched to get outside and run to the estate.

"Cindy told me what's been going on," Drew explained. "You gotta watch out, Red. Those business people can be brutal."

Of course, they might say the same about Cindy and activist folks, I thought, remembering the way the paper lanterns had become a blaze in the night. But I set the thought aside. "Thanks, Drew. I will. We'll be back sometime for another smoothie, promise!"

And with that, I ran out the door.

25

Malicious Meet

I rejoined my friends in a moment—they'd gotten a head start on me, but I was awfully fast when I needed to be. Together, we raced out of town and up the hill toward the Rises' bluff.

"Do we have any kind of plan?" I asked, as we ran along. My sandals were straining under the effort, but I was frustrated not to be there yet.

William, who had used blue familiar magic to anchor himself to me to make sure he could keep up, snorted. "What kind of plan do we need? It's pretty straightforward. Find Varsha."

"We can't just barge into the Rise estate and ask if they're holding someone captive," Officer Ebb reminded us, with a sideways glance at William. The magic made it look a bit like he had me on a leash.

"Even if the someone was last seen being trailed by goons?" William huffed.

"Of course we can," Thorn agreed. "Aren't we police officers?"

"We'd be better off asking if anyone's seen her. She might not have made it to the mansion at all," Ebb pointed out, reasonably if a bit gloomily.

"Or this all could be blown out of proportion, like with Ige this morning," I reminded everyone hopefully. "Just like you were saying earlier, William. So let's be nice!"

This last bit was added for Thorn's benefit. But Officer Thorn, naturally, was squinting at the mansion and pretended not to hear.

Fortunately, when Whitestone the butler came to answer the door, it was Officer Ebb who spoke first. "Good morning. We're here just to ask a few more questions, if you don't mind."

"Certainly. The master is—"

"Have you seen the bookseller?" Thorn interrupted.

The butler cleared his throat. "As I was about to say. The master is entertaining a guest in the library. If you would care to wait—"

But unfortunately, Whitestone's efforts were futile. Thorn was already down the hall. William, not to be outdone, was bounding after her. With an apologetic shrug and a nod, Officer Ebb and I followed suit.

Fortunately, the house was as empty as ever—it seemed the Rises' guests were content to stay in their own little cabins. Or perhaps they knew better than to get too involved . . .

". . . something like Mountain Meet Company," Varsha finished saying as we got to the door. At the sound of four large persons colliding with the door frame, she turned and noticed her increased audience. "Oh, it's Red and her friends. Did you get my note, then?"

* * *

Varsha, it turned out, had been safely visiting with Rei and Lacey since breakfast. At some point, Taiwo had joined them, and the four were quite cozy in the armchairs of the Rise library.

Well, as cozy as one could be when discussing a mysterious company and unnerving, spying goons.

Officer Ebb stepped out briefly to update his assistants with the news. William, Thorn and I made ourselves at home with cups of tea. As accommodating as the merfolk tried to be, there was nothing like tea brewed on dry land! We settled around an ancient coffee table as Ebb rejoined us and Varsha, at last, prepared to tell her story.

"It started a few days ago," she began, very practically. "Pretty soon after Red and William showed up wanting to know about Mr. Rise, actually."

My face must have betrayed my guilty feelings, because she added with a wave of her hand, "Oh, not *because* of you. I figured that out pretty quick. You two are obviously landlubbers, if you'll excuse the term, and whoever was following me was—watery.

"I started to notice wet footprints in the alley behind my shop when no one had been there, and when I went home at night, these big eyes seemed to be watching me from a shadow on the street corner. Honestly, I didn't think much of it at first, but then when I went in the next morning there was a note on my back door. A magical warning. It said *keep yourself to your own affairs,* in watery purple lettering, and then it vanished. I figured it must be magic, and that must mean it was from Clemency."

Aha, I thought. *No wonder her opinion of the sea witch seemed to change. But why would Clemency send Varsha a warning?*

"Of course, it really doesn't make sense that she'd bother to send me a warning," Varsha continued, answering my unspoken thought. "I was scared, but I didn't really understand it. I even tried writing her a letter about it, but of course she didn't write back.

"It was only last night, when something was following me again, and there was this flash in the dark like they might have a weapon on them, that I realized maybe Clemency meant that warning to *protect* me. She wouldn't use weapons when she could just use magic. So someone else must be involved. That's when I realized this was serious. I locked myself inside and didn't go out all night, after that. I decided to write some letters to my friends, just in case.

"And then this morning, I saw something following me again. Only this time, it was *two* somethings. I couldn't see any details about who they were. But with everything going on, I didn't want to take any chances. I went back into the shop this morning like usual just so I could leave the note for you, and then as quick as I could, I came here. I had a feeling the whole way like they were right behind me in the street, but I didn't dare turn around to look. As soon as I came within sight of the Rise gates, I knew I was safe. Everyone in town knows the reputation of the Rises' security."

When she finished, there was a moment of silence. Nothing but the clink of Lacey's teacup on its saucer disturbed our thoughts.

For my part, I was focused on that glint in the dark she'd seen. *Why use real weapons, indeed,* I wondered. *Knives are a far cry from quiet, sneaky poison. Maybe the murderer really is getting worried about how much we know.*

If, for example, MMC is behind this, and it really is run by someone other than Kade, then who would it be? I recalled one of us saying "gee, someone really likes Ms," upon first learning about the company with Varsha. Maybe there really is something to that—after all, it's not like there are any mountains around here. Maybe they chose that name just so the company would have certain initials. Or maybe "Mountain Meet" is itself a pseudonym for the company. If all this is the case, then it could be someone with an M name, like Moe or Mara, behind all this . . . Who'd be more likely to approve armed henchmen following booksellers around? Moe seems really riled up about sea-dwellers in general, but is that just a cover?

Apparently, my friends had more pleasant matters on their minds. In fact, Taiwo was smiling as they shifted in their seat at Rei's side. "I think it's really great you've been doing all this research for us, Varsha. Especially to keep going after seeing the first set of footprints—that's really brave!"

"It isn't done yet," said Varsha, both practical and modest. "I found the will, of course, but I can't find any official paperwork for MMC—just a few newspaper articles and mentions of it Mr. Rise had made, that's all. And anyway I wouldn't have gone as much into it if it hadn't been for Red and William."

"I'm just glad it didn't get you into too much trouble," I said.

"Yet," added William.

I glared at him, but Lacey stirred. "William makes a very good point. Varsha, I believe the threat facing you is real. Please, won't you stay with us today, and tonight?"

"It's a good idea," Thorn nodded, looking at Ebb. "At least until we know more."

"Which we will," he promised. "I'll get my assistants on it at once. We'll stake out your bookshop tonight just in case they come back.

"And that goes for you two, as well," Officer Ebb added, turning to William and me. "I want you two to stick to the Rise estate for the day. Our adversary, whoever it is, is taking matters up a notch. The best thing to do would be to stay together and stay safe."

William opened his mouth, no doubt to make a snarky comment, and Varsha had shifted on her chair, ready to speak up too. But before either of them could take the floor, so to speak, Taiwo spoke again. "I think Rei has an idea!"

We all looked to the future groom and current head of Rise Enterprises. He blushed under the pressure, but at Taiwo's urging, he said haltingly, "Varsha—we're lucky to have you here. And that you're safe. And—if you're open to it—Taiwo and I would love to invite you to our wedding."

"Really?" Varsha beamed, though not quite as brightly as Taiwo and Lacey were beaming at Rei. "It wouldn't be too much trouble, so last minute?"

"Not at all," Rei said, now smiling too. "We'd be glad to have you. And as my mother said—please feel free to stay here until all this is over. William and Red, you too. There's room enough for everyone. The Rise family looks after its friends."

26

The Rising Tide

aiwo left soon after that to meet Jeannie and the members of the Atargatis clan for their celebratory lunch. As they left, they were smiling again. I smiled, too, thinking to myself that while Taiwo could help Rei express himself, maybe Rei would bring some much-needed calm to the relationship.

And there I go again, I thought guiltily, *with those romantic thoughts William accused me of.*

Fortunately the Rise butler bustled in to distract me and everyone else. Apparently, it was lunch time at the Rise estate as well, and William and I were invited. Not to mention Officers Thorn and Ebb.

Uncle Al joined us in the dining room, though Moe and Mara were absent. Somebody's assistant came in to give their regrets, something that rang a bell in the back of my head. But why, I wondered. *Is there something about 'regrets' that I should remember? Or something about Moe and Mara together?* He seemed much too young for her, but stranger relationships had certainly happened. I puzzled throughout lunch until I realized what it was: *assistants*. Specifically, police assistants. *Jon. If he really is leaking information, then he would have told his employer all about our trip to see Clemency. How much did we say in front of him?*

It wasn't until Officer Thorn clapped me on the back that I really started paying attention again.

"Red'd be happy to help," she said loudly. "Isn't that right?"

"Umm . . ." I looked around the dining room table at a bunch of empty plates and expectant faces.

William shuffled next to me. "While Rei finishes up a meeting with Mara about the wedding, Lacey's going to take Varsha to the family office to sift through old documents. Maybe that's where the paperwork for MMC ended up."

"Hardly old, since the business was probably only started a year ago," Varsha pointed out. "It's the newer stuff I'm better with, anyway."

"There's certainly enough there to keep you busy," Lacey put in. "An extra pair of hands or two wouldn't be amiss."

"Of course we'll go," I said at once. *We're lucky Moe isn't here to complain about us prying into the family secrets,* I thought. Of everyone, he seemed the most likely to be touchy about the subject. "Shall we start now?"

* * *

"I never was much involved in the actual *business* side of the business," Lacey said by way of preamble as she led us through the halls. "I enjoyed helping with the idea side of things . . . being a soundboard, really, and a design partner, I suppose you could say."

"Did any of your ideas involve a smaller sub-corporation?"

Varsha asked. I had to hand it to her, she didn't let up on a research topic. That kind of focus would have served her well in a lab.

"Well, I did often tell Kade that he ought to consider delegating more projects," Lacey said thoughtfully, her voice echoing just barely above our footsteps. "But we never went any further than that. I didn't think he took that idea seriously, to be honest. You know how proud some people can be . . ."

"Especially when they're at the head of a massive financial empire," William said.

"I have a penpal who always says you never know what people are thinking," Varsha said, pressing the topic. "Maybe he really did hear you."

"And in that case, you're thinking MMC really was set up by Mr. Rise, like it seems to be?" I asked Varsha.

She glanced over her shoulder at me through vibrant teal glasses. "Someone with a lot of business know-how did it, that's for sure. Otherwise it wouldn't be such a mystery in the first place."

Lacey murmured something. The only word I caught was "Mara."

"We'll find out who it was," I told her gently, "but until then, we have to keep an open mind . . . even if we'd prefer not to."

Lacey stopped at a solid oak door and turned, smiling at me briefly. "How wise you are, Red. And you as well, Varsha! Yes, it's true, we don't know what others are thinking—or what their hidden talents might be. Still, I hope you can find something useful in here."

With that, she unlocked the door with a silver key from a chain around her wrist and waved us inside.

The Rise office was one of those spaces designed to take

your breath away. Simple but imposing, and far more luxurious than a working office had any right to be. The ceiling was vaulted, and easily two stories tall. The walls were whitewashed and the desk, cabinets, and chairs were all heavy, dark wood. A row of windows along the left side of the room looked out across the sea. A beautifully tiled floor stretched all the way across the room, toward the main desk at the back. And though the office probably hadn't been used since Mr. Rise's death, it smelled faintly and pleasantly of lilies.

I turned back to Lacey, who had stayed in the doorway. Seeing the question on my face, she said, "I haven't been here at all, and Rei's been too busy with the wedding. I . . . I know I should go through everything. But the lawyers already have what they need—Kade was so organized!—so I just . . . I couldn't make myself do it. I kept telling myself . . . after the wedding . . . I have to hold together until then . . ."

"It's alright, Mrs. Rise," said Varsha. "It's not like anyone realized that going through the records would be so dangerous."

Hadn't they, though? I watched Lacey's face carefully. She seemed hesitant. Of course, that could also have been due to her efforts to control her grief and the wilder side of her nature.

"It doesn't help that the wedding will go on for a while," said William. He remained sitting by the door, and his voice as he spoke to Lacey was surprisingly sympathetic. He probably didn't realize how much like Ige he sounded—bitterness aside, of course.

"Oh, it's fine," she answered with a wave of her hand. "I'm glad to have something else to think about. If it wasn't for Rei and Moe and Taiwo, I don't know what I'd do. Or if I'd be able to carry on." She drew one long breath, and then said, "Please, don't let me keep you from your work. I'll have Whitestone bring you some tea in a bit, and fetch you for dinner later if you're still working. Take as much time as you need."

The abruptness of her departure belied the gentle generosity of her voice. As the door swung closed behind her, I pursed my lips.

"Maybe we should have asked her if anything was off-limits," I realized, belatedly. "Should I run after her?"

"Let's leave her be," said Varsha, rubbing her hands together. "Better to ask forgiveness later, and all that."

"Scholars," grunted William. "Nothing more important to them than old scraps of paper."

I half expected Varsha to argue that she wasn't a scholar of ancient things, since she clearly felt strongly about the present. However, she was already distracted by the filing cabinets lining the right hand wall.

"So, you take the ones nearest the door," I called after her, seeing where she was headed. "I'll take the middle. William, are you going to take the ones on the end, or are you just going to watch?"

"I'm only doing some," he huffed, trotting to the far corner of the room. "I'm not about to exhaust all my magic for some stupid documents. If we were attacked and I couldn't do anything, where would you be?"

* * *

William needn't have worried about using up his limited store of magic for the day. We'd barely gotten into our respective cabinets before Varsha was already pulling out papers that demanded the attention of the room.

I got the feeling she wasn't used to doing work with friends nearby.

"Look at this," she called giddily after only five minutes.

"Did you find something on MMC?" I asked.

"No. It's a complete history of the Rise dealing with the Afolayan clan! How cool for Rei and Taiwo, right?"

"Yeah. Much better than the traditional present of crockery or baby clothes," William rumbled under his breath.

Ten minutes later, it was the Rises and Clemency. This, it turned out, was frustratingly vague and outdated, predating Rei's birth. But after five minutes of poring over that, Varsha once again interrupted us to exclaim,

"Here's the records on Mara's clan! They're devoted to Ran, did you know that?"

"Oh," I said, interested, "did they deal with Rise Enterprises, too?"

"It's in the details of her business listing," Varsha said, interrupting my concerns and literally shaking the file in her hands. "But I can use that to look up any other files on Ran. This could be good!"

"How do you ever get anything done?" William asked, exasperated.

"Mostly because no one comes into the bookshop in the afternoons," Varsha said easily. She plopped herself on a nearby chair and once more began to pore over the file.

I gave up the search for a moment, too, and glanced at the filing cabinets critically. At least Varsha's finds had been interesting; mine so far were invoices. Was there some kind of labeling system that might help determine which cabinets to focus on? I didn't see anything useful, but all the same I decided to move closer to Varsha. Given the rate at which she searched, it couldn't hurt.

"Do you mind if I take the next cabinet?" I asked, moving into her corner.

"Sure," she said, totally unfazed by the change in plan. "We can alternate. Do-si-do, as my penpal in Brass says."

"What, are you penpals with the entire world?" William grumbled. His voice rolled through the mostly-empty room.

"Mostly just other scholars," Varsha replied. Her nose was still stuck in the folder she'd found, and every few seconds she had to push up her glasses. "Some of them give really good advice. But it's hard having only long-distance friends. Like, who would I take to the wedding tomorrow?"

This abrupt change in topic didn't surprise me. While doing otherwise dull work, it was easy for the mind to drift. As I paged through folders on druids and goblins, I asked, "Why not ask one of your friends to come in? I know it's late notice, but maybe they could teleport."

"Most of them aren't into travel," Varsha answered. "Besides, this one that I *might* like is probably involved with someone else."

My head filled as it was with details about trolls, this didn't make sense at first. "Huh?"

"One of my penpals. I think he's cool, but he's always talking about this friend he has in town," Varsha said. "And actually it's funny you bring that up, because I'm really getting that vibe from this folder."

Once more, I gave up my search. "I'm sorry?" I hadn't thought *I'd* brought up the penpals, but even more than that, I wasn't sure how anyone could get "vibes" from a folder.

"That's what made me think of penpals in the first place. See? A lot of this folder is letters," Varsha said, holding up a stack of papers several inches thick. "Supposedly they're business letters, but once you get a feel for someone's writing style, you can start to read between the lines."

"Letters from Mara?" William asked.

"Maybe, but this person just signs their letters as Asmund M. Apparently they worked as the secretary for Ran's clan."

"Asmund," I recalled. "I *do* think Mara mentioned that name when we met her. What do the letters say, Varsha?"

"Nothing good," the scholar answered. "I mean, on the surface of it, it's just business details, like I said. But you can kind of tell, based on the context, that something else was going on. I think Mr. Rise was extorting the clan somehow."

That certainly sounded like the beginning of a motive to me, but it hardly made sense now that Mara was a successful wedding planner. *But maybe MMC is part of her new business?*

"And do the letters mention anything about Mountain Meet?" William prompted again, apparently thinking along the same lines as me.

"No. Just unfair prices and threats about reports."

Varsha turned back to her reading, apparently oblivious to the point William was trying to make about staying on one track at a time. Still confused about this business of vibes and feelings, I turned to William, but all he did was shake his ears—probably because he thought Varsha was going on a tangent.

With a sigh, I returned to my cabinet. I passed over the troll folder, which was the last one in the top drawer, and opened the middle drawer instead.

And then—for the first time—I finally got that feeling of *progress.*

The entire drawer was filled with folders about sirens.

Moe's story and his hurled insult, *sea rat,* echoed in my mind as I reached quickly for the first folder. So did Ige with his scandalous rumors about deals with sirens and Mr. Rise's death.

And, lo and behold, the folder held an inch-thick stack of papers—ship's manifestos, it looked like, and contracts drawn up and signed with watery ink. I paged through quickly, looking for anything I could readily understand, like a map. Taped to the side of the folder was a nautical map for reference, but it listed only smudged landmarks—things like "Lildly Peak" and "Port Blue"—nothing truly helpful, like, "this is where my nefarious business partners live!". Still, it *was* clear that Mr. Rise had been doing plenty of business with the sirens. The dates on the paperwork ranged from only a few months ago to two decades ago.

Despite the fact that, as Lacey had told me, Moe's birth family had fallen victim to sirens—and he still had strong feelings about them to this day.

Oh, yes, I thought. *I get the feeling thing now. And I have a feeling this will be useful!*

27

Swept Away

I pulled the folder out of the drawer, but before I could explain my find to Varsha and William, the office door opened.

"Oh, good," said William. "Is it tea time already?"

"I think it's too soon," said Varsha, pulling out of her research with a frown.

There was a pause.

The three of us looked at the door, which was open but had admitted no butler. *Maybe he's adjusting the tray or something? Or are we supposed to go get it?* I stepped forward to see if Whitestone needed help.

And when a gleaming projectile sailed through the door, glinting in the light, I shied like a wild horse.

Noises filled the room in quick succession. The door slammed closed. A click and a *thunk* indicated that the lock had been thrown. Glass shattered against the tile floor. Varsha screamed, and William barked, "*Red!*"

But I wasn't the one in danger. The glass bottle—for that's what I must have seen flying into the room—had been thrown

207

around the open door, and it landed between the armchairs in front of me. The armchairs Varsha sat in. I was several feet back, but she probably had glass shards scattered all over her robe.

And she was fast becoming engulfed in a cloud of blue smoke.

I tugged my goggles over my eyes and clapped a hand over my mouth. But my reaction was too slow to protect me fully. I still got a good, strong whiff of the smoke. It smelled like kelp at high tide. Not a smell you could forget quickly.

Especially considering someone'd just been murdered with a kelp-derived poison days before.

"William," I screamed through my muffling hand. "Open a window! Open a door! Clear out the smoke!"

Without backtalk, my companion leapt into action. As he slammed against a door set into the cabinet wall, I pulled a scarf from my belt and tied it around my face before stepping over to Varsha.

Thud. Thud. William gave up on the side door and raced for the windows. Blue smoke swirled thickly around us now. It ate up the sunlight and clung to my clothes.

"Varsha, we have to get you out of here," I murmured. I doubted she could hear me. Her eyes had glazed over and the folder had spilled from her fingers, papers covering the already glass-covered floor.

Curse it, I thought, trying to decide what was best to do. I didn't have anything on me to mitigate the smoke, not with how fast it was spreading. William was crashing into the windows with the same amount of success he'd had with the door. *They must be magic. Of course Mr. Rise would spring for unbreakable glass.* I couldn't make Varsha walk over the broken, poisoned glass; under her robes, she wore strappy summer sandals. But I also wasn't strong enough to pick her up. *Where's Thorn when you need her?*

"William," I cried again. "William, can't you open the door with your magic?"

"There's some spell on it," he huffed back. "Whose office needs this much protection?!"

We didn't have time to think about that. I shout back, "Then call Thorn! Call Ebb! *Anyone!*"

The smoke was indigo now, moving like the tide in response to my voice. My scarf was way too thin to keep it out. If I'd been in my lab, I'd have had masks.

Masks . . .

My fingers fumbled with the pouch on my belt. *Third pouch on the left. First drawer on the right. I just got that bowl last week . . . to fill with masks and gloves for visitors . . . they should be sitting right there on my workbench . . .*

I tugged the fabric free and did my best to put it over Varsha's face. It was a temporary mask, one I had treated with eucalyptus oil. *Or did I make Trent enchant it? Is it enchanted or treated? Will it work?* The strap slipped over Varsha's chin. Her tawny skin had gone pale, but I still had difficulty distinguishing it from her dark robes. Was she moving? Or had she just slumped over?

Need to open a window, I thought, my eyes heavy behind my goggles. *Maybe . . . Maybe turn on the kiln fan? Need to move the air. Maybe if I make it into the shop . . . but what if there are customers? Need to get out to the back yard . . .*

Seized by anxiety, I stumbled forward, only to trip over something and fall to the floor. The smoke down there was thick and dark, like the bottom of the sea.

But there isn't any sea in Belville. No sea in my lab. I never did like the sea very much . . .

I shifted, my shoulders wriggling on the cold tile as I tried to breathe freely. I could see shapes in the fog. The familiar shelves of my lab, the mountains of Belville. A unicorn.

It's a secret, I thought. I remembered my mother telling me long ago. *"Everyone in the family has one, Cinnabar,"* she said. *"Even if you think you don't have any magic at all. We each have our unicorn that watches over us. But we don't tell just anyone. You have to make sure you're telling the right people. Because otherwise, they will try to capture it, and you, and its magic will be forfeit . . ."*

I'm sorry, Mom, I thought. *I never could figure out who were the right people after all. I thought instead I could get away with telling no one at all . . .*

The equine face came closer, dark eyes and a twisted horn. This wasn't my unicorn. I'd seen mine before, just in flashes and glimpses. It wasn't mossy and barklike, like this one.

But I knew who this one belonged to.

Someone under a forest elf's curse.

Someone from Belville.

"Luca," I whispered. "Luca, you have to get her out of here."

* * *

I woke up to William licking my face. The smell of low tide had receded. Now, all I could smell was doggy breath.

"Ugh," I muttered, slipping as I tried to sit upright. I seemed to be leaning against a wall. "What happened? Where's Varsha?"

"You're just in the hallway. Come on, you have to get to

the garden." William was now pushing me with his snout, probably leaving bruises all over my ribs.

I rolled to my hands and knees and staggered to my feet, my head still spinning. "Varsha?" I repeated.

"Your foolish friend is getting her. Come *on*," William insisted, pushing me so hard I nearly fell over again. Instead I managed to catch myself, leaning against the wall for support as the floor gradually stopped spinning. William led the way down the hall and out a side door into another courtyard—this one much smaller than the main one—*probably*, I realized, *Mr. Rise's private office courtyard. The one behind the side door William couldn't open.*

Sure enough, as I looked to the corner of the yard, I noticed an oak door. With an iron bar across it.

I shivered. *Someone put thought into this. Although . . . Their execution of the plan was a little lackluster,* I thought, recalling the hesitation before the person behind the open door had thrown the vial in.

"Sit, sit," urged William. "I'm not picking you up again."

"It's fine. I'm fine," I told him. Another glance around the garden proved we were alone, crunching over fine white gravel amid leafy evergreen plants. I sank into a finely-made patio chair. As I focused on my hands, and on the little tea table beside me, the hallucinations of my lab back in Belville finally receded.

"You sound like you got hit by a train," he complained, shoving another chair next to mine and hopping into it so that he could pant in my face.

"I feel like it," I admitted. "I don't know exactly what that was, but—"

More feet crunching over the gravel announced the arrival

of Varsha and my "foolish friend." I hadn't given much thought to the phrase before. William might easily have referred to Officer Thorn that way. I lurched to my feet.

And as soon as he'd deposited Varsha in another nearby chair, Luca threw his arms around my shoulders. It was him I had seen in the fog, before I passed out, not a true unicorn—just my friend Luca, who must have let his hood fall away from his face as he tried to rescue us.

"Oh, Red," he cried, and I realized numbly that he seemed to be actually *crying*, "tell me you're okay! Oh, my gods, tell me you're okay. I'm so sorry I didn't get there sooner I can't believe anyone would do that I'm never letting you out of my sight again you *have* to tell me that—"

"I'm okay," I mumbled against his shoulder. The folds of his robe obscured my words. I was holding on to Luca as tightly as he was holding me. "It's fine, Luca, promise. You don't have to worry."

"Don't have to worry!" he repeated, aghast. For a moment he drew back to look at me, his dark cheeks pinched and his green eyes red-rimmed. Then he hugged me again. For once, it seemed he was without words.

But I wasn't. In the silence, I cleared my throat. "Um, Luca? If you aren't a hallucination, then how are you *here*?"

* * *

It took some time for everyone to get settled. As Luca explained brokenly that he'd borrowed a teleportation amulet from Trent and showed up at the Seaside post office not half an hour earlier, Whitestone the butler showed up, with Officer Thorn in tow. She hadn't gotten any call from William—

her communication device was still broken—but as soon as she saw us, she understood that something was wrong. She insisted on staying with us, and on shooing Whitestone away as soon as he'd laid down the tea tray.

That said, her insistences didn't meet with the warmest of receptions.

"And where have *you* been?" Luca asked her, his hands on his hips. He stood to one side, between my chair and Varsha's. William had the last available chair, so Thorn, too, was standing. However it was clear that her stature was not intimidating Luca in the slightest. "Suspecting me of murdering Owl last fall was one thing, but now I show up in Seaside and find that there have been *two* attacks on my friends and you haven't done *anything* to stop them?"

"Technically, there's only been one actual attack," Varsha corrected. Her voice was still scratchy, and she rested against the back of her chair, cradling her tea cup in shaky hands. The mask I'd tried to put on her had done a little good, at least, and she wouldn't suffer lasting damage—but her body was still in shock. I kept feeling her eyes land on me, but whenever I tried to catch her gaze, she was looking somewhere else.

"No, no, let's not sugarcoat it," Officer Thorn said. The fact that she didn't try to make some sugar-and-tea related pun spoke to how upset she really was. "Luca's right. It's clear some things have got to change. But first, let's clear up what happened, shall we?"

William, Luca, and I looked at each other. Varsha looked away again.

"Well," I said, since no one else was clamoring to narrate, "I can say for myself that I didn't notice much. Varsha and William and I were looking through the cabinets when the door opened and someone threw a glass bottle in—but they paused first. It was odd. Clearly, though, the bottle contained a gaseous poison. I'd like to test the glass shards for any residue, after the room has aired out a little. Oh—we should open the door."

"The door?" Thorn looked confused.

"Over there," I pointed to the corner of the courtyard. "There's a side door. But you can see someone bolted it from the outside."

"Well, there wasn't ever any question that someone planned this," Varsha muttered thickly.

"Still, this could be important," Thorn said as she removed the iron bar with a gloved hand and set it carefully to one side. She opened the door to the office. Most of the smoke inside had dissipated during our escape, but tendrils remained, curling out of the door ominously. Fear turned my stomach over. But, fortunately, the poison smoke escaped harmlessly into the sky.

"It was in the hallway too," Thorn said. She began pacing around the garden, ten large steps one way, then the other. "Good thing Whitestone thought to put a napkin over his face. I myself didn't even think anything of it. Just thought it was the sea."

"I think it must have been a poison related to devil's rope," I volunteered. Suddenly, the tea in my hand didn't seem so appealing.

"You're getting too close for the murderer's comfort," Thorn agreed as she paced.

"Drink it," William told me, pointing with his nose at the tea. "There's nothing wrong with it, and you still look pale."

I looked down again with a simple, "Oh."

As I complied, Thorn spun on the gravel. "And as for you?" she asked Luca shortly.

"I came because of Varsha's letter," he said. I nearly spat out my tea as it finally hit me. *Varsha's penpal! The one she mentioned by bookseller number in her note. Goddess—it's Luca! Luca must be bookseller 222.*

"She said things were getting dicey," Luca continued, "and I know you said to wait, Varsha, but I didn't like the things you were writing about people watching you. Plus, I figured Red was probably mixed up in it too, and William, and I hadn't heard from—from them, and I was worried."

"Gee," rumbled William. "Thanks."

"So I went to Trent and he got me all set up," Luca explained, again looking at Thorn. "Only, it took some time, and the spell just took me to the post office, since it's a standard teleportation spell. If I had used a more specific spell, maybe a talis—"

"Skip it," Thorn commanded, cutting off Luca's scholarly lecture. "Tell me what happened *here.*"

"Um—well, I asked around at the post office, and they told me how to get here. So I did, and then I was asking at the front door about you, Red, and Varsha, but the person kept insisting you were busy, or out, or something, and anyway I didn't get a good feeling about it."

There go these scholars with 'feelings' again, I thought, a little spark of humor stirring in me again for the first time since the attack.

"So I—um—" Luca glanced down at me, his hands flailing.

"You what?" I cocked an eyebrow at him. He fluttered his hands again, this time beside his face, and this time I caught on. "Oh!"

Luca nodded vigorously. "I don't think the Officer knows I can do that."

"Oh, right." I could see his difficulty. How to quickly—and unemotionally—explain that Luca's era of imprisonment as a beast in his ancient family's castle had left him with the strange ability to become ghostlike, particularly when Officer Thorn didn't believe in ghosts in the first place?

"The Officer doesn't know what?" Thorn demanded shortly.

"He can go invisible sometimes," William announced, as though bored with our pantomime. "Don't ask about it."

"Okay, fine. So you snuck in the house. How did you find them?" Officer Thorn asked, returning to her brisk pacing.

Luca shrugged at me, a funny smile crooking up the corner of his mouth. *Well, that was easier done than said,* he seemed to say. Aloud, he explained, "I saw someone coming down a corridor, so I just went back the way they'd come. After a while I started to hear banging and yelling, so I started opening every door I passed, and then—one of them let out a bunch of smoke, and I could hear William, and Red and Varsha were there."

"Hmm. Not too much in that that we can use," Thorn said, mostly to herself.

I rolled my eyes at Luca. He grinned. *Thank you,* I mouthed.

"Just lucky, if you ask me," William pronounced.

"Falling up," Varsha said. When Luca turned to beam at her, she smiled wanly back at him. "That's what we call it."

"Yes, well, there will be no more falling on my watch." Officer Thorn came to a stop in front of us once more. "Luca, you're telling me no one knows you're actually here?"

"Well, the butler saw me just now," Luca said reasonably.

Thorn waved this away. "For the first time, there's a chance we have one up on the murderer. And we know we have the advantage. So here's what I say: it's time we take matters into our own hands."

28

No More Love Songs

William groaned.

I blanched. "Officer Thorn, I don't know—"

"Nonsense," she said. "We've faced worse than some low-down poisoner. Just keep alert, and we'll be in tiptop shape."

Well, she's feeling more confident, I thought with a sigh.

"One way or another, they're going to attack again as soon as they realize you're all still alive," Thorn continued. "So let's make sure it's on our grounds, shall we?"

Luca frowned. "What counts as 'our grounds' in this mansion?"

"The Officer does have a point," Varsha argued.

"Of course I do. Here's what we're going to do," Thorn decided unilaterally. "We're going to keep this between ourselves. Don't even tell Ebb, okay?"

Varsha jerked back. "You can't really suspect him too!"

"No, I don't. But we've already had a scare about a mole in the police station, and so want him to act as normal as possible, to make the murderer think they have one more chance to come out. There's five of us, and we need to keep a close eye on each other. Varsha, you're with me at all times. William, you can be the go-between. That means Red and Luca, you have to stick together."

I glanced up at Luca to see how he felt about this. His face, for once, was unreadable.

Meanwhile, William snorted. "How convenient."

Thorn looked at him sharply, her pointy ears wiggling. "You have a complaint?"

"No, no. Good on you for—"

"But," Varsha broke in, "but that puts them in danger!"

"That's the alchemist that just saved your life," said Officer Thorn, pointing at me, "and a scholar who can apparently go invisible. They'll be fine. Besides, if either group encounters trouble, we'll get word to the other group via William."

"What am I, a magitech phone service?" William grumbled.

"Okay, but what are we going to do?" I asked Thorn.

"Lie low until dinner," she decided. "And stick around afterward. That way the culprit is forced to attack tonight instead of poisoning your food. We'll see who looks surprised when you show up in the dining room, eh? For now, Varsha, you're coming with me. The Rises have a nurse with her own room next to the kitchen, and you'll be needing to see her."

"I'm fine," Varsha protested.

"You're not fine," said Thorn with authority. "Come on. And Red, before you say anything, I'm going to send a note to the Afolayans by police comm, so they'll know how things stand. In the meantime, you can get more research done. All right? No more complaints from any of you. William, you're coming with us too."

William sat up. "I think *not!*"

"We need someone who can hear people coming and tell us to hide if necessary," Thorn insisted. "Now are you helping, or not?"

"Fine, but I'm coming right back afterward," William declared. He hopped down from his chair and trotted to the courtyard door. "Well? Are we going or not?"

"It'll be okay, Varsha," said Luca encouragingly.

With her mouth pressed into a very thin line, the little bookseller at last accepted Thorn's hand up and disappeared into the house.

As silence fell over the scrubby pines and patio furniture, I turned to Luca once more. And once again, the oddity of seeing him in Seaside at all sank in.

"I know it's weird and all of this is unexpected," Luca said, seeing the look on my face. "But I'm here now, and I'm going to help. I can't just go home, so don't even say it. Besides, I promised Frank some fish."

"Frank? Who's that? The mink you talked about?" I shook my head, but shaking my head hurt and jumbled up my thoughts again. "Is the mink watching your store?"

"Nope. He's right here," said Luca, grinning as he pulled his hood to one side to show a flash of white fur tucked behind his neck like a scarf.

I bit back a laugh. "He slept through everything? I guess it's a good thing he isn't watching your store, after all."

"William watches your store, and he sleeps all the time," Luca pointed out lightly as he spun the chair Varsha had vacated and took a seat. "Besides, you should be nice. He's missing a leg and he's super old."

"I'm still not sure I even know what a mink is," I admitted, smiling ruefully. "But seriously. What about your store? Are you really okay staying here overnight?"

"It's just a day or two," Luca said with a shrug. "Owl used to close the store for a full week each summer. Anyway, I would have thought you wanted company, Red!"

"I do. I mean, I *am* glad to see you," I confessed, "I'm just worried. It's dangerous here."

"You're telling me. *I'm* the one who just saved you and Varsha," Luca grinned.

"True, but . . ." I sighed. Finally, seeing that he wouldn't be swayed, I held out my hand. "Truce?"

"Truce," he agreed at once, shaking my hand warmly. "Now, what are we supposed to be doing? Looking through files? We can bring them out here to go through them."

"Yeah, good idea," I said. "And I know exactly which one to bring out first."

* * *

As soon as Luca returned with the folder I'd left on the floor in the office, I launched into my explanation. "So, Taiwo's marrying Rei, who's now the head of the family. Rei has this adopted brother named Moe. Now, Moe has been a real drag this entire time, which you might think is perfectly natural because it was his dad who died, *but* a lot of what he's had to say has been really derogatory about both the wedding *and* his dad. He especially was saying terrible stuff about sea-dwellers, by which I think he means *sirens*, not mermaids—because Lacey, their mom, told me he had a tragic run-in with them as a kid. So . . ."

"So, we're hoping this folder explains it?" Luca surmised.

"Yeah. Oh, and also—Varsha might have told you—I still

can't get over how you and Varsha know each other," I added, distracted. "Do *all* scholars know each other?"

"Mostly," Luca said, nodding. "I mean, we're not all penpals or anything. But we do a lot of business by mail. Of course, when Owl was around, no one really knew *me*. Varsha was one of the first people to reach out after he was gone."

"Aw. That's nice." I paused, thinking of her talking about her various penpals. Then I shook the thought away and concluded, "So, she probably told you all about how we've been chasing down loose ends, and one of those is the company we found, Mountain Meet. I keep thinking of it as MMC. All we know about them is they probably trade with sketchy people, which I thought might have to do with these deals with the sirens. And Moe, maybe."

Luca nodded and handed me half the papers from the folder. In companionable silence, we settled in to work.

But I had to admit that for once, I found it hard to focus. Realistically, there shouldn't have been anything more compelling in my life at that moment than finding out about this family business that had potentially led to a threat on my life and the jeopardizing of my friend's wedding. And yet . . .

I rested my chin in my hand, just for a moment. Luca looked over and seemed to know at once what was on my mind.

"Hey," he said quietly. "You know you don't have to feel bad, right? Because this was nothing. I'd go ten times as far if I had to if you were in trouble. I mean, I'd even go to other *worlds* if I had to."

I chuckled at his joke, as he'd intended. "Well, if you're sure . . ."

"I'm sure," said Luca, and for a moment his voice wasn't excitable-bookseller at all; it was ancient-royal-elf, echoes of what he'd once been. "This doesn't even scratch the surface of what I'd do for you. And I think you could probably say the same for me, right?"

"Right." It was absolutely true; so why did my cheeks suddenly feel hot? I shook my head and returned my attention to the papers in my lap. "Okay, back to work."

Of course, it was Luca who found what we needed (after laughing at me for a moment, naturally). I don't think I would have put it together without him—certainly not as fast as he did. Because the answer to my questions about Moe and the sirens wasn't one document. It was two.

"See," said Luca, waving both a ship's log and a contract at me, with the air of someone who isn't simply going to let their audience *see* without also telling a story. "I figured it had to be at the beginning. These aren't the earliest documents of trades between Kade and Calamitous Seas of Port Blue—which is the name this particular group of sirens was using. It seems like they were doing sporadic trades for a while. But all the regular business starts *after* this."

"And what is 'this'?" I asked, amused despite the dire circumstances.

"The log comes first," he answered obliquely. "It shows all the normal things they were trading, but look at this note on the side—see how someone's scrawled something in? The ship's crew brought back a person from their meeting with Calamitous Seas of Port Blue. They've made a note of how much the unexpected passenger ate."

"For billing purposes later, I guess?" I leaned in, squinting at the old paper Luca held. "Not that they gave them much, apparently. Doesn't that say 'half rations'?"

"Yeah," said Luca, eyes sparkling with the thrill of discovery as he brought forward the other paper. "Because it was a very young person."

"Oh goddess." I sat back for a moment. "Not—?"

"It seems very likely. See, if you look here—well, okay, I know the contract is kind of hard to read, since it's in cursive—but the main point is, this isn't a normal business contract. It's more about—well, it's kind of about revenge actually. There's three parties involved: the sirens, obviously, and they're basically saying how they have no responsibility, can't be persecuted, and so on. My guess is the poor child the sailors picked up had *had* a family, but the sirens had something to do with their deaths. They might have killed the child too if the sailors hadn't come in. Because, see, the sailors' part—Kade's part, that is—is talking about assuming responsibility for the child and accepting the fact that he's bound by this contract."

"I think that must be it. It sounds like what Lacey told me," I said, still absorbing the sad picture painted by such esoteric documents. "Moe does have a kind of rainbow sheen on his skin. William even said it might be a spell!"

"But the thing is, the third party, the child, doesn't seem to be named Moe," Luca realized, sifting through the papers.

I was lost in my own thoughts. *Whatever it is, I don't like it,* William had said. And then he had said that both Kade and Rei were something far from average . . .

"Red," Luca interrupted. "Is Moe short for something?"

"Oh. Um, let me think," I said, trying to refocus. "I think—think you're right—I think Lacey said it was short for Okurimono."

"A *gift,* that makes sense," Luca nodded, beaming. "At least, it makes sense for Moe. But Red, if you were thinking that

Moe was the head of this Mountain company and somehow named it after himself . . ."

"It doesn't look good, does it?" I murmured.

"Nope," Luca agreed sympathetically. "Especially because this signed testimony from Okurimono—the child, mind you—says specifically that he has no interest in business or deals, *and* that he won't seek to revenge himself on either the sirens or Mr. Rise. And magical contracts like this are incredibly binding. So he himself couldn't have anything to do with any deals, or probably any murder, either. But—doesn't it seem strange that Mr. Rise *also* didn't want Moe to seek revenge on him? I mean, he basically saved Moe. And then he also wanted him out of the business?"

"No wonder the poor kid is angry," I mused. "It does seem strange, Luca, you're right. Either Mr. Rise was very eager to keep Moe on the sidelines of his business, or he was somehow afraid of a child his sailors found at sea."

29

Be Our Guest

Soon after Luca's discovery, William joined us in the little courtyard. He had nothing out of the ordinary to report—it seemed Thorn and Varsha had made it to the infirmary just fine, and Varsha was on ordered bed rest until dinner. For the next few hours, William and Luca and I sifted through more of the Rise documents. After the deal with Moe, the logs and contracts went on as normal for years, the only change being in the type of cargo they carried.

Unfortunately, the only thing I managed to discover was that my eyes were swimming by the time the bright afternoon sun waned. Judging by the look on Luca's face, he felt the same. William had given up reading altogether and was staring up at the sky.

Just as I was about to say something, Whitestone cleared his throat.

Luca leaped about a foot. The white mink tumbled to the ground with a protesting squeak.

"Dinner will be served shortly," said Whitestone.

"Thanks," I said, though I have to admit I was mostly looking at the mink. "Hey, Whitestone, did anyone ask you about us?"

"I have been occupied solely in arranging the paddle boats to Ms. Mara's specifications for the wedding tomorrow," Whitestone informed me. "Is there anything else?"

"No, thanks, that's it."

Whitestone glided away, and Luca had already scooped up his furry neck warmer and re-situated his hood. "I guess this is the big moment, right?"

"One of two," William grunted, shaking himself. Starshine seemed to shed from his fur. "The second will be when the murderer tries to kill you later."

"That's the spirit," I quipped as I rose.

"Well, if you look at it one way, it *would* be a good thing," said Luca, falling into step with us. "Because if they don't do anything, then we wouldn't know who they are! In fact, the wedding's in a few days, right? I wonder if they'll wait and try something there instead . . ."

"I hope not," I said, thinking of poor Taiwo. "Let's just focus on one thing at a time, shall we?"

We were some of the last to arrive in the dining room. Because Jeannie and Taiwo were absent, celebrating with their immediate family, the dining room seemed less vivid than I had seen it. I felt a twinge at being here rather than with Taiwo, but it couldn't be helped. Besides, Thorn had promised to explain everything. In fact, to be honest, I was a little surprised Taiwo hadn't insisted on coming right over. Thorn's note must have been very persuasive.

In any case, that left Lacey, Rei, Moe, Mara, and Al at the Rise estate. Added to William, Luca, Thorn, Varsha, Ebb, and me, it was still a sizable party. Not that "party" was quite the right word . . .

Lacey was the first one to notice us. She looked up wide-eyed from the head of the table. "Oh, we have a visitor?"

Luca, I realized. *Hum—should we have kept him a secret too?*

Thorn elbowed Varsha—the two were already seated next to each other—and Varsha coughed. "He's a friend of mine, actually, who came to help look over the . . . documents."

"Ah, very good," said Lacey with a smile. It seemed perfectly genuine, though her eyes were still red-rimmed from this afternoon. "Please, sit anywhere you like."

"Thanks very much," said Luca, as though he really had been invited to a fancy dinner and not into a roomful of murderers. Well, just *one* murderer, most likely. But one was more than enough if you asked me. "Everything smells really good! I'm starving."

Amused by watching Luca navigate into an open seat between Mara and Moe without dropping the mink hiding in his robe, I momentarily forgot our grim mission. By the time I remembered to glance around the table, everyone had the same mildly confused or disinterested look on their face. Mara wasn't even looking up. I wondered again about the letters Varsha had found, but set it aside for now.

William and I took our habitual seats at the end of the table. And with that, the longest dinner of my life began.

It quickly became apparent why William had opted to sky gaze instead of investigate Rise Enterprises. His magic was replenished by the stars—a strange quirk of familiar-hood, one which I appreciated without understanding. Apparently, in a pinch, the evening sky could work for him as well. During dinner, his eyes shone blue each time he checked out something new on my plate or in my cup. Officer Thorn's plan must have worked as intended because nothing turned up poisoned.

Well—no food did, that is. But by the end of the entree, we were hearing poisoned words. It started innocuously.

Thorn was talking to Rei about the wedding, and Lacey piped in with a warm-hearted sentiment. "Kade would be proud of you, Rei."

There was a scoff from Luca's side of the table. It wasn't Luca, of course. But to my surprise it didn't seem to be Moe either.

It was Mara.

When she realized that we all were staring at her, she raised her face from her napkin to reveal red cheeks and stringy hair. Her makeup was probably charmed to be waterproof and tear-proof, but no amount of magic could hide the way she'd been running her hands over her face. "Don't judge me," she demanded, her voice harsh. "What a horrible family you are!"

Lacey reeled as though she'd been hit.

At her side, Al cleared his throat. "Come now, Mara, that isn't professional—"

"Professional be damned! All his life, the only thing Kade was was *professional*, and look where it got him!"

In the reeling silence, Lacey said very quietly, "It seems you didn't know my late husband very well, then."

Mara laughed—a strangled sound. "I know him for what he was if that's what you mean! I know what all of you are! Imagine—the glorious Rises, lording it over the town, and all they are is foxkin!"

I glanced down at William, who was staring hard at Rei. *Ah. Maybe this explains what William said that first night—if Mara is telling the truth. And it certainly ties into the prophecy and the hate Officer Ebb was worried about. But how would Mara know?*

Moe leaned around Luca to look at Mara, as though he was really seeing her for the first time. "Is that why Father hired you, then? Because you were blackmailing him about his heritage?"

"More fool me," said Mara, breaking into noisy tears.

Al turned to Lacey, sputtering, and with a stony face Lacey cleared her throat. "It's not a side of the business you ever saw, Al. Thank goodness for that. But yes, Kade did have a streak of vengeance in him. If anyone approached him with a secret, he always found a way to turn it back on them . . . he was clever, my Kade, if cruel at times. Mara," she added, not unkindly, "if you suffered at my husband's hands, I will not—"

But again Mara broke out, whether in laughter or in tears, it was difficult to tell. I felt like I was watching a two-bit opera. "Suffered! My whole clan has suffered! I came here thinking I could make things right, after the way he'd ruined us with his awful deals. But I never should have come here at all. He said if I exposed *him*, then he'd expose *me* as the reason my clan lost so much money in trade. They call us thieves, but we are nothing compared to *you!*"

She practically fell over the table as she spoke, her elbow crashing into her plate as she leaned to point at Rei.

Lacey stood. "That's enough, Mara. I am willing to offer you sympathy, but you must behave."

"*I* must behave!" Mara, too, scrambled to her feet. "I have tried to hold it together. I have put on this entire wedding by myself! I thought this torture might end at last after what happened to Kade, but *no!* You had to carry on with the wedding, you two-faced fox-loving—"

This time it was not Lacey, but Moe who reacted. He leapt

to his feet and swung a fist over Luca's head, catching Mara squarely in the jaw. She went down immediately.

My stomach twisted, reminded of the way Kade, too, had dropped.

Lacey came around the table to put her hand on Moe's shoulder, restraining him. When Mara didn't rise, we all looked to Officer Ebb.

He was already out of his chair and checking on her. "She'll be fine," he said, "but she reeks of wine. Might be best if we put her up in her room for—"

"In her *room*?" Moe scoffed. "You heard her threaten my brother, and my mother. And she practically confessed to the crime!"

"Nearly," agreed Thorn, one hand on her long chin, "but not actually. She could have just seen Kade's death as an out when it was presented to her."

"Either way, she had best take that out," said Lacey, quietly, "lest I finish what my son has started."

Her eyes as she looked at the woman on the floor were steely and wild. I watched her for a long moment, and it wasn't until Moe turned and put his hand on hers that I finally saw her relax.

"We'll not find out any more now," Officer Ebb decided. He turned to Whitestone, who had been observing the entire charade from the corner of the room. "Round up some people to help carry her upstairs. I'll take first shift guarding the door myself. And in the meantime . . ." he turned back to the table. "Officer Thorn is in charge."

"Right, then." Thorn actually rubbed her hands together. "Time for a change of scene, eh? It's best we leave this room as it is."

"The parlor," said Lacey absently. "We can have dessert and coffee there."

"Excellent. Come, come," said Thorn, practically pulling Al and Varsha up by their sleeves.

As the room emptied, William lingered to watch some of the Rise employees pick up Mara's limp body and carry her into the hall.

"That was a lot of passion," he murmured. "Maybe it could have been her, after all."

"Mara, you mean?" I asked. "Well, Varsha did find all those letters, remember. Seems like there was a long history there—a long time of Kade Rise taking advantage of Mara's clan. And blackmail is pretty awful."

"Mara? No." William shook himself. "Didn't you see how angry Lacey was? Murder's a crime of passion, after all. Most times, the culprit is the victim's closest friend."

On that rather grim note, William and I hustled after the rest of the party. Luca had lingered, holding open the parlor door for us. Everyone else had taken individual seats and stared uneasily at anything nonhuman.

"It was probably just the wine talking. I gave her the bottle myself. Meant it as a conciliatory gesture after yesterday. Some good that did," Al said to the fire.

"It is a good thing we have you, Officer Thorn," said Lacey to a portrait of Kade on the wall.

"Just doing my job," Officer Thorn informed a platter of small cakes.

"Thanks, Moe," Rei whispered to the floor.

Moe grunted as he contemplated his knuckles.

I exchanged a look with William. Luca had already been distracted by a small bookshelf in the corner, and Varsha seemed to be asleep.

Before I could decide what to do, Lacey rose and drifted toward me. Tugging me over to a window looking out into the garden, she said quietly, "I suppose I should explain."

I glanced quickly around. William was nearby, but no one else seemed to be listening. "You don't have to—"

"It's true that Kade, and Rei, are foxkin," she said. "The blood has been in the Rise family a long time."

"Oh," was all I could think of to say. Finally, I added, "I don't really see why it's a big deal, Lacey, if you don't mind me saying so. I mean, aside from the prophecy, of course."

At last she turned from contemplating the glass to smile at me. Tears shimmered on her cheeks. "Yes, the prophecy." Closing her eyes just as she had the first night, she repeated,

When Reynard rules Seaside
And none know his name,
And speaking the truth
Can only bring shame,
Then shall come the undrowned tide
To sweep away sickness and blame.

"Oh," I said again, and this time I got it. In fact, after Mara's outburst, a lot of things about Kade had clicked into place—including how he might think to have a literal child stranded at sea sign a contract before allowing them to live in his home. "You know, when we went to see Clemency, she admitted to us that she didn't make up the prophecy. It just sort of came through her."

"I always thought as much. But Kade never did," Lacey said with a sniff. "In fact, Kade wanted it erased from the town records. He wanted revenge. But I tried to tell him, over and over, there really wasn't anything there to get revenge *for* . . .

Vengeance is one emotion I don't fully understand. Not with Kade—and not with Mara, either. Though I do understand her shame."

"It does seem like she had reason to be upset, based on what we found in the office earlier," I confided quietly. "But I agree with you about revenge. It never seems to do much good." When Lacey was silent, thinking, I added, "What do you think? And what does Rei think? About the prophecy, I mean, and the Reynard bit especially."

Lacey heaved a long sigh. "I don't know that Rei has had time to contemplate it. I had hoped it wouldn't come up—not ever again, not now that Kade is gone. I had hoped . . ." she paused. "Do you see a light in the garden?"

* * *

"I—I think I do, actually," I said, shifting to look out. "It looks like it's by the statue that Cindy's been working on. But I would have thought that Cindy'd be with Taiwo and Jeannie and the others?"

I didn't say more. Lacey's eyes had gone steely again, and she turned to order Whitestone to send someone out to investigate.

And that was how, for the second time, a tense silence was broken by a scene at the Rise estate.

Cindy came in literally kicking and shouting, being dragged by the collar by a very grim-faced Whitestone. Two police assistants came out of nowhere to search her pockets.

"What were you doing out there?" Lacey asked, her voice cutting through the noise.

"Working on my art! My art! Not that a pampered parasite

like *you* would under—"

"Miss Red," called one of the police assistants. "Would you please come here?"

With a glance at William, then at Officer Thorn, I made my way across the room. Luca was watching too, having finally looked up from his books. Even Varsha had woken up. I had the strangest feeling of being on trial.

But it was Cindy who should have been worried. In the shadow behind the hall door, the assistant held out something from the firesprite's pockets for me to look at.

Uh-oh, I thought, before I'd even gotten my goggles all the way down. *Please don't tell me . . . it's more devil's rope.*

30

Close

The wave of tension that had swelled with Cindy's discovery broke and ebbed as she was taken down to the police station. Though she protested her innocence—and her ignorance of the poison in her pocket—at the top of her voice, it seemed everyone in the house had decided to ignore her.

Except me.

The way I saw it, whoever had murdered Mr. Rise had been calculating and extremely upset, to carry through with a crime even during a wedding. Cindy might well have been both of those things. However, I was starting to realize that the murderer must be rich—and despite what William said about commissions, Cindy seemed very much the "starving artist/activist" type. She'd probably already given whatever the Rises had paid her to a cause.

This revelation came as I was holding that vial of powdered devil's rope in my palm for a moment before Officer Ebb came downstairs to take it—and Cindy—away. Everyone around me was yelling, but all I could think was, *this is a really nice glass container. I wonder if I can keep it?*

Typical alchemist, William might have said.

But that's the thing. I knew full well that glass containers weren't all that cheap. They certainly didn't grow on trees. And yet the murderer was running around breaking them and stuffing them in people's pockets like they were going out of style. Really good quality ones, too. Not to mention that the powdered devil's rope itself had to be costing someone a pretty penny—just like Clemency had pointed out.

Someone was going to great lengths—not just murder-wise, but money-wise.

Just like someone at the head of a corporation that just made a huge deal might, I thought. But who was it? I had to admit I'd hoped that the preference for *M*s in MMC might indicate someone easy—like Moe or Mara. But Moe was out of the running, and Mara seemed too focused on her own troubles to be running around causing trouble for everyone else. So who else did that leave?

My musings were cut short as I realized that the parlor was emptying. Apparently, with all chance of a show exhausted, everyone was foregoing dessert in favor of sleep.

"The wedding's only in a few days," Lacey was saying. Her hands were clutched at her waist as people rose and said their goodnights.

Rei stopped beside me on the way out the door. "Red," he said quietly, "Just make sure Taiwo's safe, okay? And—they'll probably be really upset about Cindy. If you could . . ."

"I'll talk to them," I promised. "I figured I'd get up extra early and head over to the camp before the wedding, anyway."

If Officer Thorn let me go, and *if* we made it that long without another fiasco, which I secretly doubted.

Rei nodded and drifted out into the hall. Al followed, with a sympathetic nod of his own. Varsha murmured something to Luca and then shuffled out with Thorn close behind her.

"On your guard," Thorn muttered as she passed.

As if I could be anything else!

The parlor had emptied: just Lacey, Luca, and William remained with me. Moe had already left, unobserved. The thought made me uneasy, but I pushed that aside to smile at Lacey as she, too, swept toward the hall.

"Please, sleep well, Red," she said. "Perhaps now we will finally have peace."

From behind me, William cleared his throat. "You're sure you don't want someone to sit up with you?"

"With me?" Lacey repeated absently, before smiling down at William, understanding. "Ah, no. I will be alright. Thank you, though . . ." And in that same absent manner, she disappeared to her room.

"I don't like it," William rumbled. "I don't like any of it."

"Yeah, me neither," I said, turning to face my friends.

"Me neither, and I only just got here," said Luca lightly. "Red, you don't have to turn in yet, do you? I was hoping you could explain some things for me."

"Sure," I said, still thinking about that glass vial. "Although, we should probably go up to my room in case they want to close up the parlor," I added vaguely, meaning the Rises' staff. I hadn't seen any porters or waiters lately, but figured they must be closing up the house for the night.

William made a sound that sounded very much like a sneeze. "Sure, good reason."

"Definitely. Or someone could be listening," Luca added, looking around the darkened room.

"Why anyone would listen to the two of you, I have no idea," said William, shaking his ears before trotting out of the room.

"Is he . . . grumpier than usual?" Luca asked in his wake.

I scrunched up my nose, thinking about it. "He *has* been a little odd since we left Belville, actually. Maybe this trip was a bit much for him, and he just doesn't want to admit it."

"All the more reason to stay in town for a while after this," Luca said brightly.

I chuckled, warmth spreading through my chest. "Yeah, I guess so. Come on, we better follow him before he gets any grumpier."

Luca grinned at me and for some reason, it felt like the only nice thing to have happened all day. *For some reason? Probably because we're in a house with a murderer. Thorn would say grinning at all is foolish—*

My shoulder collided with Luca's as we both tried to make it out the door at the same time. We exchanged even goofier grins and he gestured for me to lead the way.

I think almost getting poisoned had more effect on my head than I thought, I decided giddily. Fortunately, by the time we'd traversed the dark and silent halls, I was feeling more somber.

"Alright," I said, letting Luca into my room on the second floor and closing the door behind him. William had already taken a place on top of the covers on the bed and was watching us as I tried to focus on practical things. "What did you want explained?"

"Um," said Luca. He shifted from foot to foot on the rug in front of the fire, which was blazing despite the fact that it was easily seventy-five degrees outside. I curled up on the floor next to the dresser, on one side of the fireplace, and Luca plopped down on the rug beside the room's one chair.

"I'm not even sure where to begin. But that sprite just now—Cindy—you know her?"

"Yeah, she's been around since the beginning," I said, nodding. "She's a bit—determined—and she's a really good friend to Taiwo. But—"

"They *did* date a while back," William interrupted.

"Yes, but—"

"So that, plus the fact that obviously Cindy had no love lost for the Rises, makes a pretty convincing motive," he concluded.

"I can't say you're wrong," I admitted, exasperated, "but really? Cindy? And she'd let herself get caught, just like that?"

"I thought she seemed just as surprised as the rest of us to see that vial," Luca put in.

"You can't trust everything you see," William said.

"Yes, but you can't just turn on your friends at the drop of a hat, either," I shot back. "I mean, we shouldn't take it for granted now that she's guilty. Someone could have planted that."

To my surprise, William smiled. "Hey, look. Red the pessimist is learning to stick by her friends. And strange acquaintances."

"I'm not a pessimist," I muttered.

"I wouldn't have thought so," Luca agreed loyally.

I smiled at him, releasing my annoyance with William. "So, that's that, for now. Was there anything else?"

He beamed. "Oh, absolutely. There's so much going on. A merfolk wedding! And an Afolayan one at that, and you know them! It's all really cool. Aside from the murder thing. But, um, I was wondering, what actually is supposed to happen at the ceremony?"

"You mean, aside from Taiwo and Rei getting married?" I teased him.

"Or maybe including that," Luca said, his wide smile flashing in the firelight. "I've never been to a merfolk wedding before. And I'm not really any good at modern ceremonies. Usually if I have a question about that kind of thing, I write to Varsha."

"What did she tell you about it?" I asked, a twinge in my chest. I hoped she was safe with Officer Thorn. Of course, there surely wasn't anyone safer in the house.

"Not much. She mentioned it a while back, but she didn't think she'd be invited. And you know, I think I totally forgot to mention it to her that you were going! I mean, I kind of spaced it until the last minute that you were going *here*, and this is where Varsha lives. I'm really bad at any geography more than a few miles from Belville," Luca said, ducking his head so that his hood obscured his face.

"Not surprising," William commented, "given that you literally couldn't leave Belville due to a centuries-long imprisonment."

"What William said," I agreed, "except with less reference to unpleasantries. Okay, so, from what I can gather, merfolk ceremonies are really big, but mostly a chance to get together and party. In three days at dawn is when the actual ceremony will be, and after that basically the whole day is one big party. They've got special shows they're doing, and dances, and it sounds like there's going to be a huge continuous buffet."

"And is all this happening—?" Luca waved his hands expressively.

"*On* the water," William said, a bit snidely. "Hope you don't get seasick."

"Don't listen to him," I said as Luca's eyes went wide. "I

mean, yes, the first part of the ceremony will be on the water. Jeannie—that's Taiwo's mom—she made a stage and everything, for Taiwo and Rei and the officiant, Ailelle. Most of the people watching will be swimming or in boats. But after that, everything's going to happen on the Rises' private beach."

"Imagine," William snorted, "having a private beach."

"Imagine being such a sourpuss during a wedding," I retorted, grinning crookedly at him.

"A wedding which still has a chance of being canceled due to murder!" William reminded us.

Luca was clearly still thinking everything over. "So, if it's mostly at a beach, then scholar's robes are okay? Because I didn't think to bring anything else. In fact I really didn't pack, except for—"

A knock at the door interrupted him.

William, Luca, and I frowned at each other.

The knock came again.

"Well, I'll get it," I decided, getting up and crossing the room.

I opened the door to see three people clustered in the hall. Two wore uniforms like Officer Ebb's, and one seemed to be part of the Rise staff. They certainly seemed familiar enough.

"Miss Red," they began, "sorry to disturb you so late, but these police assistants showed up asking for you. It seems your expertise is needed down at the station."

"Really?" I asked. Normally I'm happy to help, but something about this did not feel right. "Is Thorn coming too?"

"Some assistants are going for her, too," said one of the police.

I considered them. The two police assistants were tall, elfish, and reasonably well put together. And the porter . . . he seemed familiar, but I couldn't quite place him. Maybe he'd been helping at all the drama-filled dinners I'd attended.

"It really is a matter of some urgency," said the porter. "If you're feeling uncomfortable, you could perhaps take your dog with you."

I glanced over my shoulder. William was glowing faintly. I couldn't see Luca.

"It's time to go," said one of the police assistants. "Officer Ebb is waiting. Officer Thorn, too."

Uh-huh. Sure, I thought, my inner Taiwo rolling their eyes at the thought of Officer Thorn waiting quietly.

"Do you know what the matter is?" I asked the porter abruptly. "You know, in case I need to bring tools or something."

"I believe you don't need your tools," he answered. He seemed like a normal human, and he spoke quickly. "It is your expertise we need at this time."

His words echoed in my mind. *We need at this time. At this time. Aha!*

I grinned: I'd finally placed him. This was the man who had spoken to Jon on the pier! I hadn't heard much of that conversation, but his voice sounded much the same.

And he's one of the staff? I hesitated again. Finally, it clicked in the back of my mind: this was Dale, the porter I'd met on my first morning in the house. He'd ditched his name tag now, though, and he looked more determined than jittery.

"*Rred,*" a voice whispered by my ear. I recognized it at once as Luca, in his shadowy form. "*Watch out.*"

"Sure thing," I said slowly to the porter. "Just let me grab my cloak."

It was way too warm out for a cloak. I didn't need it. I didn't need anything except to get out of the way—and to watch out.

31

To The Edge

I turned from the door frame and ducked for good measure. A cool breeze rippled over my head. Dale cried out, but he was too late. The wind in the hallway whirled and all three goons were knocked back, stumbling into each other and sliding down the walls.

But of course, they wouldn't stay down for long. And the last thing I, with my itchy feet, wanted to do was let them trap me in my room. Who knew what they might take the opportunity to do—or who they might call—while I and my friends were stuck?

This, I decided, *is definitely an occasion for Officer Thorn.*

Luca shimmered back into view in the middle of them. He must have had the same idea. "Come on!"

"Time to go, indeed," William agreed. Leaving a trail of stardust in his wake, he leapt down from the bed and shoved me out the door.

"I was going," I protested.

William followed me into the hall and kicked the goon who was steadiest on his feet. "Not fast enough. Run!"

Luca grabbed at my hand and tugged me down the corridor. As we turned the corner, feet sliding over the polished wood, I panted, "That was really cool, Luca! I didn't know you could do that!"

"Me neither," he huffed, gunning for the stairs. "I've never . . . hit anyone . . . before. I hope . . . they were . . . bad guys!"

"They definitely are," William said from the back. "And they're gaining. Go faster!"

The hallway was awash with thumps and clumps as the three of us—and the three of them—dashed clumsily through the house. But none of the other bedroom doors were opening—except for Thorn's, which stood ajar. The realization hit me like a pang in the chest and for a moment time seemed to stop. *Where could she be? Is everyone else okay? Who's going to help us?*

Good thing Luca was more focused—and still holding on to my hand. "Even if we can't find her, we have to keep moving," he panted. He pulled us to the stairs, but as he turned to go up, I dug my heels in.

"Not up!" I cried. "Why does everyone always go *up?* We'll just get stuck up there!"

"Good point," Luca called back, diving for the staircase to the first floor. We tumbled down it as fast as our feet could take us.

"Where *is* everyone?" I asked William, risking a glance back as we hit the landing.

"No time to worry about that now," he said. And he was right. The goons were already at the top of the stairs.

"Let's go outside," Luca suggested, lunging to cut through the courtyard.

I hesitated. "But what about Thorn?"

"She's probably out there already, knowing her," said

William, shoving me again. "Go on, go!"

"We might even make it to the station!" Luca called back.

I almost reprimanded him for yelling about our plans when the goons might overhear us. But, seeing as they could just as easily follow us around, I supposed it didn't matter. I tucked my head down and ran.

When we get outside, I thought, *I could just run straight to the station myself. William would be okay keeping up. But Luca . . .*

He may be able to turn invisible and even attack goons, but I didn't think he'd be able to run like I did. And even if he *could* defend himself, I didn't like the thought of leaving him behind.

Luca and I hit the front door like a ton of bricks. William glowed and flashed, and the lock turned blue before opening of its own accord. Apparently, the house didn't merit the same protection Kade's office had. We tumbled out and onto the front lawn, breathless.

Breathless, but able to see. As I lifted my head, I could tell even in the dark that the big gates in front of the house were closed.

"Curse it," William rumbled. "They were ready."

"They knew what we'd do," Luca agreed in dismay.

"They've been two steps ahead of us this whole time. That's no reason to stop now," I reminded my friends. With one hand I pushed William, and with the other I tugged on Luca, taking over the lead. I herded both of them toward the side of the house, picking up speed just as the goons skidded out the front door.

We cleared the corner of the house only to collide with something very big and very warm.

"Oof!" grunted the newcomer. "Take—"

"No!" yelped William. "You fool, we're friends!"

"Aha!" Thorn pulled herself upright while the rest of us scrambled to do the same. "They came after you, too? Not to worry—Varsha's safe. Scatter!"

Seeing as three goons were hot on our heels and two large strangers were bearing down on Thorn, this seemed like good advice.

Luca disappeared on my left, and William bounded straight for the strangers on my right. Thorn barreled one way and I sprinted as fast as I could straight ahead, into the bushes.

The Rises' garden wasn't actually a maze, but it might well have been. After the crashes from William's game of chicken with the goons had subsided, a deathly quiet descended on the grounds, and everyone was swallowed up in the darkness.

But then the goons wised up.

"They've split up!" cried Dale.

"You there! Go that way!"

"You! Take the gazebo!"

"You! Aaaah!"

"A witch! A witch got me!"

Hmm, I thought, grinning to myself. *I think they found William's abandoned balloon version of Clemency.*

And with that, the crashing resumed. I took advantage of the distraction to dart amongst the shrubberies, straining for every sound, trying to figure out what was going on. I heard Thorn yell at one point, but she sounded triumphant. I thought I saw a flash of William's magic near the picnic table, but nothing came of it.

I have to be methodical about this, I thought, sliding to a halt behind an azalea. *I can't just run circles around them until dawn. We have to end this somehow . . .*

As I was trying to think of a way to devise a trap, the shadows condensed beside me.

"Just me," Luca whispered, before I screamed. "It's just me."

"Good," I breathed, trying to relax. "Do you know what's going on out there?"

"I think Thorn knocked one of them out. Maybe two. She and the porter are chasing each other around the house," he informed me.

Suddenly I was glad to be far away from that. "Okay, so that leaves at least two. Can you think of any way to trap them? I was trying to come up with a plan just now."

"I don't know the garden very well," Luca admitted. "Is there a place they could get stuck?"

"The statue!" I remembered, grinning. "Cindy's statue. It's over on the other side of the house, towards the front. It's surrounded on three sides by thick hedges. We can lead them in there, and then trap them in with it."

"Great," Luca said. "Lead the way!"

I stood and stretched, and then loped out from our hiding place. I ran more slowly than before, looking. I couldn't see William. *He might have run out of magic, especially after unlocking the door.* But I couldn't worry about him yet—I had to focus.

I loped around the garden, taking care to make extra noise. It paid off. By the gazebo, I heard a voice cry,

"There—there she is!"

And another answer,

"Come on then—after her!"

Good, I thought, smiling. *That part was easy at least.*

I leapt into a run, taking care not to get too far from them. I could hear Luca now, panting as he kept up. The two goons were heavy-footed and cursing. Apparently, chasing down victims hadn't been in their job description.

Just you wait, I thought smugly. *See how much you like it when the tables are—*

A bright light switched on over the front porch and blinded me. I stumbled to one side, knocking into Luca, who went down. The goons behind us shouted.

And, I must admit, so did I. Shouting Luca's name, I veered around in a tight circle so that I could pull him up. The goons were close by, but I wasn't thinking about them any more. There wasn't any time. There was no time whatsoever, and everything was dark, except the flashes in my eyes from that light, and the shouting, and other people's hands were tugging at Luca's robe, and then—

Something white flashed out from Luca's hood and growled like a tiny werewolf. I swear I saw teeth flashing in the night. The white form leapt, quick and sinuous as a snake, and somebody screamed.

"Frank!" Luca cried.

"Luca, get *up,*" I said, finally regaining control of my own voice.

I tugged him up and he stretched out an arm. The white thing flashed again and for a moment I thought it might attack him, too. But instead it jumped on to him and ran up to his shoulder. I kicked away the uninjured goon and pulled Luca into a run once more.

"Who . . . turned on . . . the light?" he panted.

"Don't know," I admitted. "But the statue—is right here—"

"And why, Miss Red," asked a new yet familiar voice, "would you think that the statue can help you?"

The speaker wasn't one of the goons—it was someone in

front of us. I realized this and at first I was afraid, not least because they sounded so incredibly *annoyed.* But my fear quickly became annoyance, too. Apparently, the speaker had chosen to stand right in front of Luca and me—right in the way of the statue garden.

I say "apparently" because my eyes still hadn't fully recovered from the porch light. I never saw the person at all. Before I could react to the knowledge of a new person, Luca and I both crashed straight into them. And shortly after, the goons tripped and crashed into *us.*

Again the mink was in full force, flashing white. The goons were yelling.

"Come on," I whispered to Luca, "up! Quick!"

He pulled himself from the pile, helping me get my long hair free. And while a growling Frank kept the strangers occupied, I pulled three vials from my belt.

"Solidifying Goo," I told Luca, pressing one of the vials into his hands. "Aim for the right side of the group, I'll get the left side. On three. One—

"Two—" Luca counted with me.

"Three!"

Together, we threw our glass vials of goo. I can't describe how satisfying it felt to chuck a vial at someone who had so recently ordered a poisoned vial chucked at *me.*

All three vials hit home. The mink escaped at the last minute, clambering onto Luca's shoulder with just a little of the green goo on its long tail. At first the strangers writhed in disgust, but that only helped the goo along. As it came into contact with the air, it expanded, and slowly hardened. In a minute, all three of our attackers were locked in place on the ground.

"Well done," Luca beamed, high-fiving me.

"Thanks. It's my own invention," I said with a blush, as though accepting first prize at a fair, not catching criminals. I shook my head and added, very quietly so that only he could hear, "it won't last forever. We have to get Thorn and William, and figure out who these people are."

"Frank can get Thorn," said Luca. "Right?"

"Right." A thin, whispery voice answered Luca's, and I reeled in shock. *He did say Frank could talk—I guess he's a mink of few words.* Before I could recover, the mink darted off into the night.

"Okay, then. In the meantime," I said, drawing a lightsick from my belt, "let's see who these people are."

In the glowstick's gentle light, the struggling goons fell still. Two were dressed as police assistants. But one—the one at the bottom of the pile—the one who had spoken—that one was dressed in a suit.

My mouth dropped open. "Uncle Al?"

32

Mountain Peaks

There was no mistaking the prim and proper gnome's face. But he wouldn't say a word, no matter how long I stared at him. Maybe he wasn't feeling chatty—or it was just possible that I'd accidentally Goo'd his mouth shut.

Officer Thorn, of course, would never have allowed such an inconvenience to stop *her*. She charged up to us already yelling.

"Red! Luca! Are you the owners of this critter? Why's it talking to me? Did you see the—oh." Thorn skidded to a halt at the entrance to the garden, much as we had done not moments before. "Looks like you saw them, alright."

"I think Al just came out of the house a moment ago," I said. "He must be the one who turned on the porch light. And I think—I think he must be the one behind all the goons. I bet you he owns Mountain Meet Company. Or he used to—before Kade Rise decided to try to take it over."

Muffled, angry mumbles could be heard from Al. Apparently, I *had* Goo'd his mouth shut.

Oh well, he'll have plenty of time to talk later, I thought as

Officer Thorn leapt into action.

"I remember this stuff," she said, bending down to inspect the Goo. "Nice work, Red, Luca. You two make a good team. I got the other three, of course. Well, I got two, and William's currently sitting on one of them. Pity they don't give us handcuffs in half-dozen sets, eh?"

As she spoke, she pulled a length of rope from a pocket hidden somewhere in her uniform. Winking at us, she continued, "Needs must. Give me a hand with them, won't you? No telling how long this'll last, am I right, Red?"

More muffled sounds came from Al and his hired hands, this time sounding desperate. But who were they to feel betrayed? I'd never lied to them. Or stayed in their house and murdered their business partner and hired goons to chase their guests around, either.

One by one, Thorn wrenched the criminals free and held them in place while Luca and I tied them up. By the time we were done, the angry noises had subsided into a glum silence. The night was deeper, the porch light still on. A slight snoring noise seemed to indicate that Luca's mink had gone back to sleep in his hood.

"Right," said Officer Thorn, rubbing her hands together. "Let me just give Ebb a call, and then we'll hear what Mr. Litely has to say for himself, shall we?"

"Litely?" I asked, startled.

"That's his name," Luca reminded me. "His surname, anyway. Remember? He introduced himself to me very nicely at dinner," he added, as though it was a shame that such manners were wasted on a criminal.

Litely, I thought. *Just like the peak on the "Sirens" folder map. And here I thought it said "Lildly!" I guess that explains where the idea for "Mountain Meet" came from.*

* * *

"I didn't have anything to do with any of this, regrettable as it all is," Al protested once the Goo around his face had softened up. He sat in a large armchair like a naughty child in the principal's office. Thorn stood over him, much like said principal.

"Then why were you the only one to come outside?" she asked him.

Luca, William, and I stood behind Officer Thorn. Officer Ebb and his assistants had carted away the goons, but he'd asked Thorn to talk to Al before taking him down to the station. Whether this was to have a neutral person do the interview, or to spare Al the ignominy of police attention, I wasn't sure.

We'd taken over the parlor as an interrogation room. Whitestone, when roused, quickly set to work despite the late hour. Lacey, Rei, and the others were all sleeping soundly—the effects of a sleeping draught, no doubt administered by Dale before he let in the hired muscle and closed the estate gate.

"I don't know," Al said. But as his gaze traveled over all four of us, it became less and less certain. "I just—heard the commotion, and wanted to see what was going on."

Officer Thorn put her hands on her hips.

"I thought—this is all Cindy's fault," Al tried again. "Isn't she the one who did this? She's the one who's always causing trouble. She hates the Rises. She hates Rei."

William sneezed. "Sure, Cindy seems like she has lots of disposable income for buying poisons and hiring goons."

"What would Varsha find if she looked up *you*, Mr. Litely?" Luca asked quietly. "Which company does your money come from? Is it Mountain Meet?"

I was proud of Luca for speaking up. Since we'd hauled Al into the parlor, the gnome'd adopted a holier-than-thou sort of attitude, that attitude that business execs seem to carry with them bottled up in their pockets for emergencies. It was an attitude that Luca's abusive boss, Owl, used to call on a lot. But clearly, Luca wasn't about to let the similarities get to him. I reached out and put a hand on his shoulder, readjusting as I hit something soft that seemed to be the mink's tail.

"I'm not—how did you—" Al threw up a hand in protest, but soon gave up. The hand went to his temple as he sighed. "You have to understand. All of this was in self-defense."

Officer Thorn was clearly having none of this, so it fell to me to ask the obvious question. "'Self-defense'? Was Mr. Rise threatening you?"

"Yes, and he had been for years!" the little gnome burst out. "You can't understand, any of you. You didn't know him, not like I did. He was an awful man! Once you crossed him, you were as good as dead."

Luca shivered. "Mara did say something similar . . ."

"But Lacey said you hadn't seen that side of the business," I pointed out to Al.

"Lacey is wrong," he said, not so much piquant as grim. "She doesn't remember. I've been here a long time. Kade and I were friends even before he took up the family business. Back then, I was naive. I thought we were doing great things. He *told* me we were doing great things, and I believed him. That is, until I saw him ruin a merperson's life and steal her business plans from her, taking over a monopoly on the trade of sea-gold and goods between Seaside and Ran."

So that was how his dealings with Mara's clan started, I thought. I didn't say anything aloud, because I didn't want to distract Al, but I would have bet anyone that if Varsha went back through those letters she'd found, she'd be able to corroborate Al's story.

Officer Thorn crossed her arms. "And then?"

"And then nothing," said Al, throwing both hands up. "What was I supposed to do?"

"Maybe not go into business with him," snorted William.

"By then it was too late. Besides," Al said, his gaze drifting into the shadows, "Grandmother always said, keep your friends close but your enemies closer."

Something about that sentiment rang discordantly in my mind. It wasn't that I didn't believe that he thought that—he clearly believed it wholeheartedly—it was more the fact that he'd been living with the Rises for so long. Even after Mr. Rise's death.

Was that just to keep an eye on Lacey, Moe, and Rei?

"When did the threats against *you* start?" Officer Thorn pressed again.

Al shifted. The armchair nearly swallowed him up. His suit was torn and rumpled, and his tie was askew. "It was my idea," he muttered finally. "It was mine all along. He *said* I should pursue it. He *encouraged* me!"

Officer Thorn was literally tapping her foot.

"The sea foam blade," Al said at last, when none of us spoke. "*I'm* the one who came up with it in the first place."

And when we continued to be silent, he kicked his feet against the cushions. "I thought you had done *research,*" he said, his sneer coming out more desperate than derisive. "The siren blade would have made me a fortune. All I had to do was file my official business paperwork this summer, and the sirens would deal with me—and *only* me. But then Kade turned it all against me. He said it was my project. But then he changed his mind. He came to me in the spring and he said that since I'd used company resources, company contacts, he'd be taking it all over from here . . ."

For a moment I tuned out his self-important regrets and thought. *All of this—MMC, and all the drama it's caused—has been because of a weapon?* It sounded very much like something Taiwo had reported Ige saying once—and now that we knew Ige and Jon had had a fling, it made more sense that Jon would have dropped actual intel by accident. *Ige the "alarmist" was on the right track with this one!*

"You say you came up with it," Luca was saying, coaxingly. Al was listening like a captivated child, waiting for praise. "How? When?"

"Years ago," said the gnome, petulantly. "I knew at once it'd be a success. A siren knife that turns its victim into sea foam, and disintegrates itself? Anyone would want one, and they'd have to keep buying new ones, too!"

In my head, I corrected this to, *any murderer would want one,* and *they'd have to buy new ones after they killed someone.* Yikes. Aloud, I prompted, "But it's siren technology?"

"They'd never let an outsider use one," Al said, confirming my suspicion. "Not unless they trusted them. They trusted *me.* They would have, as soon as my little business was past its probation period. But then Kade had to come in, and he took it over. Like it'd been his idea all along. He *betrayed* me!"

"And you're saying the technology was promised to MMC," I said slowly, "so why did that cause threats, when MMC was a part of Rise Enterprises, which you both worked on?"

"But it *wasn't!* MMC was *mine.* It was always just mine. But Kade couldn't stand it. He had to have everything. He took it over—because who could say no to him? Not the fools on the village council, that's for sure! And he wasn't ever going to let me in on it again, not during his life. He made sure of that. The only way I could own *my* idea was if Kade was gone," Al insisted.

"All I'm hearing so far is business rivalries, Mr. Litely," said Thorn. "That's not enough to plead self-defense."

"It wasn't a rivalry, it was my *life,*" Al exclaimed, leaping up to stand on the armchair's plush seat. "You don't understand. I'll never have kids. I don't want them, have no use for them, never wanted a family or anything else. This idea was my *world.* It was my everything. And he would have killed it before he let me run it—he would have run it into the ground! If I pushed back about anything, he'd just take it away. The moment anyone argued, Kade just decided he would take over. 'Oh, it's for the best,' he'd say, 'democracy doesn't get the work done, does it?'! He was going to run my project into the ground. He wouldn't listen to me any more. If I'd said anything else about it, he would have given it to that bumbling Rei! But it was *mine!*"

"Still not hearing threats," William muttered.

"Don't you understand?" Al was yelling now. *"To see it die would have been death to me! Better that he should die first!"*

"Uh huh." Thorn pulled out her notebook and made some notes—probably a word-for-word transcription of what amounted to a confession, if I had to guess. "And the devil's rope?"

Al eyed the notebook and snapped his mouth shut.

"Isn't it obvious?" Luca spoke even more quietly than before. "The sea-gold trade. The sirens. He—or rather, Mountain Meet—was making friends with everyone Mr. Rise offended. He made a point to do it. Your enemy's enemy becomes your friend. It's something—"Luca took a deep, shuddering breath—"It's something Owl would have done."

Al stared at Luca with round eyes.

Thorn tapped her notebook thoughtfully before turning to the gnome. "Did Mara give it to you, then?"

"Mara's a fool," Al snapped without thinking. "More drama than she's worth. I told Kade that from the beginning."

"Okay, not Mara," Thorn murmured, making a note.

"Jon," I said. Seeing that it was my turn to pick up the thread, I added, "You couldn't use a knife you had designed for a murder, right? That'd be a giveaway. Instead, you could trade for the devil's rope. But you didn't really know how to use it, did you? That's why you needed Jon—he's half merfolk, and might know the right people. He might even be the source of the wet footprints Varsha found. You needed people with access to the marine world . . . and someone to help you try different doses until it worked. That's where Dale came in, isn't it?"

"But *you* were the one on hand at the wedding, and you could do it yourself," William supplied.

Al's face twisted. "The two of them were even worse than me. Dale said he wanted to be free of Rise Enterprises—it was even his idea to use the wedding! Two birds, one stone, he said. Rei would be ruined by it all. Instead the boy's going around like his family can do *good* things, making up new mottos about looking after family friends—ha! If only he knew. But none of these goons know anything. *I* was the only one to get it right on the first try. Jon and Dale couldn't even handle an alchemist and her friends. I kept telling them they had to do more than follow people around and steal their notebooks, but did it come to anything? No, because anything you want done *right,* you have to do yourself. It's a good thing I had the charm on hand for the message about Reynard when the poison finally worked, because one of them would have messed it up."

"That took a useful turn," Thorn commented. "So, you administered the poison and created the threatening message. You had a mole in the police station and a mole in the house, and you hired them and others to scare Varsha and Red when they started getting too close. I think that about covers it, don't you, Red?"

"It does make sense," I agreed. "That's why the plan to poison us in Kade's office was well thought out, but not well executed. You told them what to do . . . but they didn't feel so good about doing it any more. Lacey told me," I added, "about devotion. She said Kade felt it for his business, and he expected everyone else to do the same. But it backfired on him, didn't it? In a way, his ambition brought everything to an end."

Al looked stunned.

A soft voice behind us coughed. "Not quite."

I turned, half thinking that it was Luca's mink talking again. (Seriously, that creature needed to explain itself—just as soon as we were done talking about murder.) Instead, in the doorway stood Rei.

"I've been here since I heard the yelling," he said almost apologetically. As we all stared, he took a few hesitant steps into the room—then stopped. He squared his shoulders and strode the rest of the way, until he stood right next to Officer

Thorn.

"Al Litely," said Rei, very formally, "my father should have seen through you from the beginning. He probably did. But he probably thought—probably thought he could handle you alone. I know that's how he was. I won't make the same mistake.

"That's why I'm going to ask Officer Ebb to see that you go on trial, and you serve out whatever punishment the judge decrees. I'm going to make sure everyone knows exactly what happened. And I'm going to rebuild Rise Enterprises, *and* Mountain Meet Company and all the other subsidiaries, from the ground up."

Al wavered. Even standing on his chair, he wasn't as tall as Rei. At first his fists clenched as though he was angry, but when he looked up, his eyes were watery. In a voice heavily choked with emotion, he said, "Thank you."

Rei stepped back and his gaze darted to me. *Not the reaction he expected either,* I thought with a smile. I nodded my support at him.

"It's—it's not for you," Rei said, finding his voice again. "It's for myself. For my family. For my new family that I'm going to make, without you or your help. Because—because *I'm not a bumbling fool, you coward.*"

For a moment, magic flashed around Rei. Just for that instant, I could see what Mara had meant when she said *foxkin.* I could see the ears, the plumed tail that ran in Rei's blood. He suddenly seemed much larger—he towered over Al. With one bound he charged toward the armchair—and then over it, as though Al and everything he touched was nothing but a mirage.

In Rei's wake, Al crumpled.

"Alright, there." Thorn picked up Al by his shoulders—literally picked him up and shook him. "There's no harm done. Nothing wrong with you. Well, nothing that some time in a cell and in front of a judge won't help."

Whistling, she tucked Al under one arm and told the rest of us, "I'm going to go see what's taken Ebb so long."

It wasn't until Officer Thorn and Al left the room completely that Rei turned back toward us. He looked normal now, and not a little exhausted.

"You did the right thing," Luca assured him.

"Thanks." Rei smiled. Somehow, he looked more like himself than I'd ever seen before. And, as if he heard my thoughts, he tugged at a small black stone ring on his finger. "I guess I don't need this any more—it'll all come out at the trial anyway, right?"

As the ring left his hand, Rei flashed and wavered, like a reflection in still water broken by a splash. And then there he was again, Rei, exactly the same as before—but with the fox ears I'd seen moments before. Somehow, they seemed to suit his pointed features much better than human ears had.

"A glamour?" Luca asked, looking at the ring.

"More like a suppression spell," William said, sniffing at it.

"Yeah—something like that," Rei nodded. "I never really understood. My father was the one who gave it to me—it was some special stone he'd made a very important deal for, he said. He said it was a good thing. But I can feel a difference when I don't wear it. I feel—more free."

"Your father was wearing that same kind of stone as a tie pin," I remembered.

Rei nodded again. "It was the only jewelry he ever wore. All his life. He said it was really for me, to give me a better chance, because of the prophecy, but . . .

"But," he resumed, stronger than before, "you know what I was thinking, while I was listening in just now? I was thinking, none of this would have happened if it wasn't for everyone keeping secrets and being afraid. My father—he wouldn't have been able to bully people like that. And Al—he might not have thought his life's work could be taken away."

William gave me a look which clearly said, *never mind that his life's work was about making it easier to murder people . . .*

But Rei hadn't quite finished. "It's even in the prophecy, too. *When truth can't be spoken,* and stuff like that. So—so I thought," he said, looking to us for support, "maybe I shouldn't do it any more. Hide who I am, I mean. I should just be myself, and—and hopefully we all can start to heal. Because I'm not Reynard. That was—that really was my father, after all."

"Exactly. But you are different," Luca affirmed. Moved, I put my arm around him—though I was more careful this time to avoid the mink.

"I'm all for it. And hey," I asked Rei, aiming for a lighter mood, "why weren't you asleep like everyone else?"

"Oh, I never drink tea before bed." Rei shrugged. "I heard all the running and I tried to go out and see what was going on, but I—well, someone knocked me over the head," he confessed. "Someone just running by, I think. When I woke up it took me a while to figure out what happened. When I realized it might be another attack, I called Taiwo. They said I should find you." With a sudden smile, he added, "they said that as long as I wasn't calling because I had cold feet, it was nothing we couldn't handle."

33

All's Well

Mere days later, Taiwo and Rei were married. The ceremony was absolutely glorious. The sunrise was beautiful—the best one we'd seen in Seaside yet. The sea was crammed full of merfolk, boats, and even a whale or two. Jeannie's platform held up perfectly, of course. And Taiwo and Rei were beautiful in their joyous blue garments—though I think that had more to do with the humongous smiles on their faces.

And above Rei's smile, his fox ears showed plainly. When he first stepped out onto the wedding platform, and everyone invited to the wedding and not a few party-crashers from town first saw him as *himself,* there was a noticeable flicker in the air.

It was like something rolled over the crowd, right over the bluff and over the town, and broke like a wave. And in its wake, the air felt a little fresher.

A little less full of prophecy.

The entire wedding party had breakfast on the beach, catered by the Rises, of course. But breakfast was far from the sit-down affair that the opening feast had been. Instead, guests and family darted back and forth across the beach, barely dodging waiters with trays full of pastries, quiches, seafood, and fruit. Jeannie cornered me by the champagne fountain with a huge smile on her face and an even bigger hug.

"You found the drink, I see," she said as she pulled back.

"Well—I figured—since it's a party—"

"You earned it! You earned it," she insisted, leaning in with her eyes bright. "Drink all you want. Eat all you want! Is there anything else I can give you? Oh, Red," she added, hugging me again and laughing, "I always knew it was a blessing when we met you."

"Aw, shucks, Jeannie," I said, feeling my cheeks grow hot. "I only do my best. If it wasn't for Officer Thorn and Luca and William—"

"And all your friends, I know," Jeannie concluded, beaming. "Did you ever think that's why we love you, Red? You bring wonderful people together. You have very good sense that way, even if you don't realize it."

Her words went straight to my heart, especially after the investigation. I passed a hand across my face, trying not to make it super obvious that I was wiping away tears.

But of course, Jeannie saw anyway. She leaned in once more. "Your mothers say to tell you hello, dear," she said to me. "I'm so very grateful you could make it and that you stayed. We all are. And—if I could tell you one thing—"

"Anything, Jeannie," I managed.

"—just remember," she said with one last smile, "that just because you're chasing one dream doesn't mean you have to throw away every other bit of good fortune."

Before I could say anything, Jeannie disappeared into the happy throng. Awash with happy feelings, I downed one glass and had another in my hands—not to mention a lot of spring in my step—as I went to rejoin William and Luca at the edge of the garden.

"Did you find Taiwo yet?" Luca asked through a mouthful of chocolate croissant. He seemed to be balancing about five plates in his hands. He handed me one, but it seemed the rest were for him.

"How could anyone find anyone in this chaos?" William murmured. "I don't even see Thorn."

"She and Ebb are hanging out on the beach by the bonfire," I said. "There's music setting up on the dock, and I think they're planning on doing a fish show later."

"Fish?" William's ears perked.

"Yeah, but," said Luca, "I know you wanted to talk to—"

"Me?" Taiwo burst into our little haven, dragging a blushing Rei behind them. "Hi, Red! Finally! Where have you *been*?"

"Talking to your mother," I said, or tried to say, as Taiwo smothered me in a hug. Clearly, hugging was a family skill in the Afolayan clan. I wondered good-naturedly if Rei would pick it up, in time. Over Taiwo's shoulder, I asked him, "How's your mom doing?"

"She's with Moe over by the waterfall," Rei said. "She likes the shade."

"She's doing just great, considering everything that's hap-pened," Taiwo added, stepping back. "I just can't believe it, even now. Red, you totally saved our wedding!"

"No, I—"

"I know, I know," said Taiwo, sounding just like Jeannie. "You couldn't have if it hadn't been for Varsha, or the police, or William, of course. Or Rei." With a smile, they linked arms with the bashful groom. "I'm just over the moon about how it all turned out. Speaking of, we're ending things with a special tribute to Mr. Rise and the new era of Rise Enterprises tonight under the moon. You'll be here, right?"

"Of course," I promised, winking down at William. He wouldn't get tired, but he knew well that I would. Luca, apparently, would be fueled by enough sugar to stay awake for another decade.

Taiwo and Rei were soon swept away by more enthusiastic guests, shouting as they left that we should eat, dance, enjoy the festivities, and so on. I couldn't help but laugh as I watched them go.

"They're really cute," Luca decided, licking the last of a cheese danish from his fingers.

"And I think Rei really appreciated you staying, too," I told him. After Al's arrest, the wedding celebration had become like a real celebration at last—a blur of comings and goings and reunions and explanations. Even Mara had stopped by at some point to take her leave before she went home.

"He told me so," Luca grinned. "We've talked here and there. We kind of—can relate about some things. I'm glad he did decide to stick with his own appearance. Oh, and Taiwo said something to me about looking after you when you're in Belville, too."

"They did? When was this? What'd you say?" I asked, stealing a piece of spinach quiche from one of Luca's plates.

Luca grinned widely. "Yesterday. I said it's bad for my nerves looking *after* you. So I've decided to just go *with* you on your adventures."

"Ha, ha, aren't you clever," I chuckled.

"You're both silly," William rumbled.

At that moment I saw Varsha wandering by and ran out to catch her. She'd recovered fully, though she still seemed a bit miffed about being left out of the big reveal. When Luca had promised to write it all down so she'd have a record of it, though, she perked up.

We took her with us to see the fish show, which had William drooling all over the dock. Around lunchtime she split off, saying she wanted to go find Officer Ebb and give him her thanks. As I turned to watch her disappear into the crowd on the beach, I could have sworn I caught a glimpse of something silvery. And on the wind, I seemed to hear,

When Reynard rules Seaside
And none know his name,
And speaking the truth
Can only bring shame,
Then shall come the undrowned tide
To sweep away sickness and blame.
Now all is well and love may reign,
And you, alchemist, will be welcome here again.

Clemency, I thought. *So that feeling earlier* was *the prophecy coming to an end, now that Rise-as-Reynard is gone and Rei is bringing out truth.* And then, though I knew she couldn't hear, I added, *thank you.*

"What's up?" Officer Thorn asked, clapping a hand on my back.

"Nothing, I just thought I saw someone. Did you—? Ah, well. Say, Ebb isn't with you, is he? Varsha just went looking for him," I said as I recovered myself.

"No, he's determined to stay by the fire. Can't decide if he likes watching it or if he's terrified someone'll try to burn down the Rise estate," Thorn said cheerfully.

"But everything's over, right?" Luca asked from her other side.

William snorted and stared out over the water.

"It is," Thorn declared. "Al and his goons are in the cells until next full moon, when their trial will take place. Ebb's thinking the judge will give them bonded time serving at a way-home and time at a station, respectively."

I nodded. Such punishments were typical, and of course ruled by all sorts of magic which made them inescapable. Who knows, the experience might help Al straighten himself out again. It wouldn't ever bring Kade back, of course, but it might help right the situation that had caused so much strife in the first place.

Thorn was still talking, naturally. "Cindy's been let out and is running around here somewhere—she helped me light the fire earlier. Said something about the ethical treatment of driftwood," Thorn added, scratching her chin. Then she changed the subject. "Pity they don't have boxes or bags so we can take some of this food home with us."

"Oh, I bet they do, and they'd be happy to send you home with some," I said, laughing.

"And what about you?" she returned. "Are you ever coming home?"

"Of course," I said, looking around at my friends. "Probably in the next day or so. Most of the festivities after the wedding are really just meant for the family, and then of course Rei and Taiwo will be going on their honeymoon.

"Besides," I added, when no one seemed convinced, "living this near the ocean throws me way off. I did it when I was little. I can't do it again. Though William seems to like it," I added, glancing down at him.

He was still staring at the shallows some distance from the dock. "It's interesting," he explained in a way which managed perfectly to imply that the rest of us weren't up to snuff. "They're about to start the high noon ceremony—"

"Is it noon already?" Luca looked baffled. He'd only barely finished eating his breakfasts. I smothered a laugh.

"—for luck and love," William continued as though we were all listening with rapt attention. "See, Taiwo's going out in the water, and supposedly if you're hit with water from their tail then you'll be blessed because *they've* been blessed with—"

I shifted my attention to the water, just in time. Taiwo and many other members of the Afolayan clan swarmed the waves, cheering and waving at friends on shore. Then, in one graceful and swift movement, Taiwo leaned back and swished their purple tail through the clear water, showering everyone within twenty yards with shimmering droplets.

"—true love," William concluded, looking up at me dourly. The drops had missed him, since he was laying along the dock to get a better view of the fish. Instead, my yellow tunic was splattered across the front and Luca was shaking water from his hood.

We beamed at each other, then turned to look at Thorn— but she had been standing far back enough that she wasn't hit.

"Looks like it's just us," I said to Luca.

"We'll have to be blessed enough for all of Belville," he agreed, giving me a high five.

Officer Thorn gave a William-like snort. "Blessed? Is that what you call it?"

"I guess we do run into a lot of trouble," I admitted. I

still couldn't shake my grin or the warm feeling in my chest, though. *That enchanted water is powerful stuff,* I thought to myself. *I wonder if I could use it in a potion . . .*

"But we always come out of it," Luca reminded me. "Did you see the way we took down those goons? I say, bring on the trouble. I know we can handle it."

"Luca, don't tempt fate!" I reprimanded, though I couldn't help laughing.

"Admit it," he grinned. "Together, we can overcome anything. Just like Taiwo and Rei!"

"Alright, alright, you win," I agreed. "You have a fair point. In the end, everything turned out perfectly."

"Not least because Rei finally found his voice," William said, looking up at me.

"True," I agreed again.

And how strange, I thought, *to think that I'd be standing here talking about our success with so many friends—friends across different places. Maybe Jeannie was right. Maybe, even if I want to think I'm still a traveling alchemist, the truth is that I've found a home.*

And that home was shared by friends I loved dearly.

Epilogue

A note from Taiwo and Rei

Hi Red!

Can you believe it? We're finally taking a moment to write to you from our honeymoon. (Take a look at the pictures! Isn't it beautiful?) By now you should be back in Belville, probably surrounded by potions and alchemical thingies. Well, I guess I can't make *too* much fun of you for it–after all, your expertise really helped us out.

And since I've already brought it up–even though I'd told myself I'd try not to–I may as well go on to say that Rei is *really* grateful. He's right here next to me as I write. He says that without you, he might have gone on to become exactly like his father. (I don't think that's really true, but what do I know?) He really does think that the weight of tradition would have pulled him down . . .

Funny how that works, right? I know you saw all the traditions at the wedding. They're supposed to be something that brings us together–that's what I would have said if you'd asked me about traditions this time last year. But as soon as I met Rei, I started seeing how traditions can keep us apart. Even simple silly things like "I'm used to living on land, and you live in water!" I mean I know, that is a *big* thing really, but also it isn't at all. In a world where we can be who we want to be and love so deeply, why wouldn't we also create our own hybrid lives?

That's what we're doing, by the way, once the honeymoon is over. Our home base will be Rei's home, of course. He's never lived anywhere else, and it *is* pretty nice, when there's not a bunch of murder suspects running around. (Kidding!) To tell you the truth, I'm actually kind of excited about having a "home base." We never really had one before–I mean, if you asked Ige he'd say "our people's home base is the sea" and that's technically *true,* but it's not really the same as having a *house,* is it.

Anyway, so we'll be at Rei's–or, I guess, *our*–estate mostly. You can write to us there–hint hint! We've already made plans to make it more merfolk-friendly. (That pier will be replaced by the *most* amazing two-level land-and-sea ballroom you've ever seen; really, you will *have* to come see it!) I still plan on traveling with Mom sometimes too, and Rei can even come with us (thanks for leaving behind your un-Drowning instructions, by the way. You'd better be extra sure they work!) And then the whole family will stop by off shore probably every summer. Believe me, we're going to stay busy!

Speaking of, Cindy finished her masterpiece–although Lacey almost didn't want to let her back on the grounds after everything that happened. I told her–Lacey, I mean–that I could totally understand her position, but also, it's not like Cindy really knew any better . . . she means well, she's just still got some growing up to do, I think. You know how it is. Even *you* changed between the years we met, and you're already pretty old. (Teasing!)

I don't have much more space, so I'd better wrap up soon. I just think it's funny how some of us are so used to changing, and some of us think we never will. When I met him, Rei thought he would never change. And I thought I would never stay the same! When I was little I used to think of myself like the ocean, always flowing. (Wow, talk about an ego, right?) Then Rei said I was his "rock" throughout the investigation and I was like, *excuse* me? Haha but I was also really touched. Now we're both a little more in the middle, I guess. And we are just having the time of our lives, I promise you that.

Got to go–Rei says hi–and thank you–love you!! See you soon or else!

Taiwo

Recipes

The recipes included here have been submitted by the residents of Belville, collected (and at times translated) by the author. Mistakes might have been made at any part of the process, but with any luck, these will bring a bit of fun and inspiration to you, our readers! Always feel free to experiment with the recipes included. And if you do, reach out to info@ellehartford.com to let us know how it went!

That said, without further ado . . .

Red's Twist on A Café Veggie Burger

The only bad thing about home-made veggie burgers is that they often fall apart. However, Red's recipe includes a duo of sticky ingredients—sweet potato and oats—to fix that. If you find you still have trouble, try blending the ingredients together more finely, or even add an egg to the batter!

Makes four patties

Ingredients:

- ½ small onion, diced
- 2 cloves garlic, minced
- Butter
- ½ large sweet potato, grated
- 1 C cooked black beans, drained
- ½ C cooked brown rice
- ¼ C rolled oats
- 1 tsp cumin
- ½ tsp chili powder
- ½ tsp coriander powder (fresh cilantro may also be used)
- ½ tsp salt
- More salt and black pepper to taste

1. Set oven to 375 and line a large cookie sheet with parchment paper.
2. Saute the onion, garlic, and butter in a medium pan over medium heat until the onion is soft. Keep an eye out for burning!
3. Add the potato to the onion and garlic, cover the pan, and cook for about 5 minutes (or until the potato is soft).
4. In a large bowl, mix together *all* ingredients. If you like your veggie burgers to have a recognizable "bean" texture, then reserve a ½ cup of the beans for now. Mix together everything else using a potato masher or large spoon. Once everything's incorporated, you can add those reserved beans and stir them in gently.
5. Divide the batter into four balls and form patties on the parchment-lined baking sheet. Aim for about ½ inch thickness. You can determine the shape based on the

kind of bun you're using.

6. Bake for about forty minutes, flipping them once halfway through.
7. Serve nice and warm with a bun or salad!

* * *

Jeannie's Veggie Sushi Tips

Jeannie knows that not everyone enjoys eating raw fish. But if you still want to try some fun sushi creations, here are some tips and tricks!

1. The basis for sushi is good rice. Whatever kind you like—white rice, brown rice, even black rice—make sure you prepare it with care, and don't be afraid to add some subtle seasonings to it as well (most common is a splash of rice wine vinegar, but even an extra dash of salt and pepper can enhance your dish if that's what you like).
2. You don't have to roll it if you don't want to! There are many types of sushi. An easy version is nigiri, which is a small mound of rice with toppings draped across it. If you like seaweed and want to incorporate it without rolling, try temaki, which is a little funnel of seaweed with rice and toppings stuffed inside.
3. Get creative. Common vegetables in sushi include straws of cucumber, asparagus, shredded carrot, or even cooked sweet potato. Common fruits are kiwi, mango,

strawberries, avocado, and crisp apple. You can get fancy with some mushrooms, tofu, or other proteins, too! The best ingredients are any that lend themselves to the shape you want: to make a sushi roll, you want straw-like or tubular ingredients; for nigiri, thin slices work well.

4. Reach for tools. If you're serious about making sushi at home, or even just having a fun night of experimenting, it's worth getting a sushi mat. Most are made of bamboo, and they look like tiny window blinds. They are used to help support your seaweed and rice as you roll it into the familiar sushi shape. You can also find bamboo paddles for shaping rice. And if you're making a sushi roll, make sure you have a sharp knife to cut it into pieces once you're done!

5. Have fun! Nothing needs to look perfect in order to taste good.

* * *

Trent's Mostly-Foolproof Travel Charm

This little travel charm is what's known as a "spell bag," to be assembled and then carried with the person it was made for—perhaps in a pocket or on a long string as a necklace. Belville's local Witch recommends putting it together during a waxing moon, preferably before the First Quarter; but if you're like a certain impulsive bookseller and you need to travel now, it should still work just fine.

In a quiet space where you can work undisturbed, collect before you:

- A small piece of chalcedony (preferably carved into an arrowhead shape for luck)
- A piece of tourmalated quartz
- Thirteen celery seeds
- A sprig of broom
- A few stalks of devil's shoestring
- A small cloth pouch and string

Calm your mind and focus on your intent. Visualize a safe arrival at your destination. Then take a moment to pick up and inspect each ingredient you've gathered: chalcedony for safe travel, tourmalated quartz for its projective powers; celery seeds to honor Mercury and ancient witches, broom to honor the wind that will hurry you along, and devil's shoestring for a bit of added luck. Hold them all in the palm of your hand and focus once more. If you have a connection to a deity, pray to them to bless this travel. Then carefully pour the blessed materials into your pouch and close it up. Hold it in your hand as you travel for a little extra boost!

* * *

William's Recipe for Peace of Mind: The Dippers

We all know by now what William thinks of recipes. Well, here he is again with another bit of advice!

"This is good for when you're traveling," says William. "But only if you're in the Northern Hemisphere, mind. If you're in the Southern Hemisphere, then you might look for the Centaur or the Cross. But for now I'm going to talk about the Dippers.

"Every schoolchild knows about the Big Dipper and the Little Dipper–that's Ursa Major and Ursa Minor, if you know what you're talking about. Once upon a time people thought of them as bears. That's what 'Ursa' means. But 'Dipper' is easy to remember, because that's exactly what they look like.

"When you look up into the sky, preferably on a clear night with no busybodies around to bother you, you can find the Big Dipper quickly. It's a big bright box. You can see the handle, too, but that's not the important part. What you want to do is look at the two stars opposite the handle, making one side of the 'dipping' part of the Dipper. They make a line. Follow that line and you'll find the handle of the Little Dipper–otherwise known as the North Star.

"So now you can always find North. Keep that in mind when you travel next . . . unless, like Red, you'd prefer to rely on a bunch of fancy maps and magitech gadgets."

The Dippers
Ursa Major and Ursa Minor

Acknowledgments

Red spends a lot of time in this story learning how to trust and rely on her friends during hard times (finally!). Likewise, this book wouldn't have come into being without the support of many lovely people!

As always, of course, I'm indebted to my family, friends, and my long-suffering partner for all their enthusiasm and kindness. In this case, I'd like to particularly acknowledge my friends in New Jersey who introduced me to beaches that later inspired Seaside! And once again, a *huge* shout-out to Richelle and Richelle Braswell Comprehensive Editing. When she says comprehensive, she absolutely means it!

Additionally, I feel so grateful to everyone who has helped me nurture and grow this series—the patient members of my writing club, the inspiring friends in the Cozy Mystery Book Club online, the heartwarming indie author community on Instagram, and the impressive folks over at the Cozy Mystery Tribe, to name just a few. Plus, naturally, all my wonderful ARC readers!

Last but not least, I'm very grateful to *you*, reading this. If you're curious about any of the goddesses referenced in the story, by the way, go look them up! They come from cultures all over the world, and there are many far more accurate and detailed resources about them than my own little book. And while you're poking around on the computer, if you'd like to leave this book a review on your website of choice, I'd be very much obliged.

About the Author

Elle adores cozy mysteries, fairy tales, and above all, learning new things. As a historian and educator, she believes in the value of stories as a mirror for complicated realities. She currently lives in New Jersey with a grumpy tortoise and a three-legged cat.

Find more stories of Red and her friends at ellehart-ford.com. And while you're there, sign up for Elle's newsletter to get bonus material, behind-the-scenes sneak peeks, and terrible jokes!

P.S. Just as a reminder, there is an extra special warm place in an author's heart for anyone who takes the time to leave a review. ♥ Even one kind sentence can do wonders!

And if you're curious about Red's next adventure, Cry Big Bad Wolf, *read on for the first chapter!*

Cry Big Bad Wolf

Chapter One
All Hallow's Eve

As I made my way across Market Square from the bakery back to my potions shop, I dodged a ghost, sidestepped a zombie, and nearly put my boot right through a carved pumpkin.

Fall in the tiny alpine town of Belville was a dangerous time.

The grassy Square, always the center of the town celebrations, was littered with decorations for All Hallow's Eve. I'd traveled all across Beyond, a world of vibrant cultures and locales all tied together by magic and fairy tales, and yet nowhere—not even in the gleaming magitech cities or the spookiest of swamps—had I seen a place that took Halloween, or more properly, All Hallow's Eve, so seriously. My somewhat bull-headed friend Officer Thorn had volunteered to oversee the decorating, perhaps because Belville's one-person police station didn't give her much opportunity for bossing people around. I could hear her voice booming from the other corner of the park and instinctively put a tree (decorated with monstrous wolf-like masks) between myself and her, thinking as I nursed my chai latte, *William probably asked me to go out and get cinnamon rolls this morning because he was hoping I'd get roped into decorating and he wouldn't have to get up and help me run the shop.*

"Hiya, Red!"

The thing about trees is they only keep you hidden from people in one direction. Caught unaware, I gave an unstealthy jerk as I wheeled to face Luca, town scholar and book seller. To be a "scholar" was a lifelong profession, which came with its own rules and protocol—and was invaluable to any town. Like all scholars, Luca wore a simple black robe and hood no matter if it was rain, sun, snow, or perfectly crisp autumn weather like today. And as usual for him, his green eyes twinkled against his dark skin as he grinned at me from under his hood.

But his smile faded much more quickly than usual, and behind his eyes there was worry as he added, "Why isn't William with you? You weren't going out alone, were you?'

"Only to the bakery and back," I said, showing him my basket of rolls—and a bonus quiche for myself—with a reassuring smile. "No one's going to abduct me in the town square. Besides, aren't you out alone?"

"Of course not. I have Frank," Luca informed me. Sure enough, a wizened white mink doing a very good impersonation of a woolly scarf lifted its head and nodded at me from Luca's shoulder.

I pursed my lips. Luca's mink had made a sudden appearance over the summer and ever since had been his inseparable companion. And while I thought it was nice for Luca to have a companion—"pet" wouldn't be the right word for an ancient, sentient mink, just as it would offend William, my dog-shaped magical familiar—I really wasn't sure how much protection it provided.

But then, appearances can be deceptive, and I had realized recently that maybe some of my preconceived notions were holding me back. Case in point: Frank had come in very handy during a fight with some bad guys at a wedding.

I shrugged away the argument, and the reminiscing. It was too early in the morning for both; I needed more chai. Or more accurately, I needed more of the caffeine my chai included.

"In any case," I said, sipping my drink, "I still think we're perfectly safe in the town square. Maybe not from all the paper ghosts and jack-o-lanterns, but definitely from roadside bandits. I'm not even *on* a road right now, for goodness' sake."

Luca fell into step beside me as I made my way toward the northeast corner of the square, where Red's Alchemy and Potions sat. "Red, you may be right—I mean, of course you're right—but it's that kind of thinking that could get you in trouble. Remember, that's exactly what got you into trouble last year at the castle, and then again last winter with the miners, too! I'm not saying you did anything wrong, exactly, and I know everything's fine now, but still—people worry about you, you know? And they aren't wrong to worry. You've been here more than a year now, Red. You know how weird and scary these attacks are for everyone here. It isn't something to take lightly. I know Officer Thorn can be— bossy, but her idea about sticking together is right. I think it's right, anyway. Just in case."

Luca's gaze on me was earnest—so earnest I had to turn away, staring instead at the crinkly red and yellow leaves under my feet. I got the feeling at that moment that perhaps what Luca was really worried about wasn't miners or robbers or even Officer Thorn, but *me*. I got the feeling—as I often had, especially since our attendance at my friend Taiwo's wedding over the summer—that perhaps what Luca was trying to say was something more like *I wish I could look out for you,* or even *I need you to stay safe because you are important to me.*

A fallen twig snapped beneath my boot. I dismissed my feelings. The cold, hard facts of the matter were that Luca had never said any such things aloud, and furthermore that he was a kind, caring, somewhat-over-enthusiastic soul to *everyone.* Not to mention he was one of my oldest friends in Belville, and had never indicated he wanted to be more.

Alchemists look for facts. That's what Paracelsus, my old teacher, would have said to me.

"Listen," I said as we approached my shop's front stoop, "I'm usually very safe, I promise. It's not like I go looking for mysteries. I've hardly even had time to leave my lab lately, what with all of Thorn's requests for ever-sticking glue and glow powder for her decorations. Today was just a blip. William woke up grumpy, and he wanted baked goods to cheer him up."

Luca stopped on the sidewalk and looked up at me innocently as I unlocked my door. "Why go buy them?"

The pure force of his faith in my baking—which is one of my favorite hobbies, but nowhere near good enough to consider actually opening a storefront—made me chuckle. "I would've made some, but like I said, I've been busy."

"I get that. I have been too. I'm putting together a display on ghost stories," Luca said absently as he glanced out at the Square.

This got my attention. The scholar before Luca, in addition to being a terribly cruel person, had always insisted that seasonal displays were "frivolous." When Luca had worked as his assistant, there had never been any such fun or levity. It made my heart swell to see how much better Luca was making his life now that he was free of Owl.

I paused before I went inside, following Luca's gaze out into the Square. Thorn and her ragtag group of volunteers marched from tree to tree, looking more like a class of trainees from the police guild than a bunch of holiday decorators. I could hear the officer yelling something that sounded suspiciously like *"Hut! Hut! Hut!"*

"Luca," I asked, my good feelings faltering again, "do you think we really will have the All Hallows celebration? What with everything that's been going on."

"I wondered that too," he admitted. "I actually looked back through the town records, because I was curious. Turns out the town council has *never* canceled a holiday celebration, not even for blizzards or droughts or one wild purple-sprite infestation. So I don't think they'll cancel one now—especially All Hallows. After all, the whole point of the party is to scare away evil spirits, right?"

\#

William, who had specifically demanded *three* cinnamon rolls still warm from the oven, ate two at the register during the first hour the shop was open. I'd arranged my shop to have an open floor plan: upon coming in through the front door, a customer was greeted with rows of waist-high shelves and displays, mostly potions arranged by specialty or raw ingredients for various kinds of alchemy. The walls were lined with more potions and books. In the back right corner, tucked under a spiral staircase that led to my apartment, was a snug nook with two plush armchairs and a pot of free tea for customers waiting for special orders—or friends who wanted to visit, more often. To the left was the sales counter, which was usually William's domain; he used curls of blue magic to operate the cash register and keep up his protective wards on the shop. Behind the register was an internal wall that separated my lab from the public space. I'd knocked out a large window so that I could see William and anyone else in the store, but I often kept the door to the lab locked. The last thing I needed was for someone to barge straight into a chemical reaction or, even worse, the ceramic kiln I kept in one corner. From my lab, I had access to a patio full of potted plants and a teeny backyard.

Punctually at nine o'clock, a rap sounded at that back door. I left my vials of specialty glue on the workbench and pushed my alchemists' goggles up over my forehead as I went to answer it.

"Hey, Sir Rowan. You know, you could come in the front. As I've told you every morning since you started work here last spring," I added with a weary chuckle, standing back to wave my part-time employee in.

"Good morning, Miss Red," he said cordially. "And as I have answered you every morning since you were kind enough to employ me, I am quite comfortable with things the way they are."

Quite comfortable, indeed, I thought to myself as I let Sir Rowan into the shop and closed my lab door behind him. I had to smile. Sir Rowan had arrived in town last winter, hard on the heels of a string of murders and all kinds of trouble at the mine. Throughout the investigation he had clung fast to his *miss* thises and his *my lord* thats and his stuffy, yet rather charming ways. Most likely a human with water-fairy blood, he still wore the armor and the habits of an actual knight, despite having settled very happily into Belville (and into a relationship with Daisy, a dragon-in-human-form who lived nearby . . . but far be it from me to gossip). I had to admit, Sir Rowan had a calming, steadfast presence that came in handy around the shop, and he knew his flowers like no one else outside of the proprietors of Belville's floral shop, A Petal in Time. Plus, William adored him.

"This cinnamon roll is extra," I heard my grumpy companion saying through the open lab window. "You could have it. If you want."

"Why, thank you, William. 'Tis convenient indeed, for I came down early this morning, and it has been a long time since my breakfast."

'Extra!' I'm so sure, I thought, shaking my head. But Sir Rowan's answer was more interesting than William's deceit. 'Came down early,' I'd learned, was Sir Rowan's discreet way of saying that he'd come to work straight from Daisy's home high on the mountain, rather than his own magical campsite outside of town. The commute was long and, of late, dangerous. Since I knew we had no customers in the shop, and Luca's worried eyes were still haunting me, I decided to ask about it.

"Hey, Sir Rowan," I called through the window without looking up from my glue. "What does Daisy think of you traveling on the roads nowadays?"

"You refer to the reports of highway robbery, I presume," said Sir Rowan, his tone measured despite the fact that he was eating a sticky cinnamon roll.

William whined. "More than just reports. You should have seen the torn up tarp Officer Thorn brought in last week while you were out. It'd been clawed to pieces."

"Indeed?" Sir Rowan sounded interested. "And what did the officer wish Miss Red to do with it?"

"She wanted me to run a few preliminary tests on some liquid found on it. I *can* hear you," I reminded them both. "Apparently she was doing it at the behest of the person who was robbed, some former mayor or something. And yes, before you ask, some of the traces were definitely blood."

"Magical blood?" Sir Rowan asked.

"I think so. Or mythical creature, maybe. Which begs my question again—aren't you and Daisy worried at all, living out in the woods?"

Sir Rowan's tone was delicate. "One would have to be a fool indeed to attempt to rob or kidnap Miss Daisy."

"More like *dead,*" William agreed with a snort. "They'd be dead."

I rolled my eyes, but I smiled too. Daisy was something of a recluse, but I'd met her a few times—enough to know that a) she was terribly shy, but almost as sweet as Luca and b) William was right. Anyone who messed with her or Sir Rowan would have one extremely angry and terrifyingly huge dragon to deal with.

"That makes sense," I said. "I just wondered if you were uneasy, that's all. We can figure out a way for you to stay in town if you ever need to."

"It strikes me that most of the targets so far have been wagons and travelers with expensive luggage—a far cry from myself and my horse," Sir Rowan said serenely. "However, I appreciate the sentiment, Miss Red."

Well, that answers that, I thought to myself as I stoppered up my last vials. *And he does have a point. The attacks of the past two weeks would just seem like normal highway robbery, if it weren't for . . .*

"Are you and Daisy coming to All Hallow's Eve next week?"

William was asking Sir Rowan.

"I am not certain. While it is our wish to be friendly with our neighbors, neither of us is particularly fond of made-up spooks."

. . . if it weren't for all the ghoulish tales.

Also by Elle Hartford

The Alchemical Tales (cozy fantasy meets cozy mystery)
Beauty and the Alchemist (book 1)
Cold as Snow (book 2)
Mermaid for Danger (book 3)
Cry Big Bad Wolf (book 4)
Cinders to Dust (book 5)
Death Pulls the Strings (book 6)
A Thousand and One Alibis (book 7)
Tangled Up in Murder (book 8)
Labyrinth of Crime (book 9)

Pomegranate Cafe Romance (sweet romantasy)
Worthy in Love (book 1)
A Tale of Rowan and Daisy (book 1.5)
Strong in Love (book 2)
Steady in Love (book 3)
Sweet in Love (book 4)

Marine Magic (cozy fantasy at the beach)
How to Care for Cursed Fish (book 1)
How to Treat Talking Beasts (book 2)

Leonine Investigations (cozy fantasy goes noir)
The Silver Deck (book 1)